THE EMISSARY OF NAIRU

INTERGALACTIC ALLIANCE
BOOK ONE

MATTHEW THRUSH

The Emissary Of Nairu

Intergalactic Alliance: Book 1

EMPIRE Publishing
20212 Champion Forest Drive, #303
Spring, TX 77379
www.empireghostwriter.com
@empirepublishing

ISBN: [ebook] 978-1-956283-36-5

ISBN: [paperback] 978-1-956283-37-2

ISBN: [hardcover] 978-1-956283-38-9

CONTENTS

1. Bex 1
2. Ben 8
3. Bex 18
4. Ben 30
5. Bex 37
6. Ben 44
7. Bex 52
8. Ben 62
9. Bex 69
10. Ben 81
11. Bex 95
12. Ben 105
13. Bex 112
14. Ben 121
15. Bex 130
16. Ophelia 139
17. Bex 149
18. Ben 157
19. Bex 167
20. Ben 176
21. Bex 185
22. Ben 197
23. Bex 205
24. Ben 215
25. Bex 224
26. Ben 233
27. Bex 241
28. Ben 253
29. Bex 258
30. Clover 268

The Cloning Of Eden   275
About Matthew Thrush   287
Also by Matthew Thrush   291

THE EMISSARY OF NAIRU

With the color of a single token, Bex and Ben's lives are changed forever. Now, instead of simply being the only human refugees on an alien planet, the Intergalactic Union will be sending them on their first mission. The only problem is that they are placed on *opposing* sides.

Blues are emissaries and *reds* are assassins.
As long as the mission stays on course, and no one veers from the Union's commands, then no one has to die. But what happens when Bex and Ben find out that their mission is to *kill* the very last humans in the galaxy—and possibly each other?

Suddenly, the two find themselves navigating both the dangerous territories of an unknown universe, and the growing feelings that they have for each other. With no way to tell which aliens to trust and which will turn on them faster than they can blink, the two find new friendships in the most unusual of places, and enemies hiding behind every corner.

When one of them is afflicted by an unknown threat, it will be a race against time to see not only if they can both survive, but if any of the planets will be spared the overreaching destruction of the Union.

BEX

"What color did you get?" Ben asks as he flips the blue plastic token onto the table.

"Red," I answer.

We look at each other for a solemn moment before the lines are called. I hold the red circle in my hand and run my thumb over the hard, cool surface. This means we won't be allowed to talk now.

I don't want it to be red.

Ben tilts my chin up with his fingers and forces a smile on his face, even though we both know there's nothing to smile about now.

"Eh, it won't be so bad," he says, trying to reassure me.

It doesn't work. I'm not stupid. I know how this works.

"We'll be able to talk to each other again once we get there," he continues.

"You sure about that?" I ask.

Before he has a chance to answer, the bells ring and the lines are called. Five of us are blue, and five are red. Blue will be the emissaries, the ones responsible for scouting the resources and talking to the natives. I would have been much better as a blue, to be honest. Red will be the scary ones, the ones they call *assassins*, charged with the equivalence of murdering our team and any of the alien species that entertain the idea of going against the Intergalactic Union. I would be less nervous about being an assassin if Ben could be with me.

It's not the fact that he and I are the only humans going that scares me. Trust me, I've gotten as used to there being as many species of beings as there are strands of dark hair on my head. It's just that the tension has been rising at the Union, and the discord among the group of us is palpable. I don't want to be on the opposite side from Ben. I'm worried.

"Come on," he says as he tugs my sleeve. "Stalling the lines won't help us."

He's right; it won't.

Ben picks up his token from the table, and then the two of us walk into the short, parallel lines that lead out of the room and into the containment pods. I've always felt that there should be a much more advanced way to do this, especially here on Nairu, one of the most advanced and powerful planets in the Union. I've never actually been inside a containment pod myself, but I've heard the stories. As soon as I found out that Ben and I had been chosen as *members*, the thing that caused me instant anxiety was the thought of having to enter the containment pod.

Ben can tell I'm nervous; he tries to hold my hand for as long as possible until our lines split. Even then, he shoots a look over at me, which translates into something like, "It'll be okay. Don't worry, Bex."

We didn't even know each other on Earth. When we were brought here, all the humans were thrown into the same room. As we waited to find out what our fate would be, some of us got to know each other.

My name used to be Rebecca. I can still remember the way my mother used to say it, with such a lilt in her voice that it sounded more like a song than a word. Even when I graduated high school, she still said my name in the same sing-song way that she did when I was five. It annoyed me then, but now I just miss her.

Ben was in that holding room with me when we arrived here on Nairu. I was scared and alone, and he was alone, too. But he seemed different than the rest of us—he wasn't scared. He came to sit next to me and asked me my name. When I told him it was Rebecca, he told me that "Bex" sounded cooler, and that's what he has called me ever since.

A clammy, nine-fingered hand pulls my collar forward and breaks me from the thoughts that I was trying to disappear into.

"Name," it says.

"Bex Fawner," I reply. I have several good friends now that are Palnarian like this guy is, but I've never quite gotten used to the extra digits on their hands and the skin that always feels as though it desperately needs a hot shower.

"Step inside, please," he says.

I turn my head to see that Ben has already disappeared into the blue side of the containment pod wing. There's nothing else for me to do but walk forward.

It's every bit as awful as I thought it would be.

I'm not claustrophobic—thank God—but the silver metal cylinder wraps around my five-foot-seven frame as if I am suffocating. Metal arms reach out from the side walls and pull my clothes away from my skin until I am standing cold and naked in an empty room that feels like it's shrinking.

Honestly, how is this even considered civilized?

Thankfully, the area opens up ahead, and as I walk forward, I can see a long, rectangular table with a pile of red folded clothes on the center of it. There are four people sitting at the table, facing me. I've learned to embrace the concept of "people" loosely. I step forward and reach for the clothes, knowing this will be my new garb for at least the next few days, but as soon as my hand touches the fabric, a hot pinch burns my left shoulder blade.

"Ow!" I shout as I whirl around to see what it is.

One of the mechanical arms is withdrawing back into the opening in the wall it came out of. I reach around and touch the still searing skin on my shoulder.

"I would suggest leaving it alone," a voice from the table says. "You've simply been marked with your tracking number in the event that you go missing and we need to assist you. Think of it as a free tattoo."

One of the others at the table attempts a grin at her remark, but the several rows of teeth in its mouth make it look awkwardly uncomfortable.

I drop my hand back down to my side and stare at the four of them.

"Please," the woman who first spoke continues. "Feel free to dress now."

She looks almost human, aside from the double pupils in each eye and the locks of hair that seem to move on their own. I've heard about her species before, but I've never met one. They're famed for being incredibly smart and volatile.

I slip the red pants over my hips and zip up the red jacket that has a single black stripe encircling my right wrist. It's extremely hard not to notice the stares as I am getting dressed. Either they find human anatomy fascinating or repulsive; I haven't been able to figure out which.

I remind myself to look in the mirror when I get back to my room so that I can see what mark I've been branded with.

"Bex, is it?" the female says to me.

I nod.

"Are you aware of what you will be doing when you leave here tonight?"

"Yes," I answer dutifully. As soon as we found out we had been selected, Ben role-played with me so I didn't botch things up. Even though I don't want to go, a botched interview after the selection only meant that you would be *dispensable*, and that was not something I wanted to be. We were lucky to have stayed alive all this time as it is.

"My job will be to ensure that everyone follows the appropriate protocol as we are scouting the chosen planet." I've rehearsed the lines so well that the words come naturally now, even with my shaky voice.

"And what happens if someone doesn't follow protocol? What happens if a native being, or even one of your team members, decides to act selfishly and not in the best interests of the Union?" she asks.

"Then it will be my duty and my pleasure to end their life." The words taste bitter in my mouth as I say them.

"Good," she says, seemingly satisfied with my answer.

I get ready to walk toward the door, which has just opened at the side of the room. I have a few hours before we will board the ship, and I intend to use that time to talk with Ben, even though we technically aren't supposed to talk to each other anymore; at least not until this is all over.

"Rebecca," she says before I can reach the door. No one here has ever called me that. I didn't even think anyone knew what my name was back on Earth.

I turn around to look at her.

"Do you know why we chose you, and why we send our select groups to new planets every eighteen months?"

I feel like this is a test I have studied for but am going to somehow manage to fail, anyway.

"So that we can all live in intergalactic peace," I say with a small, forced smile. "The Union keeps all the planets inside each of the galaxies at peace and supplies each with the necessary trade and infrastructure to survive. Without it, the system would collapse and chaos would reign over us all."

For a minute, she looks at me with her four pupils as though she is somehow able to measure the truth behind my answer. Then she smiles and waves a small hand in the air to dismiss me. It's not until I have cleared the containment pod completely that I realize I've been holding my breath almost the entire time.

I can see the other nine of us walking back toward our rooms to grab bags and make whatever final preparations are necessary prior to leaving. I've heard that these missions can take anywhere from a few days to a couple of months, depending on what type of scenario awaits at the targeted planet. I see Ben inside a small sea of other blue uniforms and start to walk toward him.

"What are you doing?" a girl with skin so translucent I can see her heart beating says to me as she steps in front of my path to block my way.

"Excuse me?"

"You can't go talk to them. They're *blue*." She looks less like she is trying to be confrontational and more like she is trying to save me from getting in trouble.

"Blue is a color," I say, "not a person. I was just going to say goodbye to my friend until we arrive on the planet."

The girl's voice becomes so hushed that I have to lean in closer to hear what she is saying.

"What do you mean *until*?" she asks.

"I mean that I know we aren't supposed to talk to members of the other color team until we arrive, so I was just going to say goodbye to my friend until we reach the planet."

The girl looks as though she is choking, and for a minute, I freeze, trying to think of what I should do to help her, despite the fact that I really don't want to touch skin that I can see her organs through. But she isn't choking; she's just completely aghast.

She tugs my arm to the side of the hall and pulls me into a corner where no one can see us. "You can't ever talk to your friend again," she whispers.

"What are you talking about?"

"Didn't anyone tell you? You're not just red for this mission; you're red *forever* now."

This is ridiculous.

I push my way past her and try to catch up to Ben down the hall. I can tell that it's almost time to go by the reflection of the several moons coming into view through the windows.

"Ben!" I shout in order to get his attention, but he must not have heard me because he keeps walking.

"Ben!" I shout again.

This time, he hears me and looks at me...right before he turns back around and disappears into a room with the rest of his team.

2

BEN

I didn't want to lie to her, but I had no choice.

I *know* Bex, and I know without a doubt that, if she had thought for a second that it would be the last time we talked, she would have blown her moment in front of the Union in the containment pod. No matter what species you are here, going against the Union means you don't show up for breakfast the next morning…or *any* morning ever again.

If Bex knew that we could never talk again, never sneak away to sit up all night, chatting in the dark bowels of the empty ship cockpits, then she would have done something rash and foolish. In this place, rash and foolish means that you are *discardable*.

The Intergalactic Union relies on complete adherence to its rules, and no forgiveness is tolerated for noncompliance. They are the supreme governing body of the systems that join the planets and galaxies together. And they are also responsible for the creation of the "invisible walls," which are enacted in order to keep the planets from warring with each other. One might say that they are the most powerful force in the universe, or at least, they think so.

I'm not entirely sure how many beings make up the Union because I have ever only seen four of them. It's the same four that appeared before us when they brought the surviving humans here to Nairu, and the same four that shifted back and forth between the red and blue containment pods during the pre-mission probe that we just went through. I know that Bex was *dreading* that part, and I wish I could have been there to keep holding on her hand the entire way through it. But we both needed to get through the initial screenings of the mission looking as if we were in full compliance.

Now that it's over, I'll work on finding a way to get to her once we reach the destination planet. There isn't a chance in hell that I'm going to just agree to not talk to her anymore. I have no intention of adhering to the rules; not when Bex is concerned.

"This way," a Palnarian points. It's difficult to tell *which* way when all his numerous digits seem to bend toward different directions.

I just follow the group of people wearing the same blue jumpsuit that I now have on. I walk with my head tilted slightly down, but my eyes up so that I can notice everything around me.

I wish I had been the one to get the red coin. Not because I want to assassinate anyone, but because I know that Bex *can't*. There's no way that she will be able to pull the trigger and kill someone, and if the time comes, *she will have to*. Fingers crossed that this will be a smooth mission with no resistance or insurgency. If all goes well, we'll be done in a couple of days and things can go back to the "abnormal normal" that they were before we were called to serve.

Complete the mission, get back to Nairu, and then figure out a way around the system.

That's the mantra playing on repeat in my head as I try to find a seat on the blue side of the ship.

I have a few ideas in mind that might work—getting one of the guys on the blue team to agree to switch places with me once we get back, and then going to one of the Rigsaru to get them to use their genetic tech and swap out our appearances. The Rigsaru enjoy breaking the laws of the Intergalactic Union. I think they like pissing off the elite…for the right price, anyway.

It shouldn't be hard to get a teammate to want to switch with me. A lot of the aliens here would sell their tentacles or third eye in order to be human. I'm not sure what the fascination is with our species, but Bex and I seem to be somewhat of a novelty among all the other breeds of alien here.

Of course, if I get caught, the consequences would be beyond severe. But since I can't imagine my life without Bex in it, I'll do whatever it takes. I just need to be smart about it.

Bex and I have been the closest of friends ever since we arrived here, and even though nothing more than friendship has happened between us yet, I *want* it to. I think I've wanted it ever since I looked up and saw her crouched down in the corner of the ship's intake room amongst a sea of scared and disheveled humans. Ever since that moment, we've been inseparable…*until now.*

I settle on the blue side of the ship and snap my seat belt into place just as I see Bex walk into the opposite section, looking for me. I purposefully turn away, knowing it will upset her but not willing to chance being seen breaking the rules before the ship has even taken off.

"This is really something, isn't it?" a double-pupiled guy says as he sits down across from me.

I try to remember what his species is called—Spewts, I think. One of the Union members is a Spewt, too. They're known for being smart and *extremely* volatile.

"I have a friend on the red team," he says as he juts out his hand for me to shake. He laughs, and his pupils seem to flicker when he does. "Guess we're not friends anymore, though. At least not on the books, anyway. My name is Soro."

I shake his hand, not saying anything in response because I can already tell that I don't really want to get to know this guy. He looks around the same age as me— twenty or so—but I know that age doesn't work the same with other species. For all I know, he could be thousands of years old.

I try not to glance over at Bex again, even though I'm dying to check on her, because I don't like the way Soro is still staring at me.

We are all called *members* now, all ten of us who were chosen for this mission. I know why Bex and I were chosen, too—we are the only two humans that the Intergalactic Union kept here on Nairu. All the other humans were given another planet to try to exist on after our species destroyed Earth. When Earth died off and the planet came to a complete ruin, the humans were rescued by the Intergalactic Union and brought here temporarily. But only two of us were brought fully into the fold. The rest were put on an empty planet to breed and attempt to restart life for themselves, essentially forgotten about and left to either die or make it work, which was done purposefully to test the resilience of the human species. I have no idea why Bex and I were spared, but I do know that our humanity is the reason we are sitting on this ship right now.

This particular mission is to scout the same planet that the other humans had been sent to. I guess the Union figured we would be able to provide some sort of insight into human behavior on this expedition. It also makes sense that we have been put on opposing sides of the team. They don't want either of us getting too sentimental about our species because that could cause rebellion—something that doesn't exist here, thanks to the Union's tight control over every corner of things. Bex and I are set against each other in order to balance each other out and make sure that we both stay on track during this mission. Clever and *cruel*.

As the seats around me fill up, I look at the members who will comprise my team until we return. In addition to Soro, who has stuck his hand out to all of us in a pushy, overtly officious sort of way, there are also three others.

One of them, a girl with a complexion that looks like cream and beautiful wings that she folds neatly behind her back, says her name is Lilybet. Another looks almost human. She has a sort of tough, punk aesthetic about her, complete with a half-shaven head that has a cerulean blue streak on it. But when she opens her mouth to talk, she speaks every language at once. It seems impossible to understand her, yet somehow, I still can. She introduces herself as Petra, which she can say in a thousand different variations of words and sounds. There are simply too many alien species to know what hers is called.

"Hey, don't I know you?" she asks the final member of the five of us as he sits down.

Three girls, two guys, I think to myself. I look over and see that the red team is balanced to the opposite. They have two girls and three guys. Everything the Union does, they do for a reason.

"Yeah, I *do* know you," Petra continues before the guy answers her. "You're that *thief,* Jabber is your name, right?"

"I reject that label," he says as he taps the side of his temple, causing his eye color to immediately change from green to black.

He's Rigsaru—good to know. I'll need to remember that for when I need to ask for a favor.

"I prefer to think of myself as an *activist.*"

"An activist?" Petra laughs. "And how exactly does stealing make you an activist?"

"I steal from the people who shouldn't have what they do. It's not right for there to be such a disparity between the living conditions of all the aliens on Nairu—or on any of the planets, for that matter."

"And do you give the disadvantaged people your contraband spoils?" she asks with a raised brow at him. There is a silver ring pierced into her eyebrow that flashes a reflection of the overhead lights when it moves.

Jabber hesitates before answering. "No. I consider the act of taking the goods away from the undeserving an appropriate act of justice."

Petra laughs again and rolls her eyes. "See?" she says as she waves her hand at him. "Just a plain old thief. You're lucky they haven't eliminated you yet. You'd better use that fancy genetic tech to change more than just the color of your eyes if you want to stay on the down-low."

Jabber doesn't seem at all fazed by her remarks. It makes me think that he has no fear of being caught and punished. He must have worked out some sort of deal with the Union. Maybe he uses his unique skillset to steal things for them, or maybe he barters his gene-altering capabilities.

On second thought, he might not be someone whom I want any favors from.

For the moment, we are all a team, and I try to get to know each of them a little. Not because I want to make friends, but because I want to know which of these people are trustworthy and which are not.

"Are you excited to be going on this mission?" Lilybet asks me. "You must be curious about what has happened with the rest of your species, aren't you?"

I think about the last time I saw my parents. Not all of the humans who were still alive on Earth were rescued by the Intergalactic Union. Some were left there to die, and some simply went "missing" after we arrived on Nairu. It was only a few dozen who were sent to the empty planet to try to restart their civilization. My parents had already died before the Union showed up in their big ship with their shiny promise to save some of us. But Bex's parents had still been alive. They were alive, and they were left behind.

"Yes," I say without any indication of emotion one way or the other. "I'm curious."

"I think it's odd that they put the other human on the red team," Petra says. I have already decided that she has a blunt and honest way about her. That makes me trust her more than the others already.

"It's not odd; it's *smart* on the Union's part," Soro interjects. "They don't want anyone getting any ideas in their heads and running off to start trouble."

"Are you *trouble*?" Jabber asks as he looks at me with different-colored eyes—red this time.

"No," I lie. "No trouble at all. I just want to achieve the mission and get back home."

For a moment, there is an awkward silence, as if

everyone is trying to read the intentions of the others—mine especially.

I run my hand through my hair, trying to act casual and at ease as I look around the room at the preparations being made for the ship to take off. My hair is getting too long now, and pieces of the dirty blond tendrils are falling into my eyes.

"Want me to fix that for you?" Jabber offers, lifting his finger toward my hair. "One touch, and I can make it longer, shorter, and you can pick any color you'd like."

"No thanks," I say. He's trying to be nice now, and I don't want to owe him anything.

"Ooo...can you do me?" Lilybet asks eagerly. "I've always wanted a new color."

"Really? Most people would kill for hair that light," Jabber says as he looks at her.

"Not my hair; my wings." She smiles as she turns and unfurls them in his direction. They look as thin and delicately iridescent as insect wings, and I wonder if they are more decorative than functional. "Just a tinge of pink, please, or maybe a shimmer of violet?"

Petra scoffs at the other woman's shallow vanity at the onset of an important mission, but Jabber goes ahead and taps the wings, resulting in them looking like they have been dusted with pink glitter.

"Pretty. Thanks!" Lilybet beams.

"Don't mention it."

The overhead speaker comes on, and a voice that sounds like one of the Union delegates from the containment pod announces that the ship is getting ready to depart.

"Here we go, guys," Soro says with excitement. He reminds me of a guy I knew back home in my borough on

Earth that used to turn turtles over in the sun, the kind of guy who enjoys things he shouldn't *way* too much.

Everyone snaps their buckles into place and sits back against their seats. While the rest of them are talking about what to expect when we get there, I steal a glance over to the other side of the ship to make sure Bex is buckled in and okay.

"You know," Petra says as she leans closer from her seat next to me. "When we get there, reds and blues are only allowed to talk as an entire group."

"They are?" I ask quietly, not wanting to draw attention from the rest of them. "I didn't think we were allowed to talk at all."

She shakes her head. "We're allowed to talk, as a *team* of all ten members. But don't let anyone catch you talking to her alone. That's a direct violation."

"I don't know what you're talking about," I say, quickly looking back toward our own side of the ship.

She grins. "Sure you don't."

"What are you two whispering about over there?" Jabber asks. "If the two of you are going to get all cozy, at least wait until after the mission. I don't want to be nauseated on this trip; the flight makes me queasy enough."

Lilybet giggles, but Soro doesn't look amused at all. He looks like he feels *threatened.*

"I thought you said you weren't going to be any trouble on this mission, human," he says in a weak attempt at posturing himself. "There are those of us, even on the blue team, who want to make sure everyone stays in line with our directive."

I've had just about enough of this asshole.

"Then maybe you didn't understand your directive," I say, making it sound like a direct attack on his intelligence.

"The blue team's mission is to act as emissaries to discover the planet's resources and bring the native species into agreement with the Union's purpose. We are not allowed to act as assassins, and doing so could greatly jeopardize your ability to collect on the generous compensation that the Union has promised to everyone here at the completion of a successful mission. Perhaps you should request a communications link with the Intergalactic Union during our ride to the destination planet so they can clarify your directives for you. We surely wouldn't want anyone to miss out on their earned payment once we return."

Soro's mouth hangs slightly open in surprise at my calm dismantling of his ego. The other three simply stare at us in silence, waiting to see what will happen next.

"Oh, and by the way," I say, now that I am ready to dig my heels into this mission. "My name is Ben, not *human*." I lock eyes with Soro for a few minutes, then lean my head back against my seat to rest until they announce we are free to move around the ship. It's a long ride until we get there.

I hear the others settle against their seats as well, and then a quiet and sarcastic quip.

"Yep," Jabber chuckles. "He's *definitely* not going to be any trouble."

3

BEX

I am beside myself when Ben turns away from me, and even though I don't want to believe what the other girl told me, I start to worry that it might be true. Even when I step into the open belly of the ship where both red and blue teams will sit for the departure, I try to look over at Ben again, and he turns away.

How can this be happening? Ben and I are a team. We were a team *long* before these stupid red and blue teams claimed us.

I follow the rest of the red jumpsuits and get settled onto our side of the ship, the *assassins* side of the ship, as it takes off from Nairu toward its target destination—the planet where the remaining humans have been left to survive on their own.

It's strange to think about how the Intergalactic Union has such an "ultimate power" to decide whether or not an entire species is capable of being redeemed and allowed to remain in existence. How can this single body of governance hold the fate over the lives of so many others? To me, it seems *wrong*.

Then again, Ben and I are only alive because of the Union's intervention. If they hadn't plucked us from a dying planet, we would be dead, too. Just like our parents.

In the minds of the Union delegates, they are *helping* by making sure that only the most viable and productive species thrive on any of the given planets in the multitude of galaxies. But isn't that how the most tyrannical regimes think? All people want to survive and live prosperously, not just the ones the Union deems worthy.

I shake the depressing thoughts from my head because none of it matters. I am in no position here to do anything other than what I am told to do. Going up against the Intergalactic Union is suicide.

I look out the ship's window as the preparations for take-off are being made. There are so many other planets out there, so many stars and moons, and so many other places with people that I'm sure I can't even begin to imagine. Sometimes I find myself daydreaming that me and Ben steal a ship and fly to somewhere else—*anywhere* else. Now is one of those times.

But now, not only don't I have a ship to steal, but it also doesn't even seem like I have my friend anymore, either.

I look over at the clump of people in blue jumpsuits all sitting together, and I can see Ben. He hasn't even glanced in my direction this entire time. I watch as it looks like he seems to be getting along with his new team.

"Hey," someone says quietly as I feel an elbow nudging me in the side of my ribs. "Pay attention."

I turn my face toward the voice and see that the translucent girl from before has taken a seat next to me.

"I'm not trying to be bossy, but if you keep acting aloof

like this, the team is going to notice that your heart isn't into the mission," she whispers as the rest of the red team takes a seat around us.

"Is anyone's?" I ask.

"You know what I mean. Everyone here has a job to do, and no one wants to screw it up."

I sigh audibly, and she looks at me with empathy. Even her eyelids are translucent, which is quite startling to look at. I haven't seen too many people on Nairu that look like her. In fact, I think she might be the only one. It makes me feel a little less lonely for being only one of two humans. I suppose it could be worse; I could be the *only* one of my kind here.

I look around at the faces of my fellow *assassins*. Apparently, we're doing introductions, and I quickly jump in, even though I don't want to.

"Peck is a weird name for a Palnarian, isn't it?" a man with double-pupiled eyes asks. He looks just like the Union woman who called me by my full name in the containment pod. Why is it that all of those Spewts seem to have such a warm bedside manner?

Peck rubs his forehead with his nine-fingered hand and looks nervous. It isn't hard to tell that he's mild-mannered and an unlikely choice for being an assassin. He doesn't answer the other guy, who I think said his name was Ransor. I wouldn't answer him, either—he's a bully.

"I'm Bex," I say abruptly as soon as I can see that it's my turn. I'm taking the other girl's advice and trying to fit in as much as I can. She and I are the only females on this team, and I'm glad that she at least seems to be nice so far. The third man on the team also seems to be okay. He hasn't said much this whole time, but he smiles politely when Vira introduces herself after me.

"My name is Aerlon," he says with a nod of his head.

He is oddly handsome, perfectly symmetrical in every way, and he looks strong. His hair is tied back in one long, blond ponytail that makes him look a bit like an androgynous unicorn. Aerlon is the kind of alien the humans back home would make those cheesy romance movies about being abducted and falling in love with the handsome alien. I can't really see any obvious features that would make him look glaringly "unhuman" aside from the fact that it doesn't seem like he's breathing at all.

Everything I have met so far has to breathe one way or another—mouths, lungs, gills, weird-looking ventilation holes in the sides of their faces or even the palms of their hands. But Aerlon has a nose and mouth just like a human and gives no sign that he is using them. No rise and fall of his chest, no air passing his lips as he talks. It's as if he is just a shell that isn't really alive at all.

As assassins, our job is not to be friends. If *anyone* on the team of ten members falls out of line, then each assassin has a duty to kill them, making it impossible for us to even make friends within our own team. But I already have a favorite out of the bunch, and not just because she is the only other female here.

Vira is smart, and she seems to know a lot about things.

While the other three guys talk about what they think the planet will look like once we arrive, I talk to Vira. She tells me all about her home world, and the more I listen to her talk, the less I am distracted by her unique physical appearance.

"I come from a star," she says as her tongue moves visibly around inside her jaw beneath her clear skin. "My home was beautiful. Everything was full of light and so cold."

"Cold?" I say as I look at the thin membrane of her see-through skin. "Didn't you freeze?"

"Oh no, I love the cold." She laughs. "All my people did."

Her face washes over with sadness, and without even knowing what happened to her species, I can tell that it was something terrible.

"I miss it," Vira continues. "Everything on Nairu looks and feels rather the same to me. The colors, the temperatures, even the people, they all blur together without any crisp edges or distinct outlines. There is no brightness here, and also no dark. There is only this stage of *in between*."

I don't really understand what she is saying. For me, Nairu is filled with more wonderous, albeit frequently alarming things and people than I ever saw back on Earth. There are more different species than I can count. And along with that diversity of people comes the varying attributes of everything else that civilizations have—food, clothing, customs, physical features, even currency. I am intrigued by Vira's underwhelming mood toward all of it. It makes me wish I could have seen the star that was her home. I bet it was amazing, and maybe even unfathomable to human eyes.

"Plus," she continues, "it's difficult to have to always be so *careful* here."

"Yeah." I nod in agreement. "It does seem like we're always being watched, doesn't it?"

"That's not what I mean." Vira pulls the top corner of her red jumpsuit down a few inches and points to her chest.

For a second, I get that freaked-out feeling, and it's hard to look away. I can see her heart beating, each of its several chambers pushing a shallow pink blood through her veins that web out into the rest of her body.

"When I am sad, my blood turns a sickly shade of midnight blue. When I'm overjoyed, it is a glowing amber color," she explains. "There is no way for me to hide it."

"What does pink mean?" I ask as I watch her blood course beneath her skin in amazement.

"It means that I am feeling nothing at all. I try to always stay void of emotion. It's the only way I can hide my true feelings about things."

"That sounds like a terrible way to live," I say with a frown. "Would it be so terrible for other people to know when you are feeling happy or sad?"

"Perhaps not. But it *would* be bad for them to see when I am feeling angry, or rebellious, or *murderous*."

I can't even picture this girl feeling murderous, but I get the point she is trying to make

"And this is even worse of a problem here," she says as she lifts one of the many braids of hair that she has piled up on her head away from her temple just enough so I can see the corner of her brain.

"Is that *me?*" I ask, looking at the tiny image playing out on the side of her skull, as if I am watching a miniature movie of myself.

"Yes, because I am talking to you now and thinking about what you are doing and how you will react. Every single thought I have is played out for everyone to see. Every image and every word are reflected on the tissue of my brain."

"Oh, wow," I gasp in awe. "That actually is truly horrible. You can never have a private thought."

"Exactly. On my home world, it was fine because it was the same for all my people, and no one meant harm to each other. But here is not the same. Here, I have to hide my thoughts or risk them getting me into trouble. That is why I always wear my hair up in braids like this." She carefully lowers her braid back down and looks at me with concern.

"I won't tell anyone," I say. "Your secret is safe with me."

"I wish I could say the same," Vira replies sadly. "But I physically cannot keep any thoughts or secrets hidden, not even my own."

We talk a bit more with the rest of our team, mostly about benign subjects, such as the food we are served for dinner on the ship and whether or not we will get issued a second jumpsuit if the mission takes a while to complete.

After the ship has reached a certain point in our trip, we are allowed to unbuckle ourselves and move around our areas. I am disappointed when the blues and reds remain on their respective sides.

Then there is a debriefing via the screens that surround the entire central area of the ship. The Intergalactic Union comes on and tells us another long, repetitive oration of our mission goals and expectations. I only half-listen to it because I've heard it a hundred times, and also because I don't really care anymore. If I think too deeply about any of this, it will draw me to the single conclusion that I am in charge of *killing* anyone who veers from their mandate, including *Ben*.

After the monologuing is over, which at least was given by one of the more attractive aliens from the Union instead of the one with too many teeth in his mouth, we are dismissed to go to our assigned sleeping pods on the ship.

"She's quite beautiful, isn't she?" Vira asks as we all get ready to head to bed.

"Who?"

"Ophelia."

"Who's Ophelia?"

Vira looks at me in a stupor. "Don't you know the names of the four Union delegates that briefed you before we left Nairu?"

I think about being in that containment pod, standing naked in front of the four people who sat behind the long desk. That seemed a lot more like an interrogation than a briefing to me.

"That one on the screen was Ophelia," she says once she realizes that I have no clue who any of the Union delegates actually are. "She's part *machine*. Then there's Mneu; you can tell him apart by the unusual number of teeth in his mouth. And Clyde—"

"Clyde? That sounds like a very *human* name," I interrupt.

"Well, I think his actual name is something like twenty-seven characters long, so they just call him Clyde. No idea where the shortened name came from, but he is definitely *not* human."

"Who is the one with the double pupils?" I ask. That is the woman I disliked the most. She has a malevolence that hangs in the air about her.

"*Pschye*. She's the most outspoken of the Union, I think. It's creepy the way that her hair moves all by itself; I don't think that's a natural attribute of Spewt. I think that is something distinctly pertaining to her."

I find it a little bit amusing that the girl with translucent skin and visible organs thinks that "moving hair" is creepy.

I head to my designated sleeping pod and get ready for bed, although there isn't much here for me to do. I have only the jumpsuit to wear, so I guess I'll be sleeping in that. They did treat me to a toothbrush, toothpaste, and a hairbrush, though. And there's a washcloth with a small bar of soap resting on the edge of the sink.

I tie my hair up into a messy brown bun on the top of my head, with long pieces already falling down around my face, and lather up the washcloth with soap. It feels good to wash my face, *normal*, almost like I am human again. Sometimes, it's easy to forget who I really am when I am surrounded by all this weirdness. Ben used to be my tether, the thing that grounded me. But now I can't even talk to him, and I feel lost, as if I am floating away beyond the ship and beyond myself.

For a moment, I look at the girl staring back at me in the mirror. I look tired.

My bright blue eyes pop, even against the dark circles beneath them. My mother used to tell me that my blue eyes were unusual. She used to say that "brown-haired girls with olive skin don't usually have such pale blue eyes." She used to tell me that I was a beautiful anomaly. But that was before I discovered that there are *so* many "anomalies" in existence, and they each have their own name.

I brush my teeth, and the mint of the toothpaste tastes good. It clears some of the hazy disbelief of all this from my head. I wonder, since the universe is constantly creating itself and birthing new possibilities and yet to be discovered places at every moment, if someday I will be able to go to a place that feels like *home* again. It's hard to be only a few years into adulthood and not know whether my future will be one of chance or not.

I turn from the bathroom and take the two steps it takes me to reach the bed. The sleeping pods are small but efficient. The Union likes when things are orderly and efficient. I think it gives them a sense of control.

Just as I sit down in the bed, I see a white slip of paper slide underneath the thin crack below the door. It looks like a note, but who could possibly be passing me a note right now? Probably Vira, since she is literally the only semi-friend that I have made here.

I stand up and bend down to reach for the paper, but as soon as I go to pull it, the note slides back under the door again.

"What the …?" I whisper to myself.

Not knowing what to expect, I open the door slowly and am shocked to see Ben on the other side of it with his finger over his lips to signal silence.

Everyone is in their sleeping pods, which means that no one is currently watching.

He steps into my pod with me and closes the door behind him.

"I snuck away to come and talk with you," he says quietly. His eyes look rather frantic. "I was worried you would be emotional and do something reckless."

"I'm surprised that you even *care*." I pout, feeling angry and indeed emotional at how he has been treating me as if I don't exist since we got through the containment pods.

"I'm sorry, Bex. Really, I am. I'm sorry I didn't tell you the truth. But if I had, then you wouldn't have gotten through the briefing."

He's probably right, but I'm still upset about being lied to and made to feel all alone here.

"Imagine how much worse that would be if I was sent on the mission and you were left behind as *disposable*. Imagine what they might have done to you."

"You're right," I sigh out. "But you really scared me. I thought you didn't want to be my friend anymore."

"Are you kidding?" Ben asks as he takes a step closer and reaches his hand up to cup the side of my face. "It's you and me against the world, Bex. Or in this case, *worlds*. I would never abandon or turn my back on you, and you should *always* remember that. But for right now, we have to go along with things to stay alive."

"What's going to happen after this, though?" I ask with audible worry in my voice.

"I don't know, but we'll figure this all out somehow…together."

Ben lingers inside the doorway for a few minutes. We don't say anything else because neither of us knows what to say. We're just standing there, staring in the dark and taking comfort in the sight of each other's faces again.

"I have to go," he says after a few minutes have passed. I can tell by the look on his face that he doesn't want to.

I don't want him to leave, either, but it's already too risky that he came. If anyone saw him here, it would be considered noncompliance, an offense worthy of triggering an assassin to follow their mandate and kill anyone who doesn't follow the rules implicitly.

All sorts of thoughts rush through my head as I look into Ben's eyes and desperately want him to stay. Things didn't feel this way before. They didn't feel so rushed and desperate. I thought that we would always have more time —more time to figure out what we meant to each other. It's a good thing that my thoughts aren't transparently viewable on my head like Vira's are. I would be mortified with embarrassment, considering that Ben and I have never acted in a way more than friends.

"Hang in there, Bex," he says as he touches the side of my arm for a fleeting moment.

When he leaves and slips down the hall quietly, I linger in the doorway of my pod for a second. I watch as Ben disappears into the darkness at the end of the hall where the blue team's sleeping pods are. But then, something catches my eye.

There's a flicker of light, something small that stands out against the dark hallway. I squint my eyes to look closer and can see Vira's eyes glowing from the doorway of her own pod like tiny luminous orbs.

She saw us. She saw Ben leave my pod.

I quickly step back inside my sleeping pod and close the door. Then I climb into my bed with my heart racing for multiple reasons as I press my eyes shut until I eventually fall asleep.

4

BEN

"What if they're all dead?" Petra asks as she pops a piece of toast in her mouth.

"Then it will make for a short mission," one of the red members replies as all ten of us sit at the long breakfast table together.

Bex sits across the table from me—blue on one side and red on the other—and sips her coffee in silence.

We are all allowed to gather together, just like Petra said, as long as it's the whole ten of us. I guess the Union thinks that the two teams will keep each other in check as long as no one gets too much alone time, and no one gets personally attached. In my opinion, that simply shows ignorance on their part. Regardless, it's the rule.

The journey to the other planet is a long one, and we still have the better part of a day on the ship together. When we get there, we are supposed to work as a team—harvest the resources, speak to the natives, and see how the humans fared with their attempt to restart a life for themselves on an empty planet. But as Petra's question poses, there's certainly a chance that we will be turning right back around and going home. If there's nothing to harvest and no one to speak with, then the mission is over. For some of the people here, that would be ideal. They just want to get back to Nairu and collect their payment. For others, it seems like a waste—a waste of time, and energy, and *life*.

I listen as everyone introduces themselves to the opposing team so we all know each other's names. I almost wish that we didn't. It will just make it worse if some of them end up getting shot by the assassins.

I watch Bex drink her coffee and stare down at the table in front of her as if her mind is somewhere else entirely. It's hard to think of her as an assassin.

"You two should both be more sensitive," Aerlon scolds. "Humans are Bex and Ben's people. How would you feel if you were about to find out if your own species met with extinction?"

Soro lets out a gruff laugh. "Spewt would never become extinct," he boasts. "We're too smart. And besides, we have representation on the Intergalactic Union. Our people are protected."

"If your people are so *protected*," I say, ignoring my own resolve not to get involved, "then why were you still forced to go on this mission?"

"*Forced?*" Ransor interjects. "Who said that some of us were forced? Most of us *chose* to come on this mission, either for money or honor. As far as I know, only you two *humans* were forced. The rest of us came here of our own free will."

I am surprised to hear that as I look around the table to see the reactions of the rest of the team. Bex looks up from her coffee. Apparently, she is just as surprised as I am.

I stare down the side of the table at the rest of my blue team.

"I came for the money," Jabber offers up without even being asked.

"Same," Petra says when I glance at her next. That surprises me. She doesn't seem like the type who would sell her soul. Maybe I was wrong about her.

I glance right past Soro because it's already obvious why he is here. He thinks this whole thing is fun. He gets to play bully to an innocent species. The Union made a mistake not putting him on the red team—he would make a great assassin. Although, perhaps that is exactly why they didn't put him on that side. He would likely kill everyone just for fun. Ransor strikes me as being the same.

"Lilybet?" I ask when my eyes fall on her last. She looks so fragile and timid that it doesn't seem plausible she would volunteer for something like this.

"My family made me come," she says, looking ashamed of her answer. "My father wants the money, and my mother wants to earn favor with the Union. I know I'm old enough not to listen to them, but there are a whole lot of people who don't even have families anymore, so I'm trying to hold mine together."

"By being bartered off by them?" Bex asks from the other end of the table.

Everyone turns to look at her, surprised that she broke her long silence, and surprised at her blunt question.

"Eh, don't mind them," Jabber says to Lilybet, as if he is trying to be her ally. "They're just upset that they didn't have a choice in the matter and the rest of us did." He turns to face me next. "You should both be grateful—you're both still getting paid."

I don't even know what to do with the currency on

Nairu. Food, clothing, and all the basic necessities are provided to us by the Union at no cost. It's not as if we are allowed to travel anywhere or indulge in anything, so what use do I have for the local currency?

"It could take several days or even more, depending on the kind of condition and demeanor any surviving humans are in," Peck says, changing the topic before it gets any more heated.

He's right. There's simply no way to tell until we get there. The assassins and emissaries are supposed to work together—ideally, for the entire mission, if everyone follows the rules. It's a fine line we are all treading of being friends and teammates, but also realizing that if anyone steps out of line, they will likely be killed by members of our own team of ten.

As tense as the situation is for all of us, it's even *more* tense for me and Bex. I keep trying not to look at her, for fear I won't be able to hide the look of care and concern in my eyes. But I accidentally make the mistake of glancing over at her during one of the more heated moments of conversation, and Ransor catches it.

As soon as I can feel him looking at me, I stare right back at him, holding his eyes in a glare. What is it with these Spewts? Why do they always seem to want to pick a fight? It's as if they thrive on controversy and conflict.

I realize that I have unintentionally just put a target on my back. If Ransor so much as *thinks* that I am breaking formation, he's going to enjoy the opportunity to put a bullet in my skull. I also now know that Bex needs to be careful of this guy. At least she has a weapon to offer some defense of herself. The blue team wasn't given weapons because our role doesn't require them. I'm glad that Soro doesn't have one, but I really wish that I did.

WHEN WE FINALLY REACH THE PLANET, OUR ENTIRE TEAM OF ten gears up and disembarks the ship to survey the situation with the humans here. Since we have no idea what we are walking into, it's at least good that we get to start out as a cohesive team. That way, I can keep an eye on Bex for now. As long as everyone stays on mission, there will be no reason for any of us to turn against each other, and no reason for a red assassin to shoot.

At first, the surroundings look pretty dismal. There is no trace of the human population that was left here. There *are*, however, signs of destruction.

"This is sad," Vira says as she pulls the collar on her jumpsuit up until it almost touches the bottom of her chin. It looks like she is trying to cover up the spidery-looking blueish veins that are spreading up her neck. "This looks almost identical to what I read about the original human population on Earth. Instead of protecting their world, they damaged it and demolished all its resources they needed in order to survive. And then they turned on each other and started to kill their fellow people in some sort of delusional power grab at individual survival."

She's not wrong. That does about sum up what happened on Earth. And I'm guessing by the looks of this desolate place that the humans here have made the same mistake. There are signs that indicate they *tried* to build a rough infrastructure and grow sustainability, but it all looks destroyed now. There are only a few remaining remnants and shambles now. And since there aren't any humans in sight, it's fair to assume that they wiped each other out, too.

"Whelp, like I said," Ransor sneered, "it's going to be a quick mission."

We all get ready to turn around and head back to the ship, but then Petra stops and points into the nearby trees.

"Look, there!" she says.

I can see what caught her eye. There's a young human girl there, watching us from behind some of the overgrown foliage.

"Hello," Petra says as she slowly takes a few steps toward the girl, but as soon as Petra makes a move to approach her, the girl runs. Petra starts to run after her, too.

"What are you doing?" Ransor shouts after her. "Come back here right now! We all need to stay together or you risk breaking protocol."

"I'm not breaking protocol, you buffoon," Petra calls back over her shoulder. "I'm getting what we came here to get."

"Stop right now, or *I will shoot*," Ransor growls at her.

Instantly, Petra slides to a stop.

"What in the hell are you doing?" Bex says to him.

I am shocked that she is confronting him. Bex doesn't have a controversial bone in her entire body. And right now isn't the time to suddenly get bold.

Everyone looks at her in surprise, and she even looks surprised with herself. Nevertheless, she continues.

"There is no reason for any of us to go turning on each other," Bex says as she instantly comes to Petra's defense. "Just because we are the red team and serving as assassins doesn't give you the right to go off the rails like a lunatic. Nobody made you the boss."

The rest of her team stares at her in astonishment, and I get ready to jump in, knowing that Ransor isn't going to take this verbal scuffle lightly. He's going to take it as a challenge to his authority and his ego, and that means that he's going to lash out. For guys like him, there's nothing worse than making them look like a fool.

Fortunately, before I have to come to her defense and put us both at further risk of being on the opposite side of this mission from the rest of the people with the guns, we are interrupted.

The scuffle is instantly dropped when we see *humans* approaching us. This time, it isn't just the young girl, but also a man and woman. This is good news—there are humans here still alive.

But there is also now a perceivable threat level between Bex and Ransor. I can see it, because while everyone else is staring at the humans who are walking toward us, Ransor won't take his eyes off Bex. He is glaring at her so furiously, he looks as if he wants to kill her on the spot. They are supposed to be on the same side of the teams here, and instead, he now looks at Bex as if she is his number one enemy.

5

BEX

"I am Amity," the woman says with a cautious smile. "And this is Ned."

The two humans stand before us, with the young gurl standing halfway hidden behind them so only the side of her face is peering around from behind Amity's thigh.

"And this is Clover," Ned says with a chuckle as he introduces the girl. "Who are you and why are you here? Are you human, too?" He is looking straight at me, so I take a step closer to them to explain.

"Yes, I'm human, and this is Ben," I say as I motion for him to walk up beside me. "He's human, too. We are all a team of members sent from the Intergalactic Union to check on you. The Union sent us here to see if your people have survived and been able to regrow your civilization on this planet." Even as I say it, I can tell they obviously haven't succeeded.

This planet, which was once empty aside from some ground cover and patches of trees—and maybe a single water source—still looks empty.

"The Intergalactic Union?" Amity asks with a look of distaste.

I don't blame her one bit. The Union is what sent her and her people here to begin with, on this plight to either survive or die, depending on their whim. I would be pissed, too.

"The Intergalactic Union *abandoned* us here," the woman says with a look of desperation. "We did our best to survive."

"And it looks like you have," Ben says as he tries to point out something positive and act the role of emissary as he is supposed to. "We aren't here to interfere. We were sent to see how you have progressed and check for planetary resources that might be useful to the Union."

"Where are all the rest of the humans?" Jabber interrupts. "We were told there were a few dozen of you."

"There *were*," Ned answers.

"Come," Amity says before anyone has a chance to elaborate on the question. "We can show you where we live and how we have survived here."

I smile at her and follow as she and Ned take Clover's hands and lead us to another part of the terrain.

As the rest of our team follows closely behind, Ben asks the other humans some more questions.

"What caused all of the destruction back there where our ship landed?" he asks. "It seems like you might have started to build some dwellings, and what looked like even a water collection and filtering system, but everything looks as though it was destroyed."

"It was." Amity doesn't look up as she explains. She watches her feet as if it pains her to tell the story of what happened here. "We tried to replenish and repopulate the planet in order to assure not only our survival, but also try to make a place that felt like home, one that would function and thrive, and maybe someday be like Earth before it fell to ruin. Things were difficult at first, for a long while, but they were heading in a positive direction. But then, just recently, the *big fight* happened."

"The big fight?"

"Yes, it pitted our people against each other, and war broke out amongst us."

"What was the big fight about?" Vira asks.

Ned looks over his shoulder at her with sad eyes full of loss, and he answers her with a single word. "*Hope.*"

Lilybet hastens her pace a bit to walk closer beside us so she can talk to the humans, too.

"It sounds odd that there would be a fight over a concept as peaceful and innocuous as hope," she says. "Hope is the kind of thing that should have brought all of you humans together in a common purpose of survival and creation of a new world."

Ned shakes his head. "Hope isn't a concept," he says, much to everyone's surprise. "It's a person."

There isn't time to ask him to expand on his strange response because we arrive at the humans' dwelling. It is nothing more than a makeshift hut with rooms made out of hanging woven fabrics that section off portions of the space. But perhaps the most surprising thing about it is that it looks empty.

Amity seems to notice everyone looking around, as if they are expecting to see other people here.

"Sadly," she says, "the big fight destroyed almost all of us who were first brought here. There are only four of us left."

"Four?" Soro asks in disbelief. "Out of three dozen? Where's the fourth human?"

Amity turns and motions for us to follow her a few steps into another section of their dwelling. She lifts a curtain covering the back corner of the enclosed space, and there, lying behind the curtained off section, is an extremely beautiful, extremely *pregnant*, and sick-looking woman.

"This," she says as she smiles sadly down at the woman, "is Hope."

None of us know what to say. We all stand there, dumb-founded, as we stare at the woman sound asleep on the bed. I don't know whether to be hopeful or horrified. And I don't know what in the world we are supposed to do with this situation. The Intergalactic Union prepared us for handling two potential outcomes. The first was that the human population was alive and productively carving out a new life here as they restored a nearly dead planet. The second was that they were all dead and there was nothing here. But the Union never prepared us for *this*. There was never any mention of the chance that the actual thing we found would be something that fell in between those other two potential scenarios. This is a different thing altogether —a withered, nearly annihilated species with just a few battle-worn people still holding onto life. And a planet in nearly the same predicament as it was before all this.

"Come, you must be tired and hungry from your journey here," Ned says. "We will share our food with you and can explain further what has happened here."

As we all sit around the small fire that Ned built, sharing the miniscule rations of food they have foraged, I feel guilty for eating any of it and taking it from their own mouths. We have food on the ship, but Amity insists that we sit and share with them, and I don't want to offend her. These are kind people. You can see it in their eyes.

The young girl still hasn't said anything at all. She sits

between Amity and Ned, but she looks nothing like either of them. They are light-skinned, and Clover is distinctly ebony. She hastily gobbles down her food—a few bits of dried meat and several nuts that she has to crack from their shells. There must be wildlife here if meat was found and hunted. But those questions about sustainability can wait. First, we are all eager to hear what has happened to the rest of the humans.

All ten of us gather around as Ned begins to explain. He talks softly in a low voice that won't disturb Hope, who has still yet to open her eyes since we arrived.

"At the beginning," Ned begins, "some of the others were too frail to survive the hardest days. Many of the women and children perished within the first week. There wasn't much food, and we hadn't found the water source yet, so we were trying our best to collect the rainwater, which was scarce. The temperatures were cold, and it took some time to build shelters. By the time we were able to get a handle on things, we had already lost quite a few. Those who remained were mostly men, with the exception of Amity, Clover, and Hope."

Ned pauses there and scowls, as if he is too disgusted by the rest of the story to tell it, so Amity takes over where he left off.

"Most of the men were focused on ensuring the survival of a bloodline, claiming it was the only true way to ensure the survival of the species. Since I am sterile, and Clover is just a child, Hope was the only one who could conceive a child."

I can already tell I don't like where this is going.

"All of the men wanted Hope," she continues. "All of them except for Ned. His wife was one of the ones who had died earlier on. The rest of the men tried relentlessly to win favor with Hope, and some of them got very agitated and impatient. Eventually, she grew fond of one of them. When he managed to impregnate her, the other men grew furious. They all fought over her, all of them wanting to claim her and her unborn child and try to breed even more children once this one was born. The man who Hope had favored was slaughtered by the others, and then they all turned to fighting each other. Everyone aside from the four of us ended up dead. Since Ned was the only man who wasn't interested in Hope, for his own reasons, he protected her and saved her life during the fight. I saved Clover here from being killed as collateral damage. Her parents were also some of the first to have perished."

"This is a terrible and heartbreaking story," Vira says. I can see her trying to pull up the collar on her jumpsuit again to hide the changing color of her blood that is matching her distressed emotions.

"What is wrong with Hope?" Petra asks. "Aside from being hugely pregnant, she doesn't look well."

"She's not," Ned answers. "She was wounded in the fight before I could manage to get her away from it and take her into hiding until the fight was over. Her wounds became badly infected, and now she is dying. We've been trying to keep her alive long enough to birth her baby. It will be the first *new* child of the human species."

"This is an absolutely incredible story," Ben says in astonishment. "To think that the four of you have survived all of this here, in this desolate place, and against all odds. You are truly a measure of strength and courage."

There is a small sound that comes from behind the curtain, and Clover jumps up to her feet.

"Hope," she says, uttering the first word that I have heard her say.

Amity nods, as if to tell Clover that she can go and bring Hope some food now that she is awake, and the girl runs off with a handful of nuts, her fingers wrapped around a small pile of the dried meat. She can't be more than ten or so, and what a traumatic existence she has had.

For a few quiet minutes, everyone eats and drinks in silence. There are some of us here who have been quiet this entire time. Peck hasn't said a single word since the humans appeared, and Aerlon seems to stare at Amity as if he cannot take his eyes off her. I wonder what is going through their heads. Mostly, I wonder what is going through Ransor's head.

I couldn't care less about his bone to pick with me, but I do care that he seems to think he is the one in charge of this mission. As he eats his meat, he looks from one of the humans to the next, eyeing them as if they are of no greater worth than the dried jerky he is shoving into his mouth.

6

BEN

At night, the planet is strangely lit by a lavender moon. I've never seen a colored moon before, although I have heard that they exist. It makes the entire surface of the world look basked in a magical twilight, which would actually be pretty cool if it weren't for the dire situation that we found these people in.

While the humans from this planet go back to their meager dwelling to sleep, the rest of us gather outside to sit and talk under the purplish light, discussing what we are going to do. We will need to report back to the Intergalactic Union soon, and I'm not sure that we are even confident in what we've found.

"We need to help these poor people," Vira says with empathy in her eyes. She seems like a decent soul. I'm glad there is at least one person on the red team who seems like someone Bex can talk with.

"Help them how?" Soro asks. "It's not as if there is much here to salvage. This is all just scraps."

"How can you say that?" Petra lays into him. "There is

plenty here to salvage. That woman in there is almost ready to birth the first new child of their species. That could be the beginning of rebirthing their entire population."

Soro scoffs at her. "Oh, please," he says dismissively. "That pathetic creature in there is nearly half-dead already. Her child won't have the substance to survive. It's honestly a cruelty that we let them drag this on any further."

"What are you saying?" Bex asks.

Soro gives her a look of annoyance, as if he has picked up on clues from Ransor that Bex is a problem and shouldn't be given any validation at all. "I'm *saying* that it's not worth our time or resources on this mission to put any more energy into trying to save these people."

His remark sparks an abrupt burst into discourse between the two teams. Everyone on the blue team—aside from Soro—wants to try to help the humans. They all initially want to bring the humans back with us to Nairu in order to save their species. But as the conversations continue, and Soro and Ransor continue to point out all the ways in which it's a bad idea—and all the ways in which the Intergalactic Union will frown on the choice to save the already feeble human survivors—some of the blue team members start to bend and lose their inclination to go against the grain of salt, especially if it could mean trouble for them. Jabber and Lilybet are the first to waiver.

"I don't think the Union will be very pleased with the decision to bring the humans back to Nairu," Lilybet says with a look of guilt in her eyes. "They told us to bring back resources and news of a thriving human population. They didn't tell us to turn this into a rescue mission."

"I agree," Jabber echoes. "If they wanted us to *help* these people, then they would have sent us here on a humanitarian mission, but they didn't. Our instructions were pretty clear, and I, for one, don't intend to break them."

Petra rolls her eyes at the both of them. "The two of you are pathetic," she scolds. "In it for yourselves, and you couldn't care less about the extinction of an entire species."

"That's not fair," Lilybet argues. "The Union will consider it *off mission* to bring the humans back to Nairu after they failed to rekindle a thriving existence. As much as we might want to bring them with us, just think of the consequences that could await us if we do."

"So, what exactly is your opinion on the matter then?" I ask, wanting them to answer clearly where they stand.

"We'll go along with whatever the entire team of members decides," Jabber says as he looks around at everyone. His eyes take an extra second or two when he looks at Ransor. Why is it that everyone is so afraid of that guy? He's nothing but a big bully.

"I agree with Soro," Ransor says, as if we all didn't already know that. "It's a bad idea."

Ransor looks around at everyone, as if he is measuring them up before continuing. "And I will remind everyone that instructions were also given as to what we are supposed to do if we found the species unable to meet the requirements of the Union. If the humans were not successful in regenerating the planet and mastering their survival, and if they are not able to become viably cooperative with the Intergalactic Union, then our instructions are to *kill* them, leave the planet as a wasteland, and go back home to Nairu."

Before she utters a single sound, I can already tell that Bex is going to be instantly triggered by what Ransor has just said. He knows it, too, and that's part of the reason he said it.

"You've *got* to be kidding," Bex hisses at him. "They are good people, and Hope is pregnant with *new life*. I am adamantly opposed to the idea of harming any of them."

"As am I," Vira says in support of Bex. "If we aren't going to help them, then the very least we can do is leave them alone and go back to Nairu without harming them."

Peck nods his head in agreement, and Aerlon sits there, strangely silent as he looks off in the direction of the human dwelling without giving any reaction at all.

The conversation continues and becomes more heated. Everyone takes sides on the issue of what we should do. There are more of us that want to either help the humans or at least leave them in peace, but those who are opposed to it are louder and more vicious about it than the others. We are divided not by the color of our team, but by our morality—or lack thereof.

I sit back from the arguing for a few moments to watch and listen. There are allegiances being broken now, with some members not agreeing with the rest of their team. And there might also be unlikely alliances forming, too, crossing the lines of red and blue to undermine the others. This is a dangerous situation.

I look across at Bex and see she can see it, too. She is carefully watching not only Ransor and Soro, but those who seek to follow the direction of whomever they fear the most. If we continue to sit here and argue, nothing will be solved and more tempers will flare. So, I offer up a temporary solution that I am surprised to hear myself say.

"We should go back to the ship and contact the Union."

I can feel Bex staring at me in surprise. I know what she is thinking, too—*the Union is not on our side*—and she is right to think that. But we need something to buy us more time. If we don't stop this argument amongst us, it won't take much before Ransor goes off the rails and starts to threaten people with noncompliance. I don't particularly want to see anyone on our team get shot tonight.

"Good idea," Soro says, as if he somehow thinks that my suggestion is in support of his position to scrap the humans.

All ten of us go back to the ship and use the communications link to bring the Intergalactic Union up on the screens. Not surprisingly, it is Pschye whose face stares back at us through the screens. She seems to have a personal interest in making sure our mission is carried out without any "issues." When she sees the entire team sitting in the central bay of the ship, looking back at her, it doesn't take her long to surmise that we have run into a problem.

Before Ransor has a chance to open his big mouth and sway the Union to his position, I launch into an explanation of what we have found. I give special emphasis on certain key points, like the fact that there is a woman with child who could bring a new phase of life for the humans, and the fact that those few humans who remain are brave, intelligent, and resourceful. Surprisingly, no one interrupts me while I verbally unpack the scene for Pschye.

When I have finished, it suddenly dawns on me how unusual it is that there is only *one* Union delegate on this communications call. Where are the other three? It is rare that the four of them aren't together when responding to a mission inquiry.

I expect that Ransor or Soro will now launch into their explanations about why we should leave the humans here, or even worse, *kill them*. But much to my surprise, they both stand there obediently silent, waiting for Pschye to respond. I do notice, though, that she seems to share a mutual glance with the both of them, and I wonder if it has something to do with the fact that all three of them are Spewt, or if there is something more that isn't discernible on the surface.

"You have made the right decision to call and seek an answer from the Union on this matter," Pschye says. "We always prefer that you clarify with us if you are confused rather than take matters into your own hands and risk *tarnishing* the mission."

Her choice of words rubs me the wrong way, as if the Union sees all ten of us as utterly disposable in the event that our entire mission failed.

"The Union's answer is this: kill all of the remaining humans in the morning, and then return home to Nairu."

"But—"

Ransor instantly squashes Bex's attempt to interject as he begins to talk over her, thanking Pschye for clearing up the matter with swift resolution and apologizing for bothering her.

Without any further discussion or chance to question the command that was given, Pschye ends the communication link, and the screens go black.

The matter is now solved, and there is no more debate. Everyone knows what we must do now, whether we want to or not, because the Union has given a directive, and *all* directives must be followed.

Ransor and Soro both grin with satisfaction as everyone stands up and gets ready to go to their sleeping pods.

"Glad that is settled," Ransor says. "Now I can sleep well."

I can see Bex getting ready to open her mouth, so I jump in to stop her, but Vira stops her first.

"It's not worth getting into another argument about," Vira says to her quietly. "The Union has spoken on the matter, and there is nothing left we can do."

Ransor looks over his shoulder at the two of them. "Yes, that's right; there is nothing left you can do, Bex. But since there are only four humans and five assassins, I'll make it easy on you. You don't have to kill one of them. You can just *watch* while the rest of us do it."

Everyone gets ready to go to their sleeping pods and rest until morning. Bex stands there, unmoving in defiance, but her defiance doesn't matter now. It won't change anything. I wish I could go to her sleeping pod again tonight and sit up and talk with her all through the night like we used to do in the ship cockpits. At least then I could try to make this all feel a little easier for her. But I can't risk getting caught. There are too many eyes watching now, and too many feelings of suspicions everywhere. Instead, I take my time walking slowly past her on my way to my sleeping pod, pausing to say a few quick words as I brush by her.

"We will finish the mission and leave," I whisper to her. "Then we can be done with this, and things can go back to how they were before."

She turns her face to me just as I get ready to walk away. "Things can't ever go back to the way they were before," she says, voice shaking. "Not anymore."

I have to fight against myself to keep walking all the way to my sleeping pod without turning around and going back to her. I want to know what she meant by that, and I want to try to talk her out of whatever is running through her head. I know that look in her eyes—she wants to do something reckless. I just hope she can wait until we get out of here and until I find a way to get around all these stupid rules. We just need to get back to Nairu, then I'll head straight to the Rigsaru and fix this mess with a new look to hide behind. Then Bex and I can talk about everything, and I will find a way for us to survive under the Intergalactic Union's thumb.

But even as I tell myself that while I get ready for bed, I know I don't believe it. I stare at my reflection in the bathroom mirror of my sleeping pod, and I know I can't let any of this happen. I can't let innocent humans be slaughtered, and I can't watch as Bex twists around herself in emotional ruin. I have to do something, but I have no idea what.

Instead of getting in my bed, I open the door of my pod and stand in the doorway, looking out into the dark, empty hallway. I just need to get some air. Staying in those pods and on this ship is restricting, and I'm starting to find it hard to have room to breathe.

I look down the hall in the direction of the blue hallway, where Bex is most likely still awake in her pod as well. And then I *see* something.

I tuck back into the doorway so I am not spotted, but I continue to peek out into the hall, trying to make out what it is and whose figure I see slipping out of the ship.

It's Aerlon.

What in the world is he doing?

I grab my jacket and follow him. We aren't supposed to leave the ship alone. We're only supposed to go as either our team of ten or our teams of five. Maybe he needs some air, too, and is taking a walk to clear his head in the lavender moonlight.

I follow him to see what he is doing, with no intention of telling the others that he is breaking the rules. But as I follow his path, I begin to see where he is heading—to the human dwelling.

He's going to go and wake the humans, and he's going to *warn* them.

7

BEX

There was no way in hell that I was just going to climb into my bed and go to sleep tonight. Trouble is brewing. I can *feel* it.

In the morning, our directive from the Intergalactic Union is to kill the four surviving humans—*five* if you count the unborn child in Hope's womb. More than half of us are against it—in theory, at least. There are some of us who will refuse, and others who don't want to kill anyone but will go along with pulling the trigger simply because they fear the consequences if they don't.

But as I stand just inside the open doorway to my sleeping pod and watch the silent hallways, I think how there are also those of us who will be driven to act against such a violent and senseless thing.

The first sign of movement I see at the other end of the hallway is Aerlon. I watch as he inches carefully down the hallway and then off the ship. I am just getting ready to follow after him when I see *Ben*.

I wait as Ben follows Aerlon out of the ship, and then I

make my move to join them. I keep a distance behind them both, not wanting either to tell me to turn around. I want to see what they're doing. If it has anything to do with saving the humans, then I want in.

When Aerlon reaches the human dwelling, he slips inside with Ben right behind him. I follow both on their heels. Aerlon doesn't know we are behind him, and both Ben and I watch as he gently touches Amity in order to wake her without causing her to be fearful. She sits up, and then stands and wakes Ned beside her as Aerlon quickly begins to warn her of what is going to happen in the morning. His voice is quiet and measured, and I know he doesn't want to wake either of the other two.

Just as he finishes telling them what the other members are preparing to do, based on a direct order from the Union, my arm nudges against something in the dwelling that causes a small creak. Both Ben and Aerlon turn to see me there, and Aerlon instantly gets a look of panic on his perfectly chiseled face.

"What are the two of you doing here?" he asks with audible worry.

"Well, *I* was following you to see where you were going," Ben says as he gives me a look. "And I guess Bex was following *me*."

"Please," Aerlon says in a panic. "You can't tell the others. They'll slaughter all of them."

"Don't worry," I say as I step forward now and stand next to Ben. "We are both on your side. We don't want the humans to be slaughtered, either."

Aerlon looks relieved, and I wonder why he would have risked his life by coming here to warn the humans to begin with. It isn't as if his life is on the line, not as long as he goes along with the team.

But then, when he glances back at Amity with a look of such utter relief, I think that I can see the answer. He cares about her. Strange. There are so many species of people on Nairu, and so many of them don't care about anything at all, that it almost seemed like caring was a distinctly human trait. Although, many could argue that the humans can be every bit as selfish and brutal as the rest of them. If nothing else, this mission so far has opened my eyes to the fact that there are other friends on Nairu who think like Ben and I do. Unfortunately, we are still outnumbered by the ones who do not.

"We need to come up with a viable plan," Ben says. "And fast. We don't have much time before morning, and by then, it will be too late."

"We could try to go further into the wild and hide," Ned suggests.

"No, that won't work. The team knows you are here. They won't return to the Intergalactic Union without having achieved the directive. They can't return from a failed mission without sacrificing their promised payment and receiving a punishment," Ben explains. "Trust me, some of those guys would rather stay here and hunt you down, no matter how long it takes, rather than go back to Nairu and tell the Union that they failed."

"He is right," Aerlon echoes. "Our only chance is to get all of you off the planet."

"Do you have another ship?" Amity asks. I can see the small glimmer of hope in her eyes that will quickly fade when she finds out we do not.

"No. But there is an escape pod on the ship that we came on."

I look over at Ben. He's got to be crazy for even thinking the idea brewing in his head will work. The escape

THE EMISSARY OF NAIRU · 55

pod is *tiny*. It's not much bigger than our sleeping pods, and there are a total of seven of us standing here. Plus, the escape pods are meant for just that—*escape*. They don't have full navigational systems and only a small tank of fuel. It's not as if they can be flown around the galaxy on a trip somewhere.

"Do you think we could detach the escape pod without waking the others?" Aerlon asks.

I can't believe they are even considering this as a good idea.

"Yes." Ben nods. "I think if we do it fast and do it now, there's a chance we can get everyone on it in time. Everyone will hear when the engines start up, but if we're quick enough, we should be able to get off the surface before they can stop us."

"This is crazy," I mutter. "We will have nowhere to go. There are countless planets out there, but we have no way of knowing if the escape pod will make it to reach any of them, or even which ones are hospitable and which are not. We would never be able to return to Nairu because the Intergalactic Union would kill us on sight for being traitors and stealing a pod."

"Do you really ever want to return to Nairu?" Ben asks.

He has a point.

On Nairu, we would now be labeled as members for the rest of our lives. I would be red, and he would be blue, and we wouldn't be allowed to be friends anymore. I know he thinks he can find some sort of workaround, but the chances of it actually working are slim. I would rather take my chances on an escape pod than know with certainty that I will lose my only true friend.

"You're right," I say. "Let's do it."

"There's another problem that we have to contend with," Amity interjects. "Hope is too weak to travel."

The four of us stand there, talking quietly for a while longer, weighing the risks and lack of options and making a plan into the wee hours of the night. The lavender sky gets a deeper hue overhead, indicating that it is time for action before it gets too dangerously close to morning. In the end, we are all in agreement. We need to take the risk and leave now. Otherwise, the humans are surely dead anyway, and likely, so are we once Ransor and the others find out what we have been plotting.

Ben and Aerlon go back to the ship to steal the escape pod while I stay with the humans and wake Hope and Clover to prepare them to leave. When it seems as if it is taking too long, I get worried.

"I'm going to go back to the ship and make sure everything is okay," I tell Ned.

"It's almost morning," he says anxiously. "Soon, it will be too late."

"I know." I look around in frustration. There won't be enough time for me to go all the way to the ship and back here to get them. They're going to need to meet us halfway. "Can you bring everyone with you toward the ship's location? Ben will bring the escape pod in this direction, but you'll need to meet us halfway."

Ned nods, and I give Amity a quick glance before I turn to leave. She looks worried, and so am I.

I run all the way back to the ship, then stand quietly outside, listening. I can hear the sounds of the escape pod being detached. It's a lot louder than I expected—loud enough to wake everyone on the ship.

"Come on, *come on*," I whisper to myself as I wait anxiously to see the escape pod come into view.

As soon as it does, and as soon as I can see Ben at the helm of it and Aerlon waving me on from the window beside him, I hear a noise coming through the belly of the ship.

"Wake up! Everyone wake up!" Soro shouts at the top of his lungs as he comes barreling out of the ship to see what is going on.

He's on the blue team. He's not even an assassin. Soro doesn't have to be ratting us out, but he is. I have a suspicion that he and Ransor were friends before this mission even started. And just because Soro put on a blue jumpsuit doesn't make him an emissary. Aggression is in his nature as a Spewt.

"What the hell are you shouting about?" Ransor yells as he comes to see what all the commotion is about.

"It's an *insurgency*," Soro tells him as he points toward the escape pod, which is slowly making its way across the terrain toward the humans.

I can see Amity and Ned coming in this distance, and I think I can make out Clover helping Hope to walk beside her.

Why can't the escape pod go any faster?

"They're trying to rescue the humans," Ransor snarls. "Go and get the others out of bed."

Vira is already walking off the ship as Soro pushes past her to rouse everyone else on the team.

"What's going on?" she asks as she rubs her sleepy eyes and looks around.

I wonder if the color gray means that she is tired, because I can see the veins in her wrist filled with streams of grayish blood that looks the color of graphite. She looks over and spots me still hiding around the corner of the ship, and then a look of horror comes over her face.

Everyone else quickly files out of the ship and gathers around Ransor, staring at the moving escape pod in shock.

"They're trying to rescue the humans," Ransor tells them. "Apprehend them!"

"We aren't assassins," Petra barks without fear. "Apprehend them yourself. Our job description is to be emissaries, nothing more than that."

Ransor glares at her with contempt, but he knows he can't argue that point because it was the Intergalactic Union that divvied out the jobs. Even he knows well enough not to go against the Union.

"Fine," he hisses. "Then stay out of our way unless you want to be labeled a traitor and shot down yourself."

I watch as the escape pod gets closer to the humans, and I watch as Ransor and Soro pull their weapons out and run toward the pod. Ransor calls over his shoulder for Peck and Vira to come on. Peck reluctantly pulls out his weapon and joins them, but Vira stays in place.

"You're a coward, Peck!" she shouts.

"Maybe," Peck says with a shrug. "But if you don't join us, then you're *dead*."

Vira looks as if she is going to cry, but she holds strong to her convictions and runs toward me instead.

"What are you doing?" I ask as she grabs me by the hand and gives away my hiding spot.

"We need to *run*," she says, pulling me alongside her and taking off toward the escape pod. "If you stay there hiding behind the ship, you won't make it in time."

She's right, and she's actually a lot braver than I gave her credit for.

The entire scene is a mess. Vira and I are running toward the pod, which is crawling toward the humans, who are trying desperately to reach it before the assassins get within range to shoot them down. The rest of the blue team just stands there, dumbfounded at the chaos unfolding. Petra starts to walk toward the rest of us, and I can't tell what she is planning to do yet. But Lilybet and Jabber just stand out of the way like obedient dogs.

As all of us converge onto a single spot, the hatch on the escape pod opens, and Aerlon jumps out to help the humans get on the pod as Ben starts to rev up the tiny vessel's engines.

A fight erupts right outside the open hatch as Aerlon tries to evacuate the humans onto the pod and escape the planet. Ransor and Soro both fire shots. Fortunately, their aim sucks, and the guns only have a few rounds each. The weapons weren't designed for battle; they were designed for single-fire assassinations. I guess the Union didn't count on the Spewt having such poor aim.

"Shoot, dammit!" Ransor yells at Peck, who still has a loaded gun. "Shoot the humans! Use those nine fingers to pull the damn trigger!"

Peck hesitates until Ransor starts to move toward him in a threatening stride.

Vira and I are almost there, and Aerlon has already helped Amity and Clover onto the ship. He is reaching down to carefully lift up Hope now. But Peck truly *is* a coward, and cowards are easily coerced by threats. Even though his heart really isn't in it, Peck aims his gun and shoots at the only human he can still see—*Hope*.

He fires once in the chest, once in the stomach, and last squarely in her head. Instantly, Hope drops to the ground, her body crumbling over itself. Instantly, the shots have killed both her and the unborn human child.

Vira lets go of my hand and runs to try to save her, but it is too late. She bursts into tears. Aerlon thinks quickly and grabs Vira, hoisting her up onto the ship instead. I stop running, even though I am only steps away from the pod. I don't even mean to. I don't even realize that my feet have stopped moving. I am simply in shock as I look at Hope's beautiful corpse spilling more blood onto the ground than I have ever seen in one place.

I can hear Ben's voice screaming at me to come to the pod, and I can see Aerlon reaching out his hand to motion me closer, but I am frozen.

Until…I hear the sound of more gunshots.

It's impossible. Peck should be out of rounds after shooting at Hope.

I turn my head to look and see Petra, with a look of absolute fury, walking backward toward me as she shoots at the rest of the team to keep them back.

"You disgusting, motherfucking pigs!" she shouts as she reaches for me and clasps her fist tightly around my arm to pull me with her. She shoots again, creating a cover for us to reach the pod until Aerlon reaches down and lifts me up into it. "Do you have any idea what you just did?" Petra screams at Peck with rage as she jumps up into the pod herself. "You gruesomely slaughtered a pregnant female in order to save your own pathetic hide, you worthless piece of shit!"

As soon as Petra is all the way in the pod, Aerlon closes the hatch, and we are all crammed together in the tight space. Ben throttles the engine to full blast and uses the limited navigational systems to steer us off this planet as I sit down in the cockpit seat beside him.

"The other ship can chase us down in a heartbeat," I say in a bit of a breathless panic. "We didn't think this through. They're going to be able to catch us before we can get away."

I can see Ransor and the others running back toward the ship to do exactly that.

"Don't worry," Petra says as she sticks the gun that she had to have stolen off one of the assassins back into the pocket of her jumpsuit. "I always make sure to have a backup plan just in case things go sideways."

I am just about to ask her what that means when I see the ship on the planet's surface *explode* into flames. I don't know how she did it, or why, but Petra saved us. It was not without cost, though.

I look over at Vira as she consoles Clover over Hope's death and the loss of the special unborn child. We may have saved these three humans, but we failed to save Hope and the baby. And we are now inside this metal pod with no certain future.

In the corner of the small pod, Ned and Aerlon sit on either side of Amity. Each of them seems to have a strange sort of protective dynamic that resonates between the three of them.

At least we managed to save *some* of them. If we hadn't, then all four of the humans would be dead, and likely a few of our teammates, too.

Ben doesn't say anything, probably because he doesn't even know what words to say that would make this situation seem any less dire. He just stares out ahead as he pilots the escape pod forward into an unknown destination.

Without thinking about it first, I reach over and hold his hand.

8

BEN

While the others on the escape pod sleep out of sheer exhaustion, Bex and I whisper together in the tiny cockpit. It reminds me a little of what we used to do on Nairu before we got sent on this hellish mission.

There weren't a lot of places for privacy without the ears of the Union eavesdropping over everything, so Bex and I would sneak into the cockpits late at night and close the hatch. Inside, all sound of our talking was kept in. We would sit there in the dark with only the glow of the overhead lights outside, and we would talk until we fell asleep. Once, we nearly got caught because we slept almost late enough for the mechanics to come and do their routine checks.

It's funny to think about how dangerous and daring that felt then, but now that we are here, in this escape pod, fleeing for our lives toward no particular destination, that doesn't seem quite so daring anymore.

"What are we going to do now that we are renegades?"

Bex asks. She sounds worried and tired, but I still can't help but smile at her choice of words.

"Renegades. I like the sound of that, actually. It's a pretty cool title to be called."

She rolls her eyes and smacks me on the arm. "Be serious. This pod only has enough fuel to travel a short distance."

"True. So, we will need to land on whatever planet we come across first. And from there, we will have to take a chance on whether the planet is habitable or not because we don't have any other choice."

"I'm not as worried about an unknown planet as I am about the rest of the team," Bex says. "I think the others will find a way to contact the Intergalactic Union, and they will get picked up. Even though the ship blew, there will still be some salvageable comm link, I bet."

"Probably so."

"They're going to regroup and come in pursuit of us," she says. I can tell that she is waiting for me to disagree. She's hoping I will disagree, but I can't because she's right.

"I have no doubt of it," I say solemnly. "The Intergalactic Union will not allow insurgency to go unpunished. They won't stop until they find and eliminate us *and* the human refugees who managed to escape the fate the Union had in store for them."

"I wish that they would just leave us alone." She sighs. "We aren't any trouble to them."

"The Union hates loose ends," I continue. "They will re-task the other members and form a new assassin mission to find and kill us."

"Well, that's reassuring," Bex says with a frown.

"Sorry," I say, trying to chuckle a little and ease the

heaviness that hangs in the air. "You shouldn't think about that right now. You should get some rest."

"How am I supposed to sleep at a time like this?"

"Just try." I hand her one of the emergency blankets sitting on the floor. "If they can all sleep back there, then you can get some rest, too. Trust me, I have a feeling you're going to need it."

Bex resists the idea for a minute, simply because she is stubborn like that and doesn't like being told what to do. Then, after a minute or two of laying her head back on the seat and having the blanket draped over her, I can see her eyes start to get heavy and fall closed.

I watch Bex as she sleeps. She's so beautiful. Even with her blue eyes covered in slumber, she is still so lovely. And even though we are now running for our lives, I'm glad we are together again.

In the darkness of the star-filled universe, I steer the pod and think about the precious cargo aboard this little vessel. There are at least four different species all stuffed into this tiny space, all of whom just want to peacefully exist.

The Intergalactic Union is nothing but a band of bullies. I wonder how they became so powerful and unquestioned. After all, there are countless other planets and galaxies, and yet, the Union gets to govern over all of it. It definitely doesn't seem right. It also seems like it will be nearly impossible to hide from them forever. Maybe if we had a ship that could travel to a new planet every few days, we could keep hiding from them indefinitely. But we don't. We only have this one tiny little space can, which will only land in one place. And that is where we will have to stay. Eventually, the Intergalactic Union will find us.

I wonder if we could find a smaller planet of like-minded people who understand that the larger and more advanced civilizations were built off the backs of the smaller ones, thanks to the Union's tight control over everything. It would be good to find a planet of people like that, and a species that would be willing to try to hide us amongst its population when the Union comes looking for us.

As I sit there thinking about it, I suddenly remember the invisible walls—a tool the Union uses in order to keep the planets from warring with each other. I've never really seen how they work, but I've heard that the invisible walls are a sort of energy shield that keeps things out of or within the confines of a single planet. Essentially, that means that if another planet were to try to invade or strike a neighboring planet, the invisible walls prevent anything from passing through and reaching the surface. Thus, they prevent damage and dissuade war.

But I wonder if the invisible walls could somehow keep the Union out, too. It's a longshot, and probably just a wishful fancy of imagination, but it would be great if we had something to hide behind.

Before I have a chance to dig too deeply into my thoughts about it, I see something come into view—a planet. I sit quietly and watch out the window as the planet gets closer and I can more clearly see its surface. Even from far away still, the planet looks like a viable and likely habitable one. We might have gotten lucky, at least until the Union finds us.

As we get closer to the surface, and I get ready to land the pod, I nudge Bex awake.

"What is it?" she asks as she opens her eyes sleepily. She

was in a deep sleep. I can tell by the way her speech is slow
and disoriented. She was exhausted, and I feel a little bad
for waking her.

"We're here," I say, looking out the window as the
planet grows bigger by the second.

"Where's *here?*" she asks.

"I couldn't tell you. But this is where we're landing, so
you might want to wake up the others. I don't know what to
expect once we land. It's probably best if everyone is as
alert and prepared as they can be."

Bex wakes Petra up first because she is the closest, lying
with her head propped up against the back of my seat.

Once Petra is awake, she helps wake the others, and
everyone eagerly looks out the window to see where we are
landing.

"Where are we?" Vira asks.

"No idea," I reply. "But we're about to find out."

When the pod lands, I reach to open the hatch so we
can all get out and take a look around, but Aerlon puts his
hand on the latch to stop me.

"I think we should wait a bit. We don't know what's out
there, so maybe it's a better idea if we stay inside the pod
for a little while longer. That way, we can look out the
windows and see if anything comes."

"What good will that do?" Petra asks. "Even if something comes, it's not like we have enough fuel to take off
and go somewhere else."

She's not wrong, but I still agree with Aerlon. We've
already suffered such losses, especially this makeshift human
tribe. It won't hurt to play it safe for a night and stay in
the pod.

"I agree," I say. "I know it's cramped in here, but there
is at least enough room for us to sit and sleep, and there's

enough food for a night if we ration it. Let's spend one night inside the safety of the pod, and then we can venture out in the morning."

"Is it nighttime here?" Vira asks as she looks out the window. "It's kind of hard to tell."

Outside the windows, the sky looks like a gray mist that seems to cover everything in a dull hue. It looks like a color of transition, as if this world is either just getting ready for dawn or just getting ready for dusk. It's hard to tell since there is no actual sun or moon visible.

"I agree we should stay inside at least until the sky clears and lightens," Amity says. "We've made it this far— we owe it to Hope not to be foolish and get killed on our first day of escape into freedom."

Everyone looks saddened by the mention of Hope's name, but Amity's point does the trick. No one protests about staying in the pod now, and I can't help but think, as dismal as a thought it is, that Hope's name was all wrong. She should have been called Despair.

"Did she have a name for the child?" I ask.

I am met by more than one set of surprised eyes. I guess it was rather random timing for me to ask, and it probably hits a nerve since it's such a fresh tragedy. But it suddenly struck me as curious and sad that the unborn baby was killed before it even got a name. I wondered if maybe Hope had one picked out already, one that she whispered to the child in her womb in the quiet early morning hours.

"Unity," Clover answers. It's the first time we have heard the girl speak since we came to find the humans. "Her baby's name was supposed to be Unity."

Sadness hangs in the air, and for a moment, everyone is silent.

Petra grumbles something under her breath about how

she will kill Peck if she ever sees the bastard again. I hope she never gets the chance to, because that would mean the Union has found us.

9

BEX

Ben wastes no time in telling Aerlon, Vira, and Petra that I have named us all renegades now. It's as if we have somehow all adopted an entirely new identity, one that Ben seems to think is a cool upgrade from the order-following, mindless minions we were on those red and blue teams. I am dying to shed that identity and take off this stupid jumpsuit, but there aren't any other clothes here, so I am stuck with it for the moment.

We all talk together for a while. We talk about our home planets, and what things were like before we all found ourselves on Nairu with the Intergalactic Union reigning over us. We talk about what happened back on the dead planet, and I can't bear the thought of Hope's beautiful body still lying in a pool of blood on the dirt.

"It was a completely senseless and needless tragedy," I say sadly. "That death didn't need to happen at all."

"It wasn't senseless," Petra says, still with anger in her eyes. "It was ruthless."

"Do you think that she would still be alive if we hadn't tried to get them onto the escape pod?" Vira asks.

"Of course not. Don't be foolish," Petra scolds.

Her attitude can be a bit harsh, in my opinion.

"If we hadn't tried to get them all on the escape pod, then none of the humans would still be alive," Petra says.

She's not wrong. And as terrible as it sounds, Hope probably wouldn't have lasted much longer, anyway. But the child she was carrying is an entirely different matter. That child was the start of new life for humanity, snuffed out before it was given a chance to be brought into the world.

"It doesn't do us any good to keep thinking about it," Ben says, and he is right.

"I agree," Aerlon echoes. "We should be thinking about what we are going to do now that we're here. There's no telling what to expect on an uncharted planet, especially not one that looks as robustly unique as this one."

The five of us sit and stare out the windows of the pod as we watch the sky change colors. I've never seen a sky like this before. It looks like somebody dumped a tray of water-color paints, and all of the colors are swirling around each other without mixing.

"I think we should stay in the pod for a full day and night cycle," Petra says. "Who knows if the native species here are daytime dwellers, or if they are nocturnal. We don't even know if they are predatory or not."

"I think there's enough food and water to last that long, if we use it sparingly," I say. "At least here we are sheltered and have a few weapons to keep things out, in case anything should try to breach the pod."

Ben nods, and the matter is settled.

We spend an entire day and night in the escape pod,

watching for any climate or native species threats from a place of safety. So far, so good.

Even within the small space, everyone finds their own corner to hole-up in. Petra sits at one end of the pod, fiddling with something in her hands. I'm guessing that she's probably rigging some other makeshift weapon since that seems to be a talent of hers. I still don't know how she managed to get a gun back on the other ship, or how she was able to rig the ship to explode. She's clever, for sure.

Ned seems like a kind soul for a human. He sits and plays a game with Clover, using only his fingers to move around as game markers. Even in the aftermath of tragedy, he seems to be able to make her smile.

I cozy beside Ben in the cramped cockpit as we face out toward the rest of the pod to watch the others.

"Have you noticed the way that Aerlon looks at Amity?" he whispers.

"Yeah, actually, I have. It's as if he is fascinated by her."

"Or perhaps he likes her," Ben says.

"Really? Do you think so?" I don't know why it surprises me so much. They both seem like good people who have been trying to do the right thing. I guess it just seems weird that an alien would find a human attractive, especially one as stunning as Aerlon.

"Yeah, I definitely think so," Ben replies. "But it's hard to tell how she feels. Granted, Aerlon isn't bad looking for an alien, but he is still an alien."

We sit for a few quiet minutes and watch them. I notice that we aren't the only ones staring. Vira is staring at me and Ben. As soon as I look over at her and smile, she looks away as if she feels bad for having invaded our privacy, not that there is any privacy in these close quarters.

"Do you remember what it was like on Earth before it was destroyed?" Ben asks.

"Yeah, a little," I lie.

I actually remember a lot, but most of my memories are of the destruction, and I try not to think about it too much. I have a handful of memories that are mostly about my mother and my high school, and those hurt almost as much to remember because of how badly I miss the way that things used to be.

"How about you?" I ask in return.

"Yeah, I can remember almost everything," Ben answers with a nostalgic, faraway look in his eyes. "But it's strange because I can't remember anything at all about when we were retrieved."

"Retrieved?"

"Yes, by the Intergalactic Union."

"Do you mean rescued?" I ask.

Ben chuckles bitterly. "That sounds an awful lot like the propaganda that they fed us when they first brought us to Nairu," he says. "Is that what they told you? That you were rescued?"

"Yes. Isn't that what happened?" I start to get the feeling that I am about to despise the Union even more than I already do. "Earth was destroyed, and all the humans left there were either dead or dying. If the Union hadn't rescued us and taken us from the surface of the Earth, then we would have died, too."

"Yep, definitely spouting the propaganda that they filled your head with," he says as he shakes his head. "That isn't what happened, Bex."

For a minute, I almost don't want to know the rest of it, but I can't help myself.

"Tell me what happened then," I say.

"The Earth was indeed a dead planet, but it was no worse off than the dead planet that we just pulled these humans from. The Union could have left us there and some of us would have survived and rebuilt."

"Some?" I ask. "That doesn't sound like great odds."

"It wasn't," Ben continues. "But neither was what ended up happening. Think about it—the Union left some of the humans on Earth to meet with whatever fate happened. And then took the rest to the dead planet that our mission was sent to. Those humans were nothing more than a science experiment for the Union."

"An experiment to prove what? What is it that the Union was trying to accomplish by moving a couple dozen humans from one dead planet to another?"

"What do you think they were trying to accomplish?" Ben asks. "They're trying to play God."

As soon as he says it, a chill runs up my spine. I already knew the Intergalactic Union liked to leverage control over the other planets and species, but this seems to cross even that line. It seems as if the Union wants to control life itself.

"What about us?" I ask. "Why were you and I spared and selected to go to Nairu and be with the Union?"

"Who knows?" Ben shrugs. "Maybe it was just random, or maybe they saw something in us they thought they could use."

"I don't know what they could have possibly seen in me," I mumble under my breath.

"I do," Ben says.

I don't know how to take his remark, but it definitely makes me feel as if there is a warmth growing from inside my chest.

"What will happen to the human species now that it has dwindled down to just the five of us?" I ask as I watch

Amity, Ned, and Clover get settled in for some sleep. Clover is too young to procreate, and by the time she is old enough, there won't be a mate for her who is her age. And it is clear by the way that Amity and Ned act around each other that they are only good friends. Ned's wife was killed, and I have no idea if Amity had a husband or not, but she certainly doesn't seem at all interested in being anything other than friends with Ned. If none of them are going to bear children to continue humankind, that only leaves me and Ben.

Of course, I don't say any of my thoughts aloud, but I don't think I need to. I can tell that Ben is already thinking the same thing. If the two of us don't continue on the human species, then our kind dies with us. No pressure or anything.

"Well," Ben says as he tries to answer my question carefully without implying anything that might be overreaching. "I suppose it's possible some of the humans survived back on the original Earth."

Good save.

I nod my head, thinking we will go with that answer for now, but the angst between us is starting to grow.

Before either of us can say anything else, there is a loud cracking noise outside of the escape pod.

"What was that?" Vira asks as she jumps up. She has pulled the collar of her jumpsuit loose in order to make it more comfortable, and I can see her blood pumping quickly through her veins. She's afraid.

Ned walks over to one of the windows and looks out. "It looks like a storm is coming. Although it's not like any storm I've ever seen before."

Aerlon goes to stand beside him. "Ben, you should come take a look at this, too."

Within seconds, we are all standing at the windows looking out, even Clover.

The noise that we heard happens again. It resembles a clap of thunder, except a hundred times louder and powerful enough to shake the little ship.

The sky changes into a deep, dark purple that lights up with a sort of phosphorescent glow every time there is a crash of light and sound.

"Where's the rain?" Clovers asks innocently.

No sooner does she pose the question, it's answered. Except, the *rain* on this planet looks more like a thick, gelatinous sludge. It's clear and shimmering, almost opalescent.

"What is that stuff?" Petra asks as she makes a face at it.

No one answers her because no one knows. But the planetary landscape outside seems to soak whatever that substance is right down into its soil.

"It's incredible," Amity says in awe as we watch the storm grow with all its threatening beauty. The sky looks as if it is being cracked open like a shell, and each time there is a burst of thunderous noise, more of the sheen-filled gel falls down to coat the surface of the planet.

The storm lasts for a while, and although it's loud and weird, it doesn't seem to be doing anything catastrophic to the escape pod, which is good. For a minute there, I thought some of us were wondering if the stuff falling from the sky was corrosive or poisonous, but it seems to be neither.

Eventually, the storm subsides, and the sky decides on a strange shade of chartreuse. If nothing else, this place is nothing short of exotically stunning, and it acts as if it is constantly changing. I'm not sure how much good waiting in the pod did us, because I have a feeling that the things on this planet might not work in cycles of day and night.

"Look!" Vira exclaims as she points at something on the ground just outside the pod. "That looks like—"

"Fruit?" Amity says, though she doesn't sound entirely convinced that she has guessed correctly.

"The whole ground is covered with it," Ben says.

The surface looks as if it is suddenly growing at a rapid pace. All the foliage that scantily covered the ground before the storm is now feverishly growing and bearing what appears to be edible fruits. It's hard to tell what is poisonous and what isn't when you have no idea what you're even looking at.

"We should go and check it out," Aerlon suggests.

With the storm gone, and hours having passed without any sign of predators or a dangerous native species, the five of us renegades leave the ship in order to check it out.

"You guys stay here and keep the hatch locked," I tell Amity as we leave the humans inside the safety of the vessel. "We'll be back as soon as we've scouted around a bit."

We each grab an oxygen mask from the pod and secure it over our heads, unsure what awaits us outside as far as the atmosphere is concerned. Once outside, all five of us stand just outside the hatch to see if the masks are still viably efficient. Sometimes the older equipment—especially the stuff on the escape pods—can be outdated and fail, but these seem to be holding up okay. My breathing feels fine and everyone around me looks okay.

"Oh, to hell with this," Petra says in annoyance. "I can't see anything with this mask on. It's too humid out here and the glass is fogging up." I look over at her and watch as she abruptly pulls her mask off from over her head.

"Petra don't!" I yell.

But she doesn't listen. Everyone watches for a few

moments to see what happens to her, and thankfully, it is nothing.

"This air smells even cleaner than the air on Nairu or the dead planet. I think you guys can take your masks off now," Petra says. "You're welcome for being the guinea pig of the group."

The first step onto the planet is a soggy one. The ground feels a bit like a sponge, but it starts to dry up quickly, making walking easier. Aerlon tastes a piece of the fruit, and I think he's crazy for just sticking it in his mouth.

"What if that is poisonous?" I ask him. "What if it kills you?"

"I'm impervious to poison," he says.

At first, I think that he's just teasing, but then I realize he's being serious.

"Really?"

"Yes. It's one of the traits of my people."

Wow. So, aside from being handsome, he's also nearly invincible, and he's got a decent moral compass. Too bad the Union isn't made up of people like him instead of the Spewt, and whatever that thing with all the teeth is.

"Uh, guys?" Petra calls from a short distance away where she has been scouting. I can hear the apprehension in her voice before I turn to see that she is surrounded by people.

At first glance, they look like they have some physical qualities that make them look almost human. They're attractive, too, but in a different and more ethereal way than Aerlon.

"I think the native species just revealed itself to us," Ben says quietly as he motions for everyone to fall back to his position and cluster together.

I don't see any weapons in their hands, but that doesn't

really mean anything when dealing with alien lifeforms. Some of the aliens can even turn themselves into weapons when they want.

"Hello," Aerlon says as he looks at one of the people who has encircled us. "We are here as visitors only. We do not wish to cause you any inconvenience."

For a moment, the people all just stand there and look at him in silence.

"Petra," he says, "you know every language there is to know. Maybe you should try some out on these guys and see if they can understand you."

"There's no need for that," one of the men says as he steps forward. "We can understand you just fine. We were just taking a moment to discuss how to approach you."

"Discuss?" Vira asks. "But none of you were talking."

"There are many ways to talk," he says with a welcoming smile. "Not all of them need open mouths to do so."

Slowly and carefully, the others with him approach us. I've learned not to be unnerved around strangers as much as I used to be, thanks to the constant exposure of new beings that the Union brings back to Nairu. Nevertheless, I am definitely still cautious and wary because one of the other things I have learned is not to trust anyone until I am positive that they can be trusted.

They seem friendly enough as they ask us questions and tell us about the planet here. The first man who spoke tells us that his people are called Fshie.

"We are refugees," Ben explains. "Fleeing a corrupted governing body that intends to kill us. We landed our escape pod on your planet in our attempt to run away with limited fuel in our tanks."

"I see," the man says as those around him seem to be

talking together with their eyes. "You are welcome to stay here for now. My people will be very curious about you. It's not often that we receive newcomers to our world, and even less often that we see such a variety of different species at once." He looks around at the small group of us, then looks back toward the escape pod as if he knows there are others still inside. "Are there more of you?"

"Yes," I answer. "There are more humans still onboard the pod."

Instantly, all their eyes seem to light up with intrigue.

"Our city is that way," he says as he motions his hand behind him. "If you would like to get the others, we will take you there. I think you will find our city to be quite hospitable. There is food, and drink, and accommodation for you there."

I look over at Ben and see that he is hesitant. His brow is furrowed with suspicion and distrust, and I don't know why. If these people wanted to harm us, they would have done so already. So far, all they are offering us is a place to stay, which we desperately need.

"Thank you," I say with a smile, trying to draw attention away from Ben's less-than-grateful reaction to their invitation.

"It is our pleasure to provide you with a temporary sanctuary," he says, and I focus on the word *temporary*. Unless they plan to refuel our tank and send us in search of another planet again, then this is where we are going to be stuck for a while.

Petra goes back to the pod to get the others while the rest of us listen to the Fshie describe their city to us. One of them is looking at Vira's translucent skin with wonderment and asking her if she is made out of the same substance that falls from the sky. Vira says *no*, then proceeds to engage in a conversation with the other woman about what exactly it is that falls from the sky. Everything feels foreign and intriguing at the moment.

"Our leader, the Minister of Life, will be very interested in meeting you once we arrive in the city," the man says as we all leave the place where the pod remains to follow these alien people.

10

BEN

E veryone, myself included, is absolutely astonished at what meets our eyes once we get to the Fshie city. The outside terrain, where our escape pod still sits, looks more like a colorful and marshy tropical wonderland. But this...well, this looks like some of the most impressive technological and scientific advances that I have ever seen.

The planet is called Brocadia, and according to our guide, whom we now know is named Talon, this city is the epicenter of life here in Brocadia. As Talon leads us through the city, we are met with the innocuous stares of many sets of beautiful eyes. The people here are rather stunning, all with deeply pigmented skin, stark white hair, and eyes the color of ebony. The group of Fshie that came and found us at our pod walks around us as if we are inside of a protective bubble. Although I'm not sure what the need for the convoy is since they all seem to be quite welcoming and friendly on the surface level.

And *that* is exactly the reason that I don't trust them. Overtly friendly species are usually the ones that wind up trying to eat humans for a late-night snack. It's that whole "lure in your prey" sort of thing.

I can tell I am the only one with my guard up right now, though, since everyone else in our group seems to be enamored by the city and counting our good fortune on having landed on such a prosperous planet with such a thriving and communicative native species.

"This is truly impressive," Aerlon says as we near the center of the city where a tall building with a towering spire sits atop the peak of a hill.

That must be where their leader resides—the Minister of Life.

"Might I ask the lifespan of your population?" Aerlon asks with intrigue.

"Lifespan?" Talon looks momentarily confused, then grins when he seems to have figured out the question. "Our people are immortal."

"Oh, wow," Petra remarks. "So, you guys only die if you become sick or wounded?"

Talon shakes his head. "We don't suffer from any of those afflictions. Our advances have made it so the Fshie are nearly invincible. It would take a tremendous force to injure any one of us."

Interesting. So, not only are these people stunningly attractive, but they are also immortal and invincible.

While everyone else seems to have a growing awe and reverence for the Fshie, I begin to worry even more. A species like this, one that is appealing and also unstoppable, is a prime candidate for being a predatorial force.

As we approach the tall building at the top of the hill, a man comes out through the wide front doors and greets us. He is adorned in thick golden robes that look almost rubbery in texture, and there are several rings on his long fingers. I assume that this well-decorated man is their leader. For some reason, I expected him to look older and wiser. Looking at the faces of all the Fshie around us, I realize that none of them look as if they have aged past a certain point of adulthood.

"May I introduce you to the Minister of Life," Talon says as he bows deeply in front of the man.

The members of our group bow, too, just to be polite. But Bex and I remain standing. There's a long human history about being made to bow down in front of oppressors, and I think we are both past the point of honoring such things.

"Talon tells me that you are refugees," the minister says.

I wonder how he was able to have told him anything since we just arrived here, but then I remember that they have some sort of nonverbal way of communication. Maybe it's a sort of telepathy or something.

"Yes," I answer. "We are hoping that we can find sanctuary here, on Brocadia."

He narrows his eyes as if he is thinking hard about my request, so I press him further in order to help sway the odds in our favor.

"From what we can see, and what we have been told so far in our short time here, it appears that your people have found solutions to many of the most crucial problems that plague other lifeforms on other planets," I say. "Death, disease, destruction—it seems you have none of those things here."

"Yes, our world has come a long way," the minister responds. "And we are very pleased with our progress."

"I'm sure. If you would allow us to stay here in peace with you, then we would be very happy to help aid in the defenses of your world. Most of us are skilled fighters, and we would join you to protect this planet as if it was our own." I lie a bit about the *skilled fighters* part, but the minister has no way of knowing that I've stretched the truth. Besides, Petra seems pretty good at fighting, so there is at least one of us with some combat experience.

"Defenses? Our planet has virtually no defenses at all," the minister says.

Several of the renegades look surprised to hear that, and I can tell I am not the only one who is starting to find all of this a bit strange now.

"But aren't you afraid of being conquered by another world who might want to steal some of your technology and the advances of knowledge that you and your people have made?"

"No," the minister answers resolutely. Then he goes on to surprise me even further. "Our people are well aware of the existence of the Intergalactic Union. I can tell by the clothing that most of you are wearing that it is the Union you are fleeing from, am I correct?"

"Yes," I answer. I wonder why Talon didn't mention that he already knew where we were from.

"We are against the corruption and control that the Union seeks to push on other planets," he says.

"Oh, thank goodness," Bex interjects. "For a second there, I thought that maybe you were going to say that you worked for the Union."

Not so fast, Bex. Don't jump to any assumptions yet. Something isn't right about all this.

She and I have always had a feeling that the Intergalactic Union was corrupt but never any sold proof of it until now. The fact that the leader of this planet is calling out the atrocities of the Union and telling us about some of the horrors the Union has committed on neighboring planets is either concrete evidence that the Intergalactic Union is a malevolent force, or he is trying to get us to trust him quickly.

"Absolutely not," the minister says with a look of disdain. "The Union has terrorized countless civilizations, all in the name of *bettering existence* for the planets around them. But the only thing that they are *bettering* is themselves. Take, for instance, the neighboring star."

The Minister of Life points his finger up to the sky, right toward an empty space that seems void of any other planets or constellations.

"Right there, in that sad hole in the galaxy, a beautiful star used to neighbor our world. The Intergalactic Union discovered the unique lifeforms that lived on that star, and the natural resources they could mine from beneath its surface. They didn't hesitate to destroy it. They kept only a sample of the precious species there for the purposes of their own curiosity—*you*." The minister looks right at Vira.

"That star was your home world," he says as Vira's face fills with shock. "Once filled with life and people just like you. Your people were close friends of ours. We shared many ideas and countless moments of discussion. They were instrumental in some of the discoveries that the Fshie made, and we willingly shared our knowledge with them in return. Your home world was a beautiful one—some might even say it was the most brilliant star in this galaxy. But the Intergalactic Union has no respect for such things. They destroyed the star, took *you* as a token to remember the alien species that once thrived there, and then set their sights on their next conquest without a moment of pause or remorse for what they did."

"It was a sad day, indeed," Talon remarks as he lowers his head in respect for the atrocity.

Everyone on our team looks at Vira, who is speechless and pulling her hair down further over her head so as not to show any of the thoughts that she is thinking. If she didn't know this before now, I can only imagine how horrible it is to hear.

"If you know all this," I say, trying to get back to the point at hand, "then how can you possibly keep your planet without defenses? The Union would like nothing more than to help itself to all the progress and innovation that you seem to have made here. With your technology, the Union could further its mission to usurp worlds at an even greater pace than it already does."

"We don't need defenses because we are hidden," Talon answers as he gives the minister time to sit down in the chair that has been brought out for him. The chair is encrusted with stones and chunks of colored rosin. The natural resources on this planet are visibly plentiful. The Intergalactic Union would have an absolute aneurysm if they could get their hands on it all.

"Hidden how?" Bex asks, reading my mind as usual.

The minister adjusts himself on the chair to get comfortable, which is slightly awkward considering that we are all still standing around him without yet being invited inside the building where we could all sit and talk together. But perhaps this is just how the customs of their people function. I've certainly seen stranger things.

"Simply put," he continues, "the invisible walls that the Union created in order to control the borders and boundaries of the other planets are nothing more than rudimentary energy fields. We were able to use our superior knowledge of such things in order to manipulate the walls and change them into the equivalent of invisibility shields in which our planet can hide behind. For now, the Intergalactic Union doesn't even know this planet exists."

"So, you mean that even if the Union flew a ship right by here, they wouldn't see Brocadia?" Bex asks in amazement.

"That is correct."

"But what if they flew a ship into the planet?" Ned asks, bringing up a good point.

Just because you can't see something, doesn't mean there aren't other ways to tell that it is there.

"We have constantly monitored systems that scan the space around Brocadia," Talon explains. "If anything were to come too close to Brocadia, then we have systems to gently move the planet out of its path."

"But you didn't move your planet out of our path," Petra says. She is wearing the same look of suspicion and skepticism that I have been.

"That is because we knew you were not a threat."

I'm not buying it. Our escape pod was an Intergalactic Union-issued vessel. If they are trying to hide from the Union, then why let a Union escape pod land on the surface of their planet? And why wait a full day before sending a scouting team to meet us?

"This is the perfect place for us to hide," Bex says as she leans into my ear and whispers excitedly. "The Union can't find us here."

Even if I am not entirely convinced that this place, and its people, are what they appear to be, there really aren't any other good options.

"We thank you for all of the information you have shared with us," I say to the minister. "And we would be very grateful to you and your people if you would allow us to stay here."

Once again, the minister looks as if he has to think hard about my request.

"I'm not sure that is the best idea," he says without any further explanation. "But I will consider your request. In the meantime, you are free to spend a day and night while I reach a decision. Talon and some of the others can show you around the city and provide you with everything you need. I am sure you would like some sustenance and the chance to get cleaned up."

He looks at the group of us from head to toe. I guess I hadn't really thought about it, but we do all look pretty roughed up and dirty from the fight on the dead planet. Vira even still has some splattering of Hope's blood on her jumpsuit.

"Thank you," I say, this time giving in to a small nod of appreciation. I would really like a decision on his part *now*, but at least this buys us a bit of time to safely regroup.

GETTING OUT OF THE JUMPSUITS AND INTO SOME REGULAR clothes feels great. I didn't even realize how much I hated those things until I peeled it off my body in exchange for some regular clothes.

Ned, Aerlon, and I were all given a room to change and a heap of shoes and clothing to choose from. I imagine that the girls in the other room were given the same.

"What do you think about him?" Ned asks as he pulls a shirt over his head.

"Who, the minister?" Aerlon asks.

"No, Talon."

I'm intrigued by their conversation now, because I

would have thought that the minister garnered the most suspicion of any of them. After all, he is the leader here.

"I'm not sure," Aerlon answers. "He seems like a decent enough man to me. Why do you ask?"

"I don't know," Ned says, shaking his head as he pushes his arm through the sleeves of the shirt. "There's something about him that is off."

"I've felt something off about all of it here," I chime in, slipping on a pair of shoes, then walking toward him. "Things seem too perfect."

"Well, they aren't that perfect," Aerlon says, "or we would have an answer to our request to be able to stay here."

"I'm not sure that we want to stay here," I say.

"Well, there's not much choice in the matter," he reminds me. "We have no place else to go. Besides, even if Talon is hiding something, this is still the safest place for us so far."

"Who said he was hiding anything?"

Aerlon looks pensive, as if he didn't even come to that realization himself until it came out of his own mouth. He turns to look at Ned right before the three of us leave the room.

"Yeah, you're right," Aerlon says. "There is something off about him."

Since none of us can put our finger on what it is, we go to meet the others. The girls have all gotten to change and freshen up, too, and their happy smiles give away how great it feels just to have some normalcy and some simple comforts, like a bath and clean clothes.

Vira looks a little uncomfortable since her new garb seems to show much more of her transparent skin. But when I see Bex, I can't help but stare. The clothing here is lovely, to match the species, and Bex looks stunning as the silken fabric hugs her curves. I try to peel my eyes away, but it takes a nudge from Aerlon to break the spell she casts.

I look over at him abruptly and see the grin that he is trying to hide. He is just about to tease me over it when Amity walks out, and Aerlon finds himself just as affixed as I was with Bex.

"Hey." Bex smiles as she walks over to me. "This place is pretty great, isn't it?"

It's hard to look at the blush-colored dress tied by a delicate string at her waist and not agree with her that this place is a utopia. But I try to stay focused.

Talon has volunteered to take us on a tour of the city. I watch him a bit more closely now that Ned has also voiced a strange feeling about the Fshie. But it is easy to get distracted by all the incredible sights.

The city is filled with towering silver buildings that reflect the colors of the ever-changing sky. Talon points out certain places of interest that his people must be the proudest of—art museums, scientific development buildings, even amphitheaters for dance performances. This is what I would imagine a perfect Earth to look like if humans hadn't driven it into destruction.

"There is one place I would like to show you that is a bit off the beaten path, if that is okay with you?" Talon asks. He looks specifically at Vira, who doesn't quite know how to respond.

"Sure," Bex answers for her. "We would love to see more of your beautiful city, wouldn't we?" She glances over at me, and I nod in agreement. Why not? It's nice to try to forget about everything that has happened. Plus, the more we see of this planet, the more I can get a feel of things here. Still, nothing jumps out at me as being out of the ordinary, and yet, things seem not quite right.

"Wonderful." Talon smiles as he continues to lead us onward.

We stop in front of a small but lovely building whose ceiling resembles that of an observatory. The building is much too small to be a window to the skies, though.

As we step inside, there is a distinct blueish glow that emanates from the center of the one-room building. There, on a pedestal carved with an intricate pattern of stars and moons, lies a small piece of what looks to be a rock.

Talon steps up to the pedestal and gently lifts the glowing rock. He cradles it as if it is a precious gem, then holds his hands out for Vira to see.

"This place is a museum of artifacts," Talon says. "It encases some of the rarest and most precious things that our people have collected."

"But there is only one thing in here," Amity says as she looks around the room. The rest of the building is empty aside from the single pedestal and the rock emanating a blueish light.

"The artifacts are frequently borrowed by members of the city to care for one at a time. In this way, we can be sure that they are always preserved. Currently, this is the artifact that resides in the building."

"What is it?" I ask.

Talon takes a step closer to Vira, still holding the piece of unusual rock in his hands for her to see. I can't help but notice that he has been extra gentle in his tone and paid extra attention to Vira during the entirety of this walk throughout the city.

"This is a piece of your home," he tells her. "The home star you are from that the Intergalactic Union destroyed.

My people tried to salvage anything we could, but this small piece of star was all that was left of your world. I am sorry for that. I thought that you might want to see it."

Vira's face floods with thoughts that seem to spill out of her brain and into the backs of her eyes. It is impossible for her to cover up all the emotions and thoughts she is thinking and feeling. She is raw and exposed as the rest of us stand around her in silence. Some of us know what it is like to be the last of our kind, and it is a burden of sadness like no other.

"Thank you," Vira says softly as her eyes fill with tears. She reaches out to place her hand on the top of the artifact and rubs her fingers over it.

"Amazing," Talon says as Vira's fingers change to match the color of the stone. It's as if she and the small piece of star recognize each other. The color floods into her forearm and up toward her shoulder. After a few moments, it has basked every inch of Vira's skin with the same blueish glow.

Vira closes her eyes and smiles, as memories of her home and her people play out across her eyes.

I still don't have any idea what Talon is up to, but for the moment, he has managed to give Vira a precious gift.

After that, we return to the center of the city and are given the opportunity to stay in the city for the night. Talon shows us to a building complete with empty rooms filled with everything we could possibly need to rest and eat for the night.

"I don't think I like the feel of this," I say to Bex as we are led toward the building where we will be allowed to stay tonight.

"What are you talking about? They have been nothing but generous and hospitable to us since we got here."

"Yeah, but something isn't right."

"I think you're being paranoid," she scoffs. "The Fshie have given us food, clothing, a place to stay comfortably, and even a tour of their wondrous city."

"And you don't think that is all a bit much?" I ask.

"No, I don't. I think it's nice. I think it's the way that civilizations should work," Bex says as if she is lecturing me. "We've gotten used to humans that destroyed the world for profit, and aliens that exploit worlds for power. I think this is how it is supposed to be. Planets are supposed to thrive and flourish, and the species on them are supposed to be kind and intelligent. I like it here."

"Okay, I don't disagree with you," I say, not wanting to argue with her. "But why don't we just go stay on the pod tonight?"

"Are you kidding? Why would we do that? Everyone wants to stay here. And the Fshie are bringing food to our rooms for us. Why would we want to go back to the pod to sleep in a cramped space with nothing but a few scraps of dried meat left from the rations?"

I try one last time to convince her, and I know it won't work because I don't have any actual proof to support my claim that something is wrong here.

"Come on, Bex, please. At least just the two of us can go back and stay on the pod just for tonight. By tomorrow, the minister will have an answer to our request, but for tonight, it can be just you and me, just like sneaking away to chat in the cockpits on Nairu. If everything is still good in the morning, then we will come back and stay in the city with everyone else."

For a second, I can tell she is thinking about it.

"No. I want to stay here," Bex says firmly. "We can't just leave and go back to the pod while everyone else stays here in the city. Think about how offensive that would look.

This is our chance to build a new home here; a chance for you and me to live somewhere out from under the thumb of the Union. I am not willing to blow it just because you have a bad feeling about something that you can't even explain. Think of what everyone has been through. We owe it to them, and to us, to give this a shot without over-thinking it."

I don't mean to get angry with her, but I do. Bex is always overthinking things, and it's usually me that talks her down. So, to hear her accuse me of making too much out of this sets me off.

"Fine," I grumble. "Stay here if you want, but I am going back to the pod."

Bex looks like she is about to say something else to me, but before she can, Petra walks up.

"I'll go with you," Petra says, not waiting for an invitation. "I never trust sleeping in a new place until I've given it a few nights."

At that, Bex glares at me and walks away. I think it's the first squabble that she and I have ever had.

11

BEX

I am so mad that I can't even see straight as I head up to my room that has been so graciously provided.

Who does that woman think she is? Who invites themselves to go back and sleep in a tight-fitting pod alone with a man who didn't even invite them? I know that Petra is bolder and has less boundaries than some of the rest of us, but still.

I'm mad at myself for being jealous, and I would never admit to it, especially since neither Ben nor I have ever admitted to having any feelings aside from friendship for each other. And I'm also mad at Ben for not giving this place a shot. He seems to be prematurely against staying here, and I just don't get why. This city is the best thing that has happened to us in a long while. Hell, this whole planet is. We went from a dying Earth, to a corrupted Nairu, to a bloody dead planet, and now we have finally found someplace nice and safe. Why can't he just be happy?

Everyone else, besides Ben and Petra, seems to be more content than I have ever seen them. Granted, I haven't known them all for that long. Amity, Ned, and Clover are smiling nonstop tonight, and that is a definite improvement from the looks of tragedy and trauma that resided on their faces before today.

Aerlon and Vira seem content, too. And Vira seems to have taken an extra interest in Talon, which I am guessing has something to do with the fact that he took her to see the last piece of her home.

I try to distract myself so I don't think about Ben and Petra together on the escape pod for the night. This is a lovely night here in the city, and we are brought the most delicious dinner that I can ever remember having. All I can do is hope that the Minister of Life finds it within his heart to let us stay here, hidden away from the Union and able to start a new life.

After an enjoyable night sitting around and talking to some of the Fshie who join us and learning about their ways and customs here on Brocadia, I am looking forward to a solid night of sleep. The rooms that they have set us up in are lavish and peaceful. There is even the resemblance of moons and stars on the ceiling of the bedroom that seem backlit with their own subtle glow. There are small glasses of cordials on the nightstand as an aperitif to help us sleep well, and plush beds stacked with soft blankets to sleep in.

How could this be anything less than delightful?

I get why Ben is wary. It does all seem to be so nice. But that doesn't mean it isn't good. I think the two of us have just gotten used to being suspicious of anything that doesn't come and smack us right in the face. However, there is nothing going on here in this lovely city, aside from a good night of sleep and a peaceful people that I hope will let us stay.

"Here you are," one of the women from the city says as she comes into my room and hands me a stack of clothing.

"What's this?" I ask. They have already given us so much.

"There is a sleeping gown for you for tonight and a change of clothes for tomorrow," she says. "If anything needs to be changed, just let one of us know."

"It's very kind of you." I smile. "Thank you."

Before I settle into bed, I walk down the hallway of the tall building to check on everyone else. It feels weird not to have Ben here with me.

This bedroom hall is several stories up in the sky, and I can see the city below from some of the windows that line the hall. I can't see the land outside the city, though—the place where Ben and Petra are probably cozied up together in the pod.

I shake my head to stop myself from thinking about it any further and say goodnight to the other humans. Amity, Ned, and Clover are all staying in one room together. They were each offered their own room, but I think they feel safer together. It makes sense, considering all that has happened to them.

Aerlon has already gone to bed, and the lights in his room are off. But Vira is still wide awake. Not only is she wide awake, but she has a visitor.

I stand just outside her bedroom door to listen. I don't want to eavesdrop, but I do want to make sure that she is safe. I blame Ben for putting all this unsettling anxiety into my head.

"Are you comfortable?" I hear Talon ask her from his position just inside the doorway where it looks as if he was just stepping inside to check on her, much as I was.

"Yes," Vira says. "And thank you for being so kind to all

of us. I hope your minister allows us to stay."

"The minister can be...fickle," Talon says. It is the first time that I notice a hint of what Ben might have been talking about. What appeared to be such a good relationship between the minister and his people now seems ever so slightly undermined by the condemning tone in Talon's voice.

Vira doesn't say anything in response, and Talon takes a step outside the doorway to leave. I push myself back into the corner to keep him from seeing me there.

"I did bring you one more thing," he says. I watch as he reaches into the pocket of his pants and as Vira steps closer to see what it is. I have to keep myself from making a small noise when I see what it is.

Talon has taken the piece of star from the museum and brought it here to give to Vira. I have no idea how their rules and laws here work, but it doesn't seem like something the minister would be pleased to see.

"I think that it belongs with you," he says as he hands it to her.

"But will you get in trouble for having taken it?" Vira asks.

"Let's just see what the morning brings," he says rather cryptically.

The blue glow shines down the hallway, and I quickly duck back into my bedroom as Talon leaves Vira's room.

I look at the small pile of clothes and pull out the gossamer sleeping gown to get ready for bed. I stand there, holding the pretty fabric and seeing how soft and comfortable it looks.

"Dammit, Ben," I grumble as I set the gown back down and reach for tomorrow's change of clothes instead. I guess I am still in a residual fight or flight mode, too, because as much as I want to let my guard down, I think I'd prefer to sleep in a set of actual clothes.

I pull the pants up over my hips and shove my arms through the shirt before laying down in the bed. Then I reach over to the nightstand to get the small glass of cordial that is sitting there. It tastes like sweet and decadent wine, and within a few minutes, I am already falling asleep.

In the morning, when I wake up, I feel incredibly rested. I can't even remember the last time I slept so soundly. I must have been even more tired than I realized.

Since I am already dressed in my clothes, I tie my hair back in a loose ponytail and wash my face before getting ready to meet up with Ben at the pod. I want to know what his plan is, depending on the minister's decision today, and a part of me also wants to make sure nothing happened between him and Petra last night. I know it's petty of me. I should be glad that the bunch of us are here and alive, but Ben is my closest friend, and then some. I can't imagine being anywhere where he and I are at odds.

"Good morning," the Minister of Life says to me as soon as I step out into the main corridor of the building.

I return the greeting and look around to see that everyone else is already awake and sitting down to breakfast at a large table set up nearby.

"I trust that you slept well?"

"Oh yes, thank you," I answer, not stopping to join them for food.

"Aren't you hungry?"

"Not yet." I smile politely. "I'm just going to go rouse Ben and bring him back here to join the rest of us."

But when I head toward the door, the minister continues to talk as if he is trying to keep me here for some reason. Every time I answer his further questions and turn to leave, he asks another. I glance over at the others, who all seem to not notice anything strange about it. Aerlon and Ned are listening to some of the Fshie explaining aspects of their technology. Amity is sitting and readying a book with Clover as they munch on their breakfast together, and the young girl looks out a nearby window. And Vira is sitting quietly, sipping on something that looks to be tea.

The only one who seems to be acting strangely is Talon. He looks anxious and uncomfortable, as if he is waiting for something unpleasant to happen.

I start to think that maybe Ben was right after all, that things aren't quite as perfect as they seem.

"Please, sit for a moment and join me for a cup of tea before you head out," the minister says as he motions with his hand toward a steaming teapot on the table.

I am just about to politely decline and tell him that perhaps I will join him for tea after I go to retrieve Ben and Petra from the escape pod when Clover suddenly jumps up from the table. Her small voice lets out a scream, and I run quickly toward the window that she is staring out of.

There, just outside the building in an open part of the city, an Intergalactic Union ship is landing on the ground.

"What is this?" I shout at the minister, no longer caring about being polite. "I thought you said this planet was hidden behind the invisible wall!"

"It was," he says.

I stare into his cold eyes. He sold us out.

"How could you? I thought your civilization was so beautiful, so advanced, and your people valued life and peace. Why would you do this? Now you have not only sacrificed us, but your own people as well. Now the Union knows you are here."

"I had no choice," the minister says most unconvincingly. "It was only a matter of time before the Intergalactic Union caught up with our technology and would be able to sniff us out. I made a deal with them to trade you renegades in exchange for an agreement that the Union would never come after the Fshie. I am sure you can understand I need to do what is best to protect my own people. Now our planet can stop hiding and stop limiting our advances through travel."

"You are a fool!" I shout at him vehemently. "Do you think the Intergalactic Union will adhere to your silly agreement? You might as well kiss your planet goodbye. Your people will be slaughtered, minus the few who are chosen as novelties for the Union's own purposes, and your city will be leveled. The Union will milk every last resource out of this place."

I don't give him a chance to respond because there is no time. I motion for the others to follow, and we all take off running toward the escape pod. I have no idea what good it will do, since there isn't enough fuel in the tanks to go anywhere else. If anything, it will only buy us a few moments of protection inside its shell before the Union peels the pod open like pulling the wings off an insect. But there is no place else for us to run in our attempt to escape the Union assassins that have come for us.

Ben and Petra meet us halfway there, running toward us from the opposite direction.

"We heard the engines and saw the ship land," Ben calls urgently to me before we slide to a stop in front of each other. "We were coming back to get you."

"I should have listened to you," I say breathlessly. "I'm sorry."

"No time," Ben says as he grabs my arm, and we all take off running toward the pod together.

"Will this thing even get off the surface?" Ned asks.

"Yes," Ben answers as we all reach the front hatch and start to climb in. "It has just enough fuel left to take off."

"And then?"

Ben pauses for a moment as he looks back at everyone. "And then there is nothing more we can do. Once the pod runs out of fuel, I won't be able to steer it at all. It will float toward whatever planet pulls it into its gravity."

"That could mean we could end up right back here," Vira says with fear in her eyes.

"Yeah, it could."

We all pile into the pod, and Ben sits down in the cockpit again, ready to get us as far away from here as a few drops of fuel can possibly take us. And then, just as almost everyone is inside, and the pod is about to take off, Amity stops just short of the hatch.

"Clover!" she cries. She turns around and looks feverishly behind her, only to find that the girl is gone.

"Where did she go?" Aerlon asks, jumping down from the hatch to reach for Amity. But Amity backs up, refusing to take his hand.

"I don't know," she says in a panic. "She was right behind me. In the chaos, she somehow disappeared. I won't leave this planet without her."

"*Ugh*, fuck," Petra says as she jumps off the pod and heads out in search of the girl. Everyone follows suit and spreads out to go in search of the girl. I swear, I am going to give that kid a solid scolding once we get out of here. Perhaps we need to keep her on a tether.

"Ben!" I call out as I see the assassins coming toward us.

He runs up beside me and scowls. I can see it, too—some of our former teammates, ones that weren't even assassins to begin with, have now been repositioned to fill in the places of the insurgents who aborted the mission on the dead planet.

Jabber and Lilybet are now wearing red jumpsuits and armed with weapons that they are brandishing in their hands.

"There she is!" Ben says.

I follow where his finger is pointing and spot Clover.

"Go get her! I'll hold them off," he says.

I toss him the gun that I was issued and run toward Clover, who looks as if she is frozen in shock and standing right out in the open. No sooner do I make a run for her, then a shot fires directly at me. I can hear it leave the barrel, and I look to see it getting ready to hit me right in the side. But before the bullet can strike me, Ned comes out of nowhere and blocks the shot.

In the split-second that I hesitate, I watch Ned fall to the ground. The shot hit him squarely between the eyes, and he is dead instantly.

I don't have time to feel anything at all. I grab Clover and hightail it back to the ship, screaming for everyone that I have the girl so they all make it to the pod in time. As soon as everyone has climbed aboard, Ben once again takes the helm to get us out of here.

Clover is crying uncontrollably and whimpering that she is "sorry" while Amity cradles the girl's head against her chest and joins in her sobs.

"Who is here?" Petra asks harshly as she pokes her gun into the pile of blankets that are bunched up in the corner of the pod. Come out!"

There is an unexpected stowaway on board—Talon.

"Get the hell off this ship right now before I blow your skull open!" Petra screams at him.

"No, wait! Please!" Talon says with his hands in the air

as he stands up from behind the blankets. "I want to help you."

"Like hell!" Petra glares at him as her fingers get dangerously close to squeezing the trigger.

"Petra, calm down," Aerlon says as diplomatically as he can. "If you fire a shot inside the pod, it will ricochet and hit us as well."

"I don't agree with what the minister is doing," Talon says with his dark eyes open so wide that they look like small abysses. "I want no part of it. I want to come with you."

"No way!" Ben hollers. He is watching out the front window as the assassins close in. Within a matter of seconds, they will be at the hatch. "Get off my ship!"

I can see Talon glance nervously over at Vira, and her eyes dart down toward the floor of the pod as if she doesn't want to get involved in it.

"I can help you," Talon says as a last-ditch effort to get Ben to concede. "I know how to make this little pod run without fuel."

"That's impossible," Petra scoffs.

"No, it isn't. It's just not technology that you know about yet," Talon explains. "You'll need my help if you stand a chance of getting away. Otherwise, your pod will fall right back onto this surface almost as soon as you get away."

I look at Ben, and his face contorts under the pressure of making a fast decision.

"Can you make the modification while we are already in the air?" Ben asks.

"Yes."

Since there is no other choice of escape, Ben concedes, and Talon sits down in the cockpit beside him.

BEN

While the escape pod is flying around in the middle of nowhere, essentially an empty pocket in this section of space, and with the Intergalactic Union ship still in pursuit, I try to figure out where we can go to find safety.

"What if we went back to the dead planet?" Amity suggests as everyone brainstorms ideas, most of which are completely undoable.

"The same planet that we rescued you from?" Petra asks.

"That isn't a good idea," I interrupt. "It's literally the place where we were escaping from, and the entire planet is desolate and without the means to survive."

"It's the perfect hiding place now," Amity continues. "The Union won't think to look for us there because they would never expect us to return to the dead planet."

She does make a small point, but that doesn't negate the other factors.

"We wouldn't survive there," I argue. "The four of you were barely able to survive when we found you, and that

was when you had Ned acting as a survivalist among you
and trying to keep the rest of you alive."

I feel bad for bringing his death up, but Ned is gone
now, and he was the one with the most knowledge of how
to sustain life on the dead planet. Amity spent her time
mostly caring for Hope and Clover. Not that I undervalue
our team's ability to survive, but we would be starting from
scratch in a place that has nothing in order to meet our
basic needs.

"I agree with her," Bex says. "We stand a better chance
of surviving on the dead planet than we do up against the
Union ship and the assassins, if they catch us."

Aerlon looks to Talon and does what he seems to do
best—stay calm in the midst of chaos and ask clever questions that will lead to solutions.

"Talon, can you use your skills to make the pod go any
faster? Or to better equip it with defenses or even *offensive*
capabilities?" Aerlon asks.

I think he is highly overestimating the extent to which
this pod is going to hold up.

"Yes, I can," Talon answers. "But in order to make
those kinds of modifications, it would require some time
and a place to land the ship to work on it. Those aren't the
kinds of things I can do in the air."

"See? This all points to us needing to land on the dead
planet to regroup," Bex says. "Besides, there aren't any
more food supplies left on the pod. "

"Fine," I say, conceding to the second poor decision I've
made in the last several minutes as I steer the pod back
toward the dead planet. I can't help but feel this is going to
be a mistake, too.

When we get there, I land the pod in almost the same
spot that we had escaped with it the last time. The first

thing that all of us see when we open the hatch and step out is the sight of poor Hope's lifeless body still lying on the ground in a pool of matted blood that has now stuck into the dirt. Amity reaches to cover Clover's eyes, but the girl pushes her hand away and stares at the dead body of her friend. It is a sign of strength and defiance, and it makes me think that one day, Clover might be a force to be reckoned with. Nothing quite births heroes like the need to avenge a great injustice.

While Vira, Amity, and Clover tend to a proper burial for Hope and her unborn child, the rest of us try to scope out and build a new place for shelter.

"I'll go look for something to hunt and some fresh water," Aerlon offers.

"I'll come, too," Petra says as she joins him.

Bex and I go back to the human's meager dwelling to see if there are any materials that we can salvage to build a new and bigger shelter while Talon works on making the adjustments to the pod. The thought of having a fast, weapon-wielding escape pod is a momentary source of amusement in my head.

"So, I suppose I owe you an apology," Bex says as we both work on untying pieces of the woven fabrics from the posts that Amity and Ned had used to shelter Hope in the back corner of the dwelling. These can be for something, though I'm not sure what yet.

"It's okay," I say. "You didn't know that the Fshie were underhanded and conniving scum."

"Not all of them," she says. "Talon seems okay."

"We'll see. I'm not going to take anything at face value. People aren't always what they seem."

"Is Petra what she seems?" Bex asks.

Her question surprises me because of how random it is.

I look over and see her trying not to look at me out of the corner of her eyes. Is she jealous?

"Petra has saved our asses on more than one occasion now," I say, trying to ignore the emotion behind her question that I might be misinterpreting. "So, yes, I think she is probably worthy of our trust now."

Bex makes a remark under her breath that I can barely hear or make out—something about "one night in a pod together, and suddenly I would hand over the reins to an alien."

"Are you jealous?" I ask, blurting it out because I'd rather address the issue than hear Bex mumbling snide remarks.

"Of what?" she asks indignantly. "Of a hard-ass, punk girl with blue streak? I don't see anything there that I need to be jealous of. Just because she speaks a million languages doesn't make her special."

"Oh my gosh, you *are* jealous," I say. I can hear it in her voice now. I don't know whether to be flattered or to laugh at how ridiculous she sounds, or to let Bex know that Petra could never, ever compare to her. No one could ever compare to Bex; not for me.

"No!" she says quickly as her cheeks begin to flush. "Don't be stupid. I just think that it's odd that she wanted to be alone in the pod with you."

"She didn't want to be alone in the pod with me," I try to explain. "She simply didn't want to stay in the city with the Fshie. And can you blame her? Look at what ended up happening."

"So now you're coming to her defense?"

"Okay, this is ludicrous," I say as I toss the fabric I was holding onto the ground and reach out to take Bex's hand. I don't even know why I do that; it's almost like an innate reaction. "I don't want to get into a spat with you, Bex. Nothing happened in the pod with Petra."

For a second, I wait to see if she is going to continue to be upset, but then she simply smiles and draws her hand away to keep scavenging for supplies. I think we've made amends, which is good because I absolutely hate being at odds with her.

After Hope has been buried, and a rough excuse for a shelter has been built, we go to check and see how Talon is progressing with the modifications to the vessel.

"It's beautiful," Bex says to Amity and Vira as she looks at the grave on which Clover is setting a few withered flowers.

They managed to find a few nearly dead blossoms and built a small fence around Hope's grave with sticks. It actually isn't beautiful at all, but the sentiment behind it is.

"Have Aerlon and Petra come back with food and water yet?" I ask.

Talon shakes his head, then he motions for me to come over and see what he has done so far.

"This is all pretty incredible," I say as I look at the modifications he has made without any sort of tools here at his disposal. I get ready to ask him how he knew to make certain adjustments and what kind of effects these are going to have on the pod, but am interrupted by Petra and Aerlon, who come running up to us with a look of terror on their faces.

"What's happened?" Bex asks just as I am turning around to see what is going on.

"Get in the pod!" Aerlon shouts. "Now!"

He grabs Amity and Clover and shoves them in through the door as he and Petra follow closely behind. I grab Bex and head for the hatch right as I see an enormous predator barreling toward us. I have no idea what kind of creature it is, only that its massive jaw is hanging open and drool is pouring over its sharp teeth. It looks like it wants to eat us all alive.

Vira is the closest to its path, frozen in fear.

As soon as Talon sees what is about to happen, he makes a move that I think is going to get Vira out of harm's way. Instead, Talon does the unthinkable.

He stands in front of Vira as if he intends to protect her from this beast, which is at least a hundred times his size, and then he transforms.

Bex and I stand in the center of the hatch and watch in shock as Talon transforms into a beast that is even bigger, even more terrifying-looking than the creature. His black eyes bulge, and instead of just two of them, his face is now covered with two rows of eyes like a spider. His white hair has turned into a bristly fur with ends as sharp as spear tips. In a matter of seconds, he has torn the predator to pieces.

"Well, there's something that none of us saw coming," Petra says as she hangs her head out the hatch to see the tail end of Talon's violent slaughter of the beast. "I guess it turns out that, in addition to being highly intelligent and advanced, the Fshie are also quite a deadly and dangerous species."

As soon as the predator has been put down, Talon transforms back into his original form. He turns to make sure that Vira is okay and looks at her sadly, as if he is ashamed of himself and of what he is. Then he goes right back to working on the pod without saying a word to anyone.

Slowly, everyone else comes back outside, and even Petra seems sensitive to the fact that Talon just wants to pretend like that didn't happen and no one saw what he can turn into. Considering he just saved our lives, everyone obliges and goes about tending to other things. Petra and Aerlon managed to collect some water, and surprisingly, even some fish, which they dropped as they ran here. Amity helps them recover it.

As Bex and I start to build a fire to cook the fish upon, I watch out of the corner of my eye to see Vira walk up and stand beside Talon near the pod. She talks to him gently and thanks him for saving her, seemingly unrepelled by his temporarily vicious form.

"I think I might have been wrong about him," I say quietly to Bex.

"Who? Talon?" she asks. "I'd say you were spot-on. You said that there was something off about him, and I would say that shapeshifting into that giant monster definitely constitutes as being off."

"Yeah, maybe. But I don't think he's a monster. I am actually starting to think he might have a pretty good heart, unlike the Minister of Fshie."

After a while, everyone comes to sit together by the fire, even Talon. We all savor the fish that was caught, and I am glad to hear that there is a running stream with fresh water nearby that even has a bit of life in it still. Maybe this planet isn't quite so desolate as I thought.

13

BEX

For the first few days on the dead planet, things actually seem to be going okay. Granted, creating a livable habitat where one didn't exist is a daunting task, but there are no further aggressors or predators...yet.

None of us wander too far away from the camp we've set up, just in case that giant beastie had friends, which it probably does. For now, it feels safer than anything else has felt in a while—and at least the Intergalactic Union hasn't found us. I'm starting to think that Amity was right that the Union will never think to look for us here. If that's the case, then I would honestly be fine with staying here forever. Anything is better than having to go back to Nairu, receive some terrible punishment, and be separated from Ben for the rest of our lives. Although, if the Union got their hands on us again, they would probably kill us before any of that happened, anyway.

Talon covered the ship with a net that Amity and Vira wove from the wide leaves of some of the native trees to camouflage it just in case anyone tried to scope the planet's surface from afar.

"I'm starting to wonder why the Union always referred to this planet as dead," Aerlon says. "There are trees, water, even fish and other living things here. It's far from dead, in my opinion."

"I think the Union calls anything that doesn't serve their purpose dead," Ben says.

"Then that means we are dead, too," I say.

I didn't mean for it to sound quite as dark as it did, but it's the truth. None of us serve a purpose for the Union anymore. In their eyes, we are unredeemable, and if anything, they would consider us an obstacle to their goals. That makes us as good as dead to them.

"Well, thankfully, they can't find us here," Vira says in her attempt to be positive.

"That's wishful thinking," Petra chimes in with her blunt assessment of things. "The Intergalactic Union can find us here. It's simply a matter of whether or not they will."

"Well, as long as we try to stick close and stay hidden, and as long as we don't squander the very few fragile natural resources that remain here, like the humans before us did, then I think we stand a chance at making this work."

That is the first upbeat thing I've heard Ben say this entire time. I smile at him because I like the thought of making a new home and a new future. Even if it is in a place like this. At least we have each other, and friendships are forming amongst our little group of renegades and refugees. Everyone is getting along surprisingly well, despite our differences in species and opinions on some things.

I watch as Clover plays in the dirt, drawing pictures of

animals with a stick that she found. She seems more at ease now, and I think it's because she is happy to be "home." It's impressive how resilient children are, clinging to anything that doesn't get pulled away.

Another thing that impresses me is the way that here, when we are not forced to try to govern other species or subjugated to obey them, it almost seems as if the differences between our people don't matter all that much anymore. Amity is human, and Aerlon is not, and yet their friendship seems to be blossoming into something much more intimate. They share glances and brush hands when they walk past each other, and I notice how they are always making sure the other is okay and nearby.

An even more surprising relationship that seems to have developed is the one between Vira and Talon. Both are alien beings, and both couldn't possibly be more different. Vira's entire body shows *everything* about herself, and Talon's transforms into an ungodly creature, yet both seem to be inherently gentle and affectionate toward each other.

"Whelp, I'm going to go get started on that water filtration system so we can use it at the stream and sift out any crap that we've been drinking," Petra says as she starts to walk toward the trees that encircle the little body of running water. "If we're thinking about staying here, then we better start digging our heels in."

For a minute, I stay with the others and watch as Petra walks off. Then I get up and follow her.

"You come to help?" she asks as I walk up without saying anything.

"Yeah."

She shows me how to use some cloth sections from the old jumpsuits in the pod and a handful of stones to make a rudimentary filter. She explains the basic principle of making a bigger model that could function as a whole system instead of having to do this each time we draw water from the stream.

"We don't know what else uses this water source," she explains. "And when it rains—if it rains here—we don't know what is in the atmosphere that is being carried down into the water. In order to make sure we stay safe and don't get sick, we need to have a better way to filter the water." She reaches for a metal piece that looks a bit like a large straw with a piece of mesh at the end of it. "Talon made me this. I think it might work."

It's impressive listening to her talk while she figures out how to piece bits of things together to make something. I guess this is how she pieces together bombs and guns, too. It's interesting and adaptable. Maybe that's part of her species' traits. It would make sense since she is so adept at picking up languages, too. Petra is really quite a fascinating woman, if I could just get over my jealousy of her.

"So, I guess that night in the pod on Brocadia was pretty quiet until morning, huh?" I try my best to tiptoe around asking her flat-out what she and Ben did on the night that they spent alone together.

"I mean, yeah, it was quiet until morning when the ship touched down," she says. "Those engines were so loud that they shook the pod."

"But *until* then was pretty quiet?"

Petra stops what she is doing and looks at me. There really is no graceful way to get at the question I want to ask her.

"You're jealous, aren't you?" She grins. Her grin makes me eve more jealous and angrier.

"No," I say quickly. "What would I have to be jealous about? That's ridiculous."

"You know," she says as she brushes off her hands and sits down to talk to me, "one of the things about knowing countless languages is that I am really good at picking up patterns and nuances in speech. A person who is telling the truth would have answered that question with a simple *no*. But a person who was lying and trying to cover up the fact that they are indeed jealous would answer just as you did. Helpful word of advice for when you might attempt to lie again in the future—less is more."

I am embarrassed and can feel my face getting hot. I'm embarrassed about getting caught in a lie, and I'm embarrassed about being jealous.

"I can assure you that Ben and I did nothing at all that night except talk about our mutual distrust of the Minister of Life and go to sleep."

"Really?" I ask, knowing she didn't need to answer me and reassure me at all.

"Yes, really." Petra smiles.

I feel a little better now.

"Oh, and he did keep waking me up all night with his constant pacing around that little pod because he was so worried about you," she adds.

"He did?" Okay, now I feel a *lot* better.

"Yeah, he wouldn't shut up about you." Petra goes back to working on the water filtration, and neither of us say anything for a little while as I help her. But just as we are getting ready to leave, she has one more nugget of advice.

"If you have feelings for Ben, you should tell him. We aren't guaranteed any *tomorrows.*"

Later that night, while we are all lying on the woven mats that Amity helped to make for us, I cannot sleep. I look over and can see that Ben's eyes are still open, too. So, I get up to go lay beside him. I always feel better when I talk to Ben, and sometimes even when I am just sitting beside him. But lately, every time I get *too* close to him, I feel as if I can't breathe. By the question that he asks, I think that he must be feeling that way, too.

"Do you ever wonder why we haven't gotten together?" he asks as I lay down beside him and he lifts his arm up for me to lay my head on his shoulder.

I wasn't expecting him to ask such a blunt question. To be honest, I wasn't really expecting him to be thinking about this at all—about us. Still, even though I am caught off guard, I recognize that this is a chance to have a real conversation with Ben about how we both feel.

"I don't know," I answer honestly. "I guess that maybe it's the thought of not ever wanting to lose each other that has kept that last, final piece of distance between us as a sort of self-preserving barrier."

I wait for him to say something, holding my breath so I don't get overrun by nerves. But instead of saying something, Ben tilts his head down and lifts my chin gently toward him with his finger. Then, as everyone around us is peacefully sleeping, he kisses me.

It feels like the moment in some of the books I used to read—that magical moment when everything changes.

I've kissed plenty of guys before back on Earth, but none have ever made me feel like this. No kiss has ever felt this soft, and urgent, and recklessly necessary.

I press my lips back against his and feel my heart pound against the inside of my ribcage, as if it wants to get loose. With my hand pressed flat against his chest, I can feel the laboring restraint of his breathing, too. For a small moment in time, I feel as if I am thinking about nothing and everything at once. If I had the same unconcealable form that Vira does, then I would look like a frenzied tangle of thoughts and emotions. But one emotion overpowers the other—the feeling that I just want to stay here, in this kiss with Ben, as the rest of world goes on without us.

But way too soon, the kiss is over, and Ben slowly pulls his mouth away. I want more, but we are here, out in the open, sleeping amongst a crowd of alien friends on this shell of a planet. The time for another kiss will have to wait. At least it happened, and now we know. We've just taken a chunk down out of that barrier. Now I feel like knocking the whole damn wall down.

I curl up against his chest as Ben wraps his arm around me.

"Goodnight, Bex," he says.

This time, I have no trouble falling asleep.

In the morning, I have a renewed sense that things are going to be okay. I don't feel jealous, or worried, or anything other than happy and safe. Who would have thought when we went through that containment pod and were funneled out into red and blue sides of separation that Ben and I would wind up here, in each other's arms, on a nearly empty planet?

I linger with my eyes closed for a while, listening to Ben's steady breathing and not wanting to move an inch until he wakes up and I have to. But when I finally do open my eyes, I gasp in shock at the sight of three people standing over us. Jabber, Lilybet, and even Ransor are there.

It must be a nightmare, I tell myself. There's no way that the Union found us here, and no way that we wouldn't have heard them coming until they were literally standing over us.

The three assassins stand there silently and unmoving, as if they are apparitions, making me doubt even further whether I am awake or still asleep. But when I turn my head to look around, I can see that all the others are tied up.

I nudge Ben in the side, wondering why he has not yet already woken up, and then I stare up into Ransor's cold eyes.

"Good morning, Bex," Ransor hisses with eyes so narrowed that all four of his pupils seem to smoosh together. "Miss me?"

A sick feeling pits in my stomach as I realize this is no dream. Why did this have to happen right now? Just when I dared to let myself hope that things could get better and we would be safe? Just when I started to think that maybe we could all start a new life somewhere outside the reach of those who would seek to rule over us and destroy us.

I look up at Jabber and Lilybet—those sellouts. They are even worse than the Union delegates themselves because they know what it's like to be on the other side of oppressive power, and they chose the path of cowardice in order to save their own necks.

Ben finally starts to move beside me and opens his eyes. I was getting worried that maybe they had knocked him out or something, but maybe he was just in a deep sleep, having good dreams about that kiss, which will now probably be our last.

"What the—"

Before Ben can get to his feet, Jabber thrusts him back down against the ground with the heel of his boot. He's been completely indoctrinated now—no longer just a blue, but now a full-fledged assassin.

Ben looks over at me quickly to make sure that I am okay, and I state the obvious simply because I need to say it aloud in order to believe it myself.

"The Intergalactic Union has found us."

14

BEN

The first thing that comes to mind once Ransor and the other assassins have managed to tie up me and Bex is Talon.

He could stop these guys.

But when I look over at the rest of our small tribe of friends and allies, I can see that they have already knocked Talon out and subdued him. Apparently, the assassins, or at least the Union, are aware of Talon's violent abilities. He's no good to us unconscious.

"So, what's the plan here?" I ask Ransor, glaring at him with as much spite as I can bring to my face, knowing that Ransor will tell me everything because he's the kind of idiot that will monologue all his plans just to hear himself talk. This guy likes an audience, and he likes to be feared.

Ransor sits down near the dying fire and picks some of the scraps of fish from the sticks we used to cook them on. He chews the flesh slowly, then makes a rancid face.

"This is what you've been eating here?" he chides. "At least you can look forward to having a last meal that is better than this crap." He stands up and walks around the little camp in a slow circle, as if he is showing off his strength at capturing a small, defenseless camp of people while they slept.

What a great conqueror he is, I think to myself sarcastically. One day, I would really love to send his alien eyes rocking back into his skull with a solid punch to the face.

"Well, let's see," he says as he begins his predictable monologuing. "The Fshie will get dropped back off on his own planet and hand-delivered back to the Minister of Life in order to face the consequences of his actions. He can be punished in his own world, which I hear is quite beautiful and also quite harsh."

He pauses both his walking and talking to look over at Amity and Clover, who are both glaring at him ferociously. Those two are turning out to be a lot fiercer than I thought they were. Instead of looking scared, they look as if they want to skewer Ransor over the fire like one of the fish from last night's dinner.

"These two humans can be left right here on this dead world to die without any more of the Union's time wasted on them," he says with disgust, as if the mere sight of them is repulsive.

"And the rest of you—you failed assassins and emissaries—you will be brought back to the Intergalactic Union."

"I have to admit," I say as I try to pry some more information out of his daft skull, "I didn't expect that part. I'm surprised that you aren't just going to kill us here on the spot. I know you want to."

Bex shoots me a look, as if warning me not to egg him on, but I'm poking the hornets' nest on purpose.

Ransor grins at me maliciously as he starts to answer,

then quickly corrects himself from telling me *too* much. "The Union has much bigger plans for you. Consider it a punishment to fit the act of your betrayal, for which a simple death is too small."

That wasn't helpful at all. It didn't tell me anything.

"All right, motley crew, let's go," Ransor says as he directs Jabber and Lilybet to help us all to our feet so they can funnel us onto their ship. All of us, that is, except for Amity and Clover.

I watch as Aerlon tries to wrestle his way out of the bindings they have put us in. He looks back at Amity with distress and tries to knock out Jabber with his elbow in order to get to her. It's no use. If he keeps resisting like this, Ransor is going to lose his patience and kill him, anyway, despite the Union's directive. Guys like Ransor have a short fuse that can blow at any moment. Besides, the Union might have even given him a leeway clause to put a few of us down if we cause too much trouble.

"Aerlon, stop," I call to him. "You aren't helping Amity this way. There's nothing that you can do."

Ransor chuckles and smiles as he walks onto the ship, pleased, I am sure, to see that we are in a position of forced submission.

As I get closer to Aerlon while we walk toward the ship's hatch, I speak to him quietly.

"They're better off here," I say. "Amity and Clover have a much better chance of survival being left here than being taken to Nairu. The Union would kill them on the spot and claim they are a failed species. At least here, they are home. They'll figure out a way to get loose from the bindings and go back to trying to survive. They're smart and strong— they'll make it."

"But what about that *thing* that attacked us? What if there are more of them here on this planet?"

I look over as I see Talon being carried onto the ship, still unconscious, and I think about how he defeated that predator the last time.

"I highly doubt that if there are any more of those creatures on this planet, they will be back anytime soon," I tell Aerlon. "I think Talon sent a pretty clear message the last time. Right now, we need to focus on keeping ourselves alive if you want any chance of coming back here and seeing Amity again."

Aerlon subdues his anger and follows my advice. The only chance for any of us now is to find a way to get away from the Union again. This time, though, it will be much harder because they already know we are against them.

With Amity and Clover left behind, the ship takes off. The assassins make a quick stop back on Fshie now that it is no longer hidden by the invisible wall.

"Stupid mistake," I whisper under my breath. That whole planet is toast as soon as the Union gets around to having their way with it.

Ransor drops Talon off as Vira looks distressed in the corner of the ship. She's right to be worried. I would imagine that Talon's punishment from the minister is going to be a weighty one. But just as I told Aerlon, there's nothing we can do about it for now.

Now it's just us renegades here on the ship as we head back to Nairu, forced to leave our newly made friends behind and go on to face our own dire straits of what is likely to be the Intergalactic Union's unadulterated fury at our betrayal.

On the ride there, I try to talk to Jabber and Lilybet,

thinking that if I can just appeal to their moral conscience, that perhaps there is still a chance for us to escape this mess.

"How does it feel to be an assassin?" I ask Lilybet. "Do you feel powerful now?"

She looks down at her feet and tries to ignore me, but I can see the subtle twisting of her face. She feels guilty, and rightly so.

"Leave her alone," Jabber scolds. "If you want to pick on someone, you can pick on me."

"Oh, how noble of you to come to her aid," I quip. "I guess you only come to the rescue of females who are fellow traitors. And not those who had been trying to save your sorry ass."

"*You're* the only traitors here," Jabber hisses. "And I can save my own ass, thank you very much."

Ransor laughs at my futile attempt to sway the others. Even though I can tell that Jabber and Lilybet feel visibly bad and ashamed for what they are doing, they're both much too scared of Ransor and the Intergalactic Union to switch sides now.

"You might as well stop trying," Ransor says with a smirk. "No one is going to come to your rescue here. You and Bex are going to wish that I just killed you instead of bringing you back after you see what the Union has in store for you both."

"You're bluffing," I say as I try to get him to tell me more. But this time, Ransor doesn't budge. He rides the rest of the way in silence, which worries me. It means that whatever the Intergalactic Union is planning, it's worse than I can imagine.

All of us sit there quietly since there's nothing else to do. I sit beside Bex and reach out my pinky finger to touch the side of her hand.

"Everything is going to be okay," I assure her. I'm not really sure that's true, but I always tell her that regardless. It makes us both feel better, even if it is only words. Deep down, I think we all know how screwed we are.

When we arrive on Nairu, we are met by Pschye as soon as we step off the ship. She is accompanied by a new Union delegate, one that I have heard mention of but have never seen myself.

"Welcome back," Pschye says sharply. "The lot of you has caused us quite a bit of a headache." She smiles with tight lips, and I know we are definitely in for it. "Ophelia has generously agreed to help me with your reconditioning."

"And by *reconditioning*, do you mean torture and punishment?" Petra asks as she glares at Pschye with a vengeance that could kill.

"I mean Ophelia has been brought in to help bring all of you insurgents into compliance," Pschye answers her as she returns Petra's look with one equally as vicious. "Be it the hard way or not."

"Renegades," Bex says softly.

"Excuse me?" Pschye asks, turning around to look at Bex with contempt. "What did you say?"

Bex straightens herself up in order to meet Pschye's posture. "We are called renegades," Bex growls at her in a sort of calm confidence I haven't seen her have before now.

Pschye's face contorts in anger. I am sure she received quite a scolding from whoever is in charge of the board of Union delegates. None of us have ever seen the "big boss" of the Intergalactic Union, but I'm pretty sure there is one. Otherwise, why would the delegates look nervous whenever things don't go exactly as planned? If I were to guess, I think there's a powerful head to this snake. Maybe someone who stays behind closed doors and pulls the strings like a puppet master. One day, I'd like to find out who it is and their entire purpose for this Union. It can't simply be to just conquer all the planets in the galaxies. What good would that serve someone who is never seen? There has to be another goal here; I just don't know what it is.

All of us are quickly separated, taken by a different henchman of the Union to separate holding cells to wait our consequence and rehabilitation—whatever the hell that means.

I struggle and try to resist being pulled away from Bex, ignoring my own advice that I gave to Aerlon about how pointless it was to resist, but this is different. This is Bex.

The Union lackeys are quick to put us down with stun guns that make it so I can't feel my muscles anymore, and then we are carried away, unable to stand or even speak until the effects of the stun wears off.

I am tossed into a steel containment room and left alone for what seems like days. Food and water are slid through a small rectangular hole in the door that is too small for me to stick anything but a hand through. I sit there thinking about Bex and the tease of a kiss I was able to have before all this happened.

Maybe if I hadn't slept so soundly on the dead planet, I would have heard the assassins coming and been able to get us to a safe hiding place on the other planet before we were captured. Maybe if I hadn't kissed Bex and allowed myself to feel so comfortable and at ease, none of this would have happened. I should have kept my guard up.

Even as I have those thoughts, and even as I sit here worrying about what is happening to her now and if she is okay and in a steel box like me, I still hold onto the memory of that kiss as if it is the one, single thing keeping me going. I'm not sure I would have traded it.

Finally, after I have paced the perimeter of this small cell so much that my boots have nearly dug a small divot into the stone floor, the door opens.

I expect to see a guard, or maybe even Pschye again, but as I try to adjust my eyes to the bright, artificial light that pours into the cell, I see Ophelia.

"Hello, Ben," she says with a wicked smile as she steps inside the cell.

Brave move. I could probably take her, even in my weakened state of confinement.

I look closer at her for the first time. I hadn't really noticed before—mostly because we were being separated and I was worried about Bex—but Ophelia is different than other Union delegates. She is part machine.

"What are you doing here?" I ask, deciding to refrain from trying to attack her when I see the shiny metal arm that she has on one side, and the eye that seems to be automatically adjusting to look at me with different filters.

I don't know what she can do, or what she is capable of. I've never seen anything like her.

"I came to retrieve you and get you out of this prison cell," she says with a perfectly pitched voice. "Unless you'd like to stay in here, of course."

"Where is Bex?"

"I'm not quite sure," she says, looking as if she knows but doesn't want to tell me. "But she isn't my concern. You are. I have been specially assigned to you. I suppose you could say that you are my new pet project."

She takes a step closer to me, and I am taken aback by her form. She is beautiful but strange, and the seams where her pinkish flesh seem to meet with the sharp hardware infused into her body look almost painful.

"I have a whole new purpose for you," she continues as she reaches the tip of a cold, metallic finger out to tap the side of my temple. "You're a smart human, aren't you? That is why you've been chosen for such an honor, even though you've been so naughty."

"What honor?" I ask, ignoring the rest of her condescending comment.

"I'm going to help refine and reform you, make you into something worthy of admiration. Granted, it is no small task, to say the least. I am sure that I can do it, though. I have special skills to meet the job."

I stare at her silently. She's monologuing, too. What is it with these power-bloated people and their need to hear themselves talk so much? I wonder if her tongue is flesh or machine. Either way, I think I'd like to rip it out. Instead, I wait for her to get on with it.

"You see, I have the special task of executing your punishment," Ophelia continues. "It's such a clever mix of things that will break you. I am going to recreate you, Ben, in order to make you a delegate of the Intergalactic Union."

15

BEX

When Pschye comes into the room I've been confined in, I lunge at her with the intent to strike her down. I don't even care anymore what happens to me. I'm sick of having things torn from my hands and taken away.

I don't get far with my attempt before a couple of guards rush into the room and restrain me.

Too bad. I would have liked to see if Pschye could defend herself.

"Nice to see that you are so full of energy and vigor," she says snidely. "How about the two of us sit down and have a chat, woman to woman?"

She waves her hands for the guards to leave us, and they hesitantly let me go. They linger for a moment to see if I am going to make another attempt to attack her, but it's all pointless. So, I sit down at the only table in the room instead.

Pschye comes to sit down across from me, and the guards leave.

"What do you want with us?" I snarl at her. "Why has

the Union chosen to keep us all alive and not just killed us already, like you would have done with anyone else who went against the mission team? That's the rule, is it not? To kill anyone who betrays the team or defies the Union's directive?"

Pschye nods. "Yes, that is indeed the rule."

She stares at me for a minute, as if she is trying to decide what, and how much, to tell me.

"We have plans for you," she says, avoiding giving me a straight answer.

I am constantly unnerved by her double-pupiled eyes. I have yet to meet a Spewt that hasn't proven to be a despicable coward or simply a terrible person.

Instead of telling me what our fates are going to be, she stands up from the table and instructs me to come with her. Since I obviously have no choice in the matter, considering there are a handful of less than friendly guards just outside the door, and since I am sick of being stuck in this room, I follow her.

"Where are we going?" I ask once we get into the corridor.

Pschye doesn't answer—no big surprise.

We walk through the Intergalactic Union station, and then all the way out into the open air of the planet of Nairu. The air is thick and heady. It must have just finished storming here.

"Have you ever traveled out into the open country of Nairu?" Pschye asks.

"No," I answer, wondering why she cares. "I've been outside on this station before, but I've never gone all the way out into the open lands."

"Perfect." She smiles, seeming pleased with my answer. "It takes a lot of effort and resources to support and fund the missions the Union deploys. Of course, we do it all in the name of betterment, not just for our own society, but for all the civilizations on all the planets and life in the universe."

"You'll have to forgive me if I doubt that," I scoff. "I highly doubt that anything the Intergalactic Union does is for the betterment of anyone but yourselves."

For a moment, Pschye looks slightly less evil, staring far off in the distance at something I cannot see.

"I think you have a lot to learn still," she says as she starts to walk forward.

I walk alongside her as we head out into the open lands of Nairu, because what better thing do I have to do? Everyone has been separated, and I don't know where anyone, including Ben, is being held. My greatest chance of finding out any information is to stay with Pschye and see if I can get her to tell me anything at all. She seems weird this time—different—but I still don't trust her.

"Do you see double with those extra pupils?" I ask while we walk.

I am partly intending to be rude and disarm her into getting angry with me, and partly trying to make chitchat to keep myself from trying to kill her again. Even if I succeeded in killing her, which I doubt I would, it wouldn't get me far. She is only one Union delegate, and this entire planet is beneath their rule.

But Pschye doesn't seem angry or offended by my remark as I hoped.

"No," she answers factually. "But we do see clearer. I can see things that your lacking human mind could not hope to process."

I frown because this exercise in futility is getting me nowhere.

After not too long a walk, we arrive at what looks to be the equivalent of a working farm. There are several resources being managed here, and the people toiling away on the farm look no better off than slaves.

"Bex!" a voice shouts out.

Up ahead, I see Vira running toward me. Beside her, Petra is there, too.

"What is this?" I ask as I suddenly realize that this walk isn't just a leisurely stroll. Pschye has brought me to this place for a reason.

"This is the farm where you will be staying for the rest of your mortal life now," she answers with a coldness in her voice like no other. "You will slave away on this work farm in order to support the furthering of the Intergalactic Union's missions. With every crop you harvest, and every livestock you slaughter, you will know that you are feeding the bellies of those assassins who will do the things you and your insurgent team failed to do. With every fabric you weave until your fingers bleed, you will know you are clothing the very Union delegates whom you so erroneously disobeyed."

I can feel the hatred swelling in my chest as my blood pushes against my veins.

"You see, *this* is why we didn't kill you," she sneers. "Death isn't a sufficient punishment for those who seek to undermine the Union and its noble purposes. Instead, you will spend the rest of your life in misery, working to help the very governing body you despise so much."

"Like hell I will," I growl at her.

"Oh, you will," Pschye says with a sinister smile. "And you will see, in time, the entire reason you are here."

"What the hell is that supposed to mean? Where is

Ben?" I scream just as Vira reaches my side. Petra is not far behind her.

Pschye turns to leave without answering me, and I reach to grab her wrist.

"Let her go, Bex," Petra says as she places her hand on my shoulder.

"What? Why? We could take her right now! There are no guards here. The three of us can easily kill this snake!"

"You don't know everything yet," Petra says. "Let her go."

I turn to look at her in disbelief. Since when does Petra back down from a fight, and since when would she want to spare Pschye?

"Listen to her, Bex," Vira says with a shaking voice. Her skin is a strange color I haven't seen before, so I have no idea what kind of emotion she is conveying.

I grumble to myself and let Pschye's arm go with a sharp snap of my hand.

Pschye stands there, looking pleased as she rubs her arm. I hope it leaves a bruise. Then she turns and walks away without ever telling me where Ben is.

"What the hell?" I ask as I turn to look at both Vira and Petra, unable to hide how upset I am. "Why would you stop me? I am heading right back to that Union station right now to find Ben."

"You can't," Petra says as she points off toward the perimeter. "There are guards stationed nearly every ten feet. There is no escaping the work farm. It's also laden with all sorts of kill traps in place for when the guards go on their breaks."

All the more reason they should have let me kill Pschye when I had the chance.

"Where's Aerlon?" I ask as I look behind them to see if

any of the other people slaving away on the farm resemble his perfectly chiseled form.

"We don't know for sure," Vira says, "but we've heard rumors that he has been put back on the members team as an assassin."

"That's impossible." I shake my head. "None of the other assassins would trust him now, and I doubt the Union would trust him not to sabotage another mission, either. Why would they risk it by allowing him back on a team?"

Petra shrugs. "No idea, but there's a lot of chatter here on the farm and word gets around. Some of the aliens are more forthcoming than others. That's all that we've heard about him. We heard about you, too—that you were kept in seclusion for a few days until Pschye was ready to deal with you."

"We didn't know if you would be brought here, though," Vira interjects. "I'm glad to see you."

This isn't the time for warm reunions.

"What about Ben?" I ask anxiously. "Have you heard anything about him?"

The two of them exchange a glance, and I can immediately see that they know something—something they don't want to tell me. I try not to panic, even though I feel as if my heart is stopping.

"What have you heard?" I press. "Tell me."

They stay silent.

"Tell me!" I demand again.

Vira looks absolutely miserable. Her face is a sick shade of chartreuse, and her braids are tied up tight enough that I can see a few of her cloudy gray thoughts dripping down behind her eyes. I can't make out any images in them, though. It's as if she doesn't even want to think anymore.

"We did hear something," she says, then stops.

"It's not good, Bex," Petra picks up for her. "Word has it that Ben has been chosen to be Ophelia's new pet."

"Ophelia? The Union delegate that was there when we got off the ship with Pschye?"

"Yeah." Petra nods. "She's a force to be reckoned with. Even worse than Pschye, from what I've heard. She's part organic alien lifeform and part machine. Sort of like a cyborg, I guess, but way more deadly."

"What does she want with Ben?"

The two of them look at each other again.

"Okay, look, you two seriously need to stop that," I scold. "If we have any chance of getting out of this mess, then all three of us need to be on the same team. You can't keep things from me."

"She's right," Vira says as she looks sadly over at Petra.

Petra gives her a nod. "You tell her then. I don't want to get punched in the face."

By the time Vira turns to me and finally opens her mouth, my nerves are so shot that I feel like I am either going to have a panic attack or take someone out.

"Ophelia is grooming Ben to be a Union delegate himself," Vira says.

I am in shock. I am in too much shock at what she has said to even process words for several long minutes as I stand there, and the sky opens back up with rain.

"We should go inside the building," Vira says.

"No." I shake my head adamantly without moving. "Ben will never go along with being anyone's pet. And he will never go along with being part of such a horrible and corrupted system. He won't do it. The Union and Ophelia are wasting their time. Ben won't switch sides and turn against us."

The sky rumbles with what is Nairu's equivalent of

thunder, except on this planet, the sound actually cracks the sky and loosens more rain to fall in big heavy drops that pummel the top of my head.

"Bex," Petra says in a tone that is calmer and quieter than I have ever heard her use before. "I know how much Ben means to you, and I know you mean just as much to him. But sadly, I don't think he will have a choice. The Intergalactic Union is hell-bent on making us all pay for turning against them, and they seem especially focused on making you and Ben suffer. There's no telling in what ways they could get him to obey."

I still keep shaking my head feverishly, as if I cannot stop. "He won't break," I say. "He's tougher than they think."

"*Bgh'sgharti alune nahorem,*" Petra says, as if it is some sort of gibberish chant. She reaches out and places a hand on the top of my shoulder. "That means *everyone can be broken in some way.* It's a language that is no longer used because the species it stems from was annihilated by the Union years ago. They thought they couldn't be broken, too."

I stare at her as tears well in my eyes, and I get angry at myself for wanting to cry.

"I'm not trying to say that we should just roll over and die," Petra says. "But I do think we need to be realistic if we want to survive this."

For a moment, I stand there and think about her words, from both of the languages, and what they mean. Then…it dawns on me.

I tilt my head up toward the sky, which is now storming intensely, soaking the three of us to the skin. I let the deluge wash away the tears from my face. When I finally look back down again, I can feel the resurgence of defiance that is building up its very own storm within me.

"Bex?" Vira asks as she looks at me with concern. "Are you okay?"

"We should go inside now," Petra repeats. "We need to get out of this storm."

"Why?" I ask as a smile slowly grows on my face at the realization I have just found. "The storm, along with those words you just said, have given me the greatest idea of all."

"What idea?" Petra asks with a furrowed brow.

"You said that everyone can be broken in some way," I repeat. "*Everyone*, right?"

"Yeah, that was kind of the point of the saying."

"Then that means the Intergalactic Union and every one of its delegates can be broken, too," I say, feeling the water drip from the sides of my smile. "And I intend to break every last one of them."

16

OPHELIA

The thing with having so many cybernetic parts is that it's a constant effort to keep everything oiled and running smoothly.

I reach into one of the drawers in the vanity in front of me and rummage around for which hand I am going to adorn myself with today. I have so many now. So many appendages to go with my outfits, and moods, and whims.

I look into the mirror and stare back at my face. I am constantly amazed at how beautiful I am, and I am continually reminded that every sacrifice I have made up until this point has been worth it in order to gain this much power.

I choose the hand I want to wear and begin to affix it clumsily to the half-organic stump of my arm. Just as I think that I need a third hand just to attach my own self together, there is a knock at the door.

"Madame Ophelia," the guard bellows from the other side of the slab. "Your pet has been cleaned up and is ready now."

"Wonderful." I smile to myself in the mirror. It would

seem that my "third hand" has arrived right in the nick of time. "Bring him in."

The door opens, and the guard shoves Ben through the door with a solid push that sends him stumbling over his feet.

"My, my," I say as I look him over. "Don't you clean up nicely."

This disheveled human who needed a bath and a solid attitude adjustment now stands before me all cleaned up and dressed in proper Union attire. He almost looks presentable, although there is a wild side to him that makes my blood rush through the portion of my body with organic veins.

Ben looks at me indignantly, but then he seems distracted by the hand that is still sitting on the vanity.

"What are you?" he asks with increased intrigue. "Are you part human and part machine?"

"Oh no, dear." I laugh. "I am no part human, I can assure you of that. But I *am* part machine. And at the moment, I could use a bit of help with this." I motion toward the hand, then toward my handless arm that needs tending to.

"Is this why you've brought me here, so I can tend to your broken parts?" he asks defiantly.

"As I have already told you, you are my pet and my charge," I repeat. I wonder why humans are so daft and require so much hand-holding to get them to follow simple directions. "Today will be the first day I teach you how to act as a delegate to the Intergalactic Union." I reach down and pick up the hand to attach myself. I no longer want his help since he is obviously so averse to being respectful.

"Of course, I don't want you to get the wrong idea," I

continue. "This whole thing is not an honor on your behalf. It is a punishment."

"A punishment?" he asks with a roll of his eyes, as if I said something incompetent, or humorous even. "Is this how you *punish* all those who break the Union's rules? You clean them up, put them in Union attire, and then bring them on board? You must have a very complex issue with loyalty."

"Let me make this startlingly clear for you since you seem to lack the brainpower to see things for yourself," I hiss, quickly losing patience with his attitude. He may be handsome, for a human, but he lacks any impressive qualities that would make him a fit delegate. I am going to have my work cut out for me.

"Your job in the Union will be to oversee the strict compliance of your friends, who have all been assigned other positions here on Nairu. You will squash anyone who attempts to rebel, as you tried to do yourself. If any of your friends get out of line or disobey their new stations in life here, then you will see to it that they are harshly punished."

"And if I don't punish them?" he asks.

Oh good. I was hoping he would ask that question. I like it when I get to elaborate on the fun bits.

"Then it will fall to me." I grin. "And I can assure you that my idea of punishment will be much, *much* worse than what you will be tasked with doing."

This is a glorious day. I love it when I have a new purpose to set my attention on, and breaking this human is my newest intention.

I twist the mechanical hand onto my arm, then dig the small screwdriver out of the drawer. While Ben stands there gawking, I screw the piece into place.

"You're bleeding," he says as he points to the place where the artificial wrist meets the nub of my flesh.

There is a bright red stream of blood that runs down my forearm and drips off the tip of my elbow and onto the top of the vanity. I've always been rather perturbed that I bleed in the same color that humans do, but I suppose we all have our flaws, no matter how minute.

"Of course I am," I answer with indifference as I finish turning the screws from the metal piece through my flesh and into my bone.

"I would have thought that a Union delegate would have a more advanced way of attaching a prosthetic than literally screwing hardware into your body," he scoffs.

"Then you are a fool. What is better than affixing something in such a steadfast and painful way than screwing it into your very bones? I change body parts out as often as I change outfits, and each time I do, it requires pain. Pain is the only way in which we learn strength, and I can see you have not been taught enough of it. But, don't worry; I intend to cure you of that lacking."

Once fully attached, the advanced technology in my hand integrates itself with my nervous system, and I am now able to sense the slightest touch on my smooth, metal fingertips. Or play the most intricate melody with the bow of a violin gliding with sheer agility in my hand.

I am a beautiful balance of advanced and refined technology, and brutally wrought frailty that comes with having flesh.

"Are you ready?" I ask as I stand up, ready to begin the day of training with my new little project.

"For what?"

"To begin your training. We will start with grooming you to act more like a delegate and less like a layperson."

"I refuse," he says, as if he is trying to make a martyr of himself.

This is a dumb hill for him to die on since nothing at all will come of it.

"I don't think you understand that there is no opportunity for you to refuse here, Ben. This is not a choice you have been given; it is the punishment that you will serve and suffer."

"Well, I won't do it. I won't abide by your training, and I won't punish my friends, and I most certainly will not become a delegate of the Union," he says stubbornly.

Instead of lowering myself to argue with this miniscule lifeform, I simply smile because I have chosen this hand that I am wearing for precisely this reason.

I have several different limbs to act as my "accessories" to various tasks and needs, and something told me I would be needing this one today. Perhaps it was the look of stubborn defiance that he gave me the first time I saw him, or maybe it was simply because I was hoping for a chance to rough him up a bit myself. I despise insurgents.

I step closer to him as he stands there in the center of my room with his prim and proper Union suit adorning the body of a human that doesn't seem to fit it well. I reach out a single finger to place against the lower part of his chest.

Before he can move away, I sweep my finger quickly against his shirt and cut into his skin with one of the blades hiding inside the cyborg finger om my hand. The blade is sharp enough to cut through bone if I want it to. But this time is just a warning.

It cuts his lovely shirt and slices his skin open like butter, releasing a deluge of blood onto his new outfit that he clearly despises, anyway. It most certainly hurts him, although he doesn't react much more than a slight wince. I can tell he is just trying not to give me the satisfaction of a reaction as he glares at me.

"For each act of defiance, and each refusal to do as you are told," I say with a punitive tone, "you will receive a new scar. And trust me…it will leave a scar."

He glares at me without saying a single word—*good*. At least he has stopped his incessant arguing.

"Come with me," I say as I walk toward the door. "I am going to show you to your new post."

Ben follows behind me, not bothering to cover or clean up the cut on his chest as we walk down the hallways of the station. We reach a large room at the end of the hall framed by two closed, black double doors.

"Welcome to your new position," I say as I push open the doors to reveal a large room with walls covered in screens. There are a few people sitting at their stations and monitoring the activities that they have been assigned to. All along the walls are secrets revealed for Ben to see. Mouthwatering morsels of knowledge and insight into the Union's business that is sure to tempt his curiosity.

"All of these screens monitor the things and people that the Union is watching both here on Nairu and around the galaxies," I say with a flourish of my hand. "The intricacies of the Intergalactic Union's most prized plans are revealed in this room."

"Then why would you show me this?" Ben asks, finally relenting to speaking to me again. I knew he couldn't stay silent in here. "If these are Union secrets, then you are risking your security by showing them to me?"

I can't help but laugh at how foolish this human is. "You are such an insignificant piece of this puzzle," I say. "One tiny cog in a great machine. Do you really think the Union is afraid of anything that you could possibly threaten to do?

Take a look around. Maybe it will help offer you some perspective."

I stand and wait as he walks closer to look at some of the images on the screens and thumb through some of the files and notebooks on the desks.

"It's fine," I say when one of the other workers begins to protest. "He can look at whatever he likes—he's with me."

Instantly, the worker nods and goes back to her work, leaving the papers for Ben to look at.

"I don't understand," Ben says after a few minutes of reading. "How could this be true?"

"Which thing?"

He holds up a file and points to the screen in front of the woman. "You said that the goal of the Intergalactic Union was the betterment of everyone," he snarls at me. "But according to this stuff, the Union is doing the exact opposite." He walks over to me and pushes the file up against my chest, as if he is smacking me with it.

Apparently, I have not yet instilled a healthy fear of punishment in him—something I will need to work on.

"Those documents indicate you are wiping out planets and populations. This stuff all points to the fact that the Union deems civilizations as disposable."

"True," I say, handing the file back to him and running my metal hand dangerously close to his heart. "I don't need to look at this. I already know all of the Union's secrets."

"These secrets are much worse than even I imagined," he says with disgust.

"You're missing the forest for the trees," I say, an old adage that stemmed from his species, I believe. "There is a much greater force pushing everything toward the future. The Intergalactic Union seeks power to harness that force, and it seeks to prevent itself from dying out. This is a mission of self-preservation to ensure that the great entity of the Union thrives and survives forever. And if we need to do a little destruction and engage in a bit of corruption in order to do so, then so be it. Try to use your feeble little mind to see the big picture."

"How is that a big picture? It's shallow, and egocentric, and a very narrow view of your own survival. You think that just because you save a few sample species here and there that you're somehow making amends for all the life you are wiping out like some sort of parasite?"

"You'll come around," I say, not wanting to entertain his argument any longer.

"Why would you risk showing me all this and letting me have all this information when you know I am against the Union and all that it stands for?"

"Like I said before, you cannot do anything to stop this," I answer. "In fact, you will be a key component of helping to drive our success."

"Don't hold your breath," he grumbles.

"You are special, Ben, and one day you will know why. But until that time is revealed to you, I would greatly appreciate that you simply cooperate and not make this any harder than it needs to be." I try to sound rational and calm with him, imposing a new approach to see if he will be more malleable to reason. "The universe is constantly creating itself, and the discovery of new and uncharted planets is infinitely possible. We will need your help in order to further our goals."

"I thought you said I wasn't of any value to you or the Union."

"No," I correct him. "What I said was that there was nothing you could threaten us with, which remains true.

But you *are* of value to us, and that is why we need you to cooperate."

"I'm not going to cooperate with you," he growls, still glaring furiously at me. "I won't do a single damn thing to support anything that the Union does. I want no part in any of it, and I demand to see Bex before I take another step anywhere with you."

I can feel the flesh covered side of my face flush with the heat of anger, and I know without looking that my beautiful cream complexion is turning a shade of scarlet. I have lost patience with him.

"You will cooperate," I snarl. I can feel my lips curl around the metal curve of my left cheek. "And it is exactly because of Bex that you will do as you are told. Let me show you."

I walk up to one of the screens myself and use my fingers to pinch against the glass and change the camera angle.

"There are cameras placed in every corner of Nairu, including the work farms," I say as I smile viciously at him. I know I am going to enjoy seeing his reaction to this delicious morsel of torment. "I bet you never even knew that there were work farms on Nairu, did you?" I don't wait for him to answer. "Well, your precious Bex is here," I say as I zoom in and point to her on the monitor. "Looks like she is hard at work, toiling away, doing manual labor already."

Ben is suddenly unarmed as he stares longingly at the screen.

"Is this her punishment?" he asks. "She has to be a slave while I get dressed up in fancy clothes and indoctrinated into the governing body? Why the discrepancy when we both committed the same infraction of insurgency? If anything, I should receive the harsher punishment. I'm the one who drove the stolen ship."

"Oh, don't worry my dear, you *are* receiving the harsher punishment, I can assure you. You are going to be the very thing that Bex hates—one of us. And if you refuse, trying to act all noble and plan some sort of great escape and rescue of your friends, then their deaths will come swifter than you can possibly imagine."

"What are you talking about?"

"Look," I say as I change the camera angle again. "See that assassin there? The one in the red jumpsuit that stands just out of sight of your little girlfriend while she works? That is the assassin who has been assigned to watch over Bex continuously. In the event that you refuse to do as you are told, that assassin will be given the command to kill Bex on the spot. And don't for a second think that any of us would hesitate to do it. We would rather keep you alive than her. She is simply our collateral for making sure you are compliant."

I can see the look on his face change from one of indignant anger to one of helpless nausea. This last part is going to be the most fun of all.

"The last thing that I will show you for now"—I grin —"simply because you deserve a bit more anguish today for being so difficult. Maybe it will teach you to be more agreeable tomorrow for your second day of training."

I zoom all the way in so the assassin's face is now visible on the monitors. Then I turn to look at Ben so that I can fully enjoy his reaction as he stares at the screen and sees who we have recruited as the assassin to do the job of killing Bex if necessary—Aerlon.

17

BEX

The work farm is hard labor. We are being treated like slaves, but I don't complain or even care, because my sights are set on something far more important.

I am going to find out who is at the very top of the Intergalactic Union, and I am going to break them.

I have already figured out that the work farm is closely monitored by cameras. I can see them everywhere—inside the meager dwelling, the barns, even hovering in drones above the fields. I assume that we are being constantly and carefully watched over by the Union in the event that we try to escape or otherwise wreak havoc. I can just picture Pschye sitting there at her thin little desk with her equally-as-thin-lipped smile as she watches me toil over the fields to feed her stomach and the looms to weave her stupid dresses. There isn't even a need for most of this now. With the technology that the Union possesses, machines can do these jobs in far less time and with far greater efficiency, but that is not the point. The point is punishment and humiliation.

Over our meager dinner, after a hard day of slaving on

the farm in yet another rainstorm that made me soggy all the way down to my undergarments, I decide it's time to break the hell out of here.

"I've been watching the guards," I whisper to Petra and Vira as they eat the chunk of stale bread and salted meat that we were given as rations. "I know when each of them takes their breaks, and I know their shift rotation by heart. There is a gap of a few minutes between the shift change overnight. *That* is the time to escape."

"You can't escape here," Petra says again. "There are kill traps set everywhere. You step on one of those, and you're dead."

"I know where they are."

"That's impossible. You can't possibly know where all the traps are."

"I do. I've been watching the pattern that the guards walk. They carefully avoid the places where there are kill traps. I know the rotations by heart and the safe patterns of ground at the edge of the work farm."

"Please don't tell us that you're going to risk trying to escape." Vira frowns. "I don't want anything to happen to you."

"I am going to try to escape—tonight," I say in a hushed voice. "And I need the two of you to stay behind and cover for me. I promise I will come back to get you if I don't wind up getting caught and killed."

"And there's no way we can talk you out of this foolish plan?" Petra asks.

I shake my head.

"All right, we'll help," she answers for them both. "But if you manage to survive this, you had better not forget about us and leave us here to rot."

"Of course I won't!" I say, surprised that she would even think that.

We wait until the shift change. It's just a few minutes before the next rotation, so we don't have much time. I sneak toward the border of the work farm while Vira and Petra watch from a distance to make sure that the guards don't come back early without me knowing. But the one thing I didn't plan on—which I probably should have, knowing how vile Pschye is and that she would have a back-up plan to keep me trapped here—is the assassin. Just as I am almost about to step off the work farm and avoid the traps and guards as I run out of here in the cover of darkness, I see the form of the assassin with his red jumpsuit lit up by the moonlight.

I should have known better. I should have been prepared for this. Pschye assigned an assassin to watch my every move and likely kill me on the spot if I try to escape or step out of line. The Union might have wanted to keep me alive for some future purpose, but I know that if I become too much of a problem to outweigh my worth to them, then the assassin likely has already been given instructions to put me down if I cause a problem.

But I am already here.

I look behind me and see Petra and Vira delaying the guards that have come back early. Now is the only chance I will get. So, I make a run for it.

I have to escape this work farm, infiltrate the Union station, and find whoever is in charge. If I don't get out now, then it will all be too late.

From there, I don't really have any other plan. I didn't really get any further with it other than to kill whoever it is that is leading the Union. I figure that if I can cut off the head of the snake, then the delegates will be far easier to break. And I want to break them all. Pschye already looks like her resolve or allegiance has been wavering a bit, and I have no idea why. She seems to truly enjoy her evil ways and position of power.

I give one more quick glance over my shoulder, and then I run as fast as I can, hoping I might luck out and that the assassin might not be a fast or an accurate shot if he tries to aim at me.

But before I can get too far, a shot is fired that narrowly misses me. As much as I am grateful for the miss, it is highly unlikely that one of the assassins missed on accident. The Union ensures that all assassins aim to kill as if their own lives depend on it, because they do.

I stand there and look at the assassin as he walks slowly toward me with the gun still in his hand while both Vira and Petra come running to help me at the sound of the fired shot. Everyone converges on the same spot at once, and all three of us stand there in shock when we see the face of the assassin in the moonlight.

"Aerlon?" Vira asks quietly. She looks at him in astonishment, as if she isn't sure whether to be happy to see him or gutted to see that he is the assassin.

We stand there in the twilight staring at him until Aerlon finally speaks.

"I missed the shot on purpose," he says in a hushed voice. "I wanted to get your attention because we all need to talk."

"I'll say," Petra mumbles under her breath.

"Come, follow me." He turns to sneak off with us to find somewhere private to talk.

"Should we follow him?" Vira asks. "Can we even trust him, now that he is an assassin?"

I shrug. "Maybe not, but I want some answers."

All four of us walk toward one of the empty barns used to store machinery for the work farm, and Aerlon breaks the lock to let us inside. As soon as we get inside and he closes the door behind us, he launches into telling us about everything that he knows and has found out.

"My punishment was to be assigned as the assassin that would keep Bex in line or kill her if she tried to escape or cause trouble. The Union knew that not only didn't I want to be an assassin in their new schemes, but that Bex became my friend. It was as if they were trying to craft the perfect punishment that would upset me the most."

"Yeah, that is definitely not a surprise. They've done the same to all of us, I think. But why wait until now to reveal yourself to us?" I ask.

"I'm still trying to get a feeling on what's going on here," Aerlon answers. "I've been watching the other guards and watching the delegates back at the station. They're up to something—something big—but I don't know what it is yet. When I saw you trying to escape tonight, I realized that I had to get your attention and couldn't wait any longer. What are you trying to do, Bex? If they catch you, they'll kill you."

"I know that. But I have to find Ben. Have you seen him?"

"No."

"I thought that they sent you on another mission off of Nairu," Vira says. "We heard you were made an assassin, but we also heard that you were sent on another mission to another planet."

"That was just a cover. They wanted to make sure that no one figured out that I was still here and assigned to keeping an eye on Bex." He turns to look at me with caution in his eyes, but there is also something else there. I dare to think that it might be hope. "Bex, the Union might seem unstoppable, but it's not. I have seen cracks in their armor."

"What kind of cracks?" Petra asks as she leans in closer to listen to him carefully.

Before Aerlon even answers, I tell him that I have seen them, too. I can't really explain what they are because they are more like feelings, subtle nuances, like the way that Pschye seems discontent. Or even the way that the guards here at the work farm have a gap in their rotation. One would think that an entity as powerful as the Intergalactic Union wouldn't make small mistakes like that, mistakes that could cause them big trouble if they aren't careful.

"I can't really explain it," Aerlon says, echoing my own thoughts. "But I can see there are kinks in what they want to portray as a seamless appearance."

"Aerlon," I say as I focus back onto my plan of getting out of here, "do you know if there is a higher-up? Someone who controls the delegates in the Union? Or is it just the panel of delegates that runs things here?"

"There is definitely someone in control of it all," he answers.

I can feel the excitement rise in my chest because this is what I'm hoping for, that there is a kingpin, a master of command, and someone that the other delegates like Pschye have to answer to. It could explain her air of dissatisfaction with things. I don't see her as the kind of person who is content to follow rules; I see Pschye as the one who wants to run the entire show herself.

"It always amused me that they call themselves delegates, and that whole bunch of them calls themselves a Union," Petra scoffs. "They are the most power-hungry and vile bunch of people, who I am sure would be just as willing to stab each other in the back if they thought it would launch their own goals. To label themselves as a diplomatic body is more than hypocritical."

I nod in agreement, but want to hear more about what Aerlon knows.

"I don't know much about who it is," he says. "I've never seen the man, never heard anything of importance about him, and don't even know where in the station he resides. But I do know that he exists."

"How?"

"Because every day, I am required to go back to the station to give a report to the Union, to update them about you three and if anything of pertinence has happened here on the work farm. The other day, when I went to give my report, I heard arguing inside the room I was supposed to go inside to meet with the delegates. It was Pschye and that cyborg woman."

"Ophelia?" Petra asks with a look of disdain. "She's pure evil. I don't care if she is part machine, part alien, or part goddess—that creature is as malevolent as they come."

"Agreed," Aerlon says quickly before continuing. "I couldn't tell what it was that they were arguing about, but I could tell that the matter was something of importance, and something that they needed to report to *him*. Ophelia was making a big fuss about it not being her job to give their leader bad news and that Pschye should be the one to tell him. And Pschye's voice…well, it sounded nervous."

"I can't even picture that vile woman being nervous," Vira says as she shakes her head. "She is the most impenetrable and scary person that I have ever met." The color of her face turns dark with fear.

"I wish I had more information to tell you," Aerlon says. "And I wish that I could have figured out what it was that the two women were arguing about, but one of the other delegates came up behind me and pushed me into the room. They accused me of eavesdropping and interrogated me for several minutes to make sure I hadn't heard anything. Then they threatened to go back to the dead planet to find and murder Amity if I didn't mind my own business and do my job." Aerlon's face drops. "I hardly believe she would still be alive now, anyway," he says with a pervasive sadness.

"We have to still hope and believe that she is," I reassure him as I put a hand on his shoulder. "After all, if we can stay alive in this place, then surely Amity and Clover are still managing, too."

"Yeah, at least they don't have to contend with the Union," Petra adds. "I'd choose a big predator any day over one of these covert and even more lethal predators that hide behind viciously pretty faces."

Her comment, although well-meaning, didn't help matters because it just jogged Aerlon's memory of the dangerous beasts on the dead planet that Amity is dealing with now, alone.

"Oh," he says after a few minutes in which we all take a moment to recollect our thoughts. "There is one more thing that I do know about whoever it is that is leading the Intergalactic Union."

"What is it?"

"His name," Aerlon answers. "I heard them mention it while I was outside the door before I got caught. Matheus."

18

BEN

I just can't wrap my head around the fact that Aerlon would be willing to be an assassin against Bex. Although, I doubt that he simply agreed to it. It's much more likely that the Union threatened him in some way that he couldn't deny. Maybe they convinced him by telling him they would go back to the dead planet to retrieve Amity and do something atrocious to her, like dismember her limb from limb—assuming that the giant creatures on the dead planet haven't already beaten them to the task. Whatever the reason or the blackmail, I still can't picture Aerlon lodging a bullet in Bex. He doesn't seem like the kind of guy who could live with himself after doing something like that.

But people change, especially when they are confronted with terrible options that they never thought they would have to consider. The Union changes the rules on everything, including the rules that would keep most people decent.

"Are you excited about your first interaction with the

Union today?" Ophelia asks with enthusiasm when she comes to my room in the morning.

I have been given a small, nearly bare room in the same hallways as hers. There is a bed, a table, and a window that is affixed shut so I can't open it. The door doesn't lock, and there is a bathroom through a small door off the room so I do not need to venture out into the hallway past the guards until Ophelia comes to fetch me. This is the way that the Union wants things—controlled.

"I thought I interacted with the Union when you took me to see all the screens and threatened Bex's life if I refused to comply."

"No, tsk," she says with a sharp snap of her tongue, as if I am too far beneath her to understand what she's saying. "Those people were merely workers, not delegates. You might want to get better at recognizing positions of power. You won't make much of an impression if you can't tell the difference between the servants and the dignitaries."

"I don't give a shit about making a good impression," I say. "I have agreed to do what I need in order to protect Bex, but I don't need to enjoy it."

Ophelia rolls her eyes, and it's the first time that I can see some of her internal wiring. When her one mechanical eye rolls upward, it exposes the tiny web of wires beneath it. She's a strange paradox of uniquely beautiful and horribly unnerving to look at.

"Well, this is your second day of training, and you are lucky because there is a gala event today that will be the perfect opportunity for me to introduce you to the other delegates. Do try to be on your best behavior. It won't do you or Bex any good to make enemies here."

By now, I would think that she would already know they are all my enemies.

When we walk into the large ballroom, there are several delegates there already, many more than I thought existed.

"I thought there were only four of you," I say quietly as I turn to Ophelia.

She is dressed in a white silk gown that hangs over the curves of both her organic and mechanical features in a flattering way that shows she is trying to make herself look appealing to someone here.

"There are only four of us on the Intergalactic Union board of delegates," she says. "But all the other people here are supporters in some way. Some are wealthy contributors, benefactors, and some are politically powerful and hold influence on other planets. You don't need to mind yourself with most of them, though. It's really just the four of us in the Union that you should concern yourself with."

No sooner does she finish talking that the other three Union members see us walk in and approach. I am already way too familiar with Pschye, and I detest the vile woman. And unfortunately, I already have the pleasure of knowing Ophelia, too. But the other two are less familiar to me.

The other two delegates are both male. Drelax, I have seen before. He was there during our first mission initiation before we left Nairu. His appearance is unmistakable, thanks to his several rows of teeth that are so crowded inside his mouth that you can see the ridges of them even when his mouth is closed.

The other is Clyde. I've glimpsed him only once before, and I've never heard him speak. I don't even know if he does speak, although I'm assuming that he would have to in order to be in the Union. Clyde is rumored to have godlike strength, which goes hand in hand with his appearance of being more that of a giant beast than a man. He is covered in coarse fur and towers above even the tallest person here.

Down by his ankles hangs a tail that I've heard sometimes doubles as a lethal whip.

None of these people are to be trifled with.

For a while, I stand there and listen with glassed-over eyes as the four of them talk about things of unimportance. I want to hear about things that will give me answers and help me rescue Bex. Instead, they act like gluttonous fools, talking about their delicious foods and shiny things. To think I once at least gave the Union credit for being a powerful governing body when now they sound like nothing more than the spoiled elite.

"You certainly cleaned him up well," Pschye sneers as she looks at me.

"Thank you." Ophelia beams. "I keep him on a tight leash."

If she continues to act like I am some sort of leashed dog, then I am going to wind up losing it and biting her like the rabid animal she thinks I am.

I look around the room while I continue to only half-listen to what they are saying about me. I honestly don't even care anymore; I just want to find Bex. Maybe she's here. Maybe they brought her in to help serve food, like a servant, or to watch as they parade me around like a shiny new toy.

But I don't see her. I only see other people talking and eating, and some of them are staring over at me as if I am a circus oddity. One man in particular seems as if he can't stop looking at me from the opposite side of the room.

I hear one of the delegates hint that there is something *unique* about me, and I turn to finally open my mouth and engage in the conversation.

"What is it that you find unusual and special about

me?" I ask the four of them. "Is there something that sepa-rates me from all the other humans you killed?"

"You make us sound like murderers, Ben," Clyde says in a low growl. His voice is everything I would have imagined it to be—low, strong, and predatorial.

I get ready to open my mouth and tell them that they indeed *are* murderers, even though I know I probably shouldn't. However, Ophelia grabs me sharply by the side of my arm to prevent it. She looks as if she is simply holding my arm like we were dates at prom, yet I feel her metal finger digging into my skin and know she is giving me a warning.

Their conversations continue, and I have a feeling they are tediously dragging their nonsensical conversation out as a test to see how long I will stand there obediently. I hate them all. All I can think about is trying to find a way to get back to Bex and the others, if there are still any of the others left who haven't yet been killed or betrayed us by now.

"Stay," Ophelia barks with taunting sarcasm as the dele-gates move to go and refill their glasses with a golden, bubbly liquid that I am sure is potently alcoholic.

"You're just going to leave him alone?" Clyde asks her in surprise.

"I'd hardly say he is alone in a room full of people," she says. "And Ben knows better than to disobey me. He has already been warned of the consequences of going against a command I give him, and he wouldn't dream of it. Isn't that right, Ben?"

I don't say anything because I don't need to. The answer is obvious as I stand here in the middle of this lavish event and watch them walk off to a table not too far from me that is laden with decanters of drinks. The entire ordeal is humiliating and demeaning, and it is meant to be.

I try to put my attention on my surroundings so I can fight the urge to run from the room, knocking people out of my way to find Bex. Instead, I look at the thick, red velvet curtains hanging against the walls. They look expensive, like something that might decorate a castle back on Earth, when Earth still existed and castles still remained in some of the more historic places. Here, they don't look quite as beautiful, because all I can imagine with the deep, rich crimson color is the sea of blood the Union has caused in all of its planetary invasions and slaughter of innocent species.

"It's a lot to take in, isn't it?" a voice says from beside me.

I turn to look and see a man standing there with his hand out to offer me one of the cocktails he is carrying. I hesitate as I look at the glass.

"Don't worry," he says with a small smile. "If the Union delegates haven't poisoned you by now, then you certainly don't need to worry about me lacing your glass with anything."

I chuckle because he is right, and then I take the glass.

"Thank you," I say as I take a sip. "Ophelia either doesn't care or doesn't understand how human bodies work because I haven't been given anything to eat or drink since last night."

"I would wager that it's a bit of both," he says. "At least your first drink of the day is a good one, then." He lifts his own glass to his lips and takes a sip.

The man looks almost human to me, but not quite. His eyes are deeply sunken into his skull, and his skin has a strange yellow tinge to it. He must be some kind of alien I haven't seen before. Considering there are so many different kinds, it really doesn't matter, anyway. The more important thing is that he seems to have a distaste for the Union, too.

"Are you a recruit here, too?" I ask.

"I would hardly call you a recruit," he says without answering my question. "Everyone knows who you are, Ben."

"Why is that?" I ask, still trying to figure out what it is about me that has garnered so much interest from the Union and the people here.

"Haven't you heard? You're special." He grins.

For a second, I am about to ask him what he knows and what makes me special, but I can tell by the look on his face that he is simply trying to tease me about rumors he has heard—or at least, I think that's what he is doing. Regardless, he seems to be the most kindred spirit that I have met here so far.

"Do you know anything about the sinister plans that the Intergalactic Union is trying to carry out?" I ask, hoping I haven't read this guy totally wrong.

"Sinister plans? No. What are they?" he asks as if he genuinely doesn't know.

I spend a few minutes telling him about the things I saw in the room yesterday and the stuff Ophelia told me.

"You see, they are trying to keep themselves from dying out," I say as I bring the explanation full circle. "They don't care who they hurt or enslave. All they care about is making sure the Intergalactic Union succeeds and survives. It's the secret reason behind all this overreach of power."

He is pretty quiet while he listens to me, even for several seconds after I finish talking. It looks like he is contemplating something as he finishes off the drink in his glass before responding.

"That truly is interesting," he says. "It seems the Intergalactic Union may have its priorities muddled."

"That's an understatement," I scoff.

From the corner of my eye, I see Pschye watching our conversation. When she sees me looking back at her, she acts as if she is going to come this way. The other guy notices it, too, and is quick to close our conversation and leave.

"If you ever need my help," he says before walking off to rejoin the rest of the crowd. "Just ask."

"How would I find you?"

"You can just ask anyone here in the station for me by name—Matheus."

Matheus slips into the crowd right before Pschye and Ophelia show back up. They took their time getting drinks, allowing me to have the rather mysterious conversation with Matheus. Surprisingly, neither of them even asks me who I was talking to, or about what. They just continue to carry on where they were.

I nod my head in answer to a few random things they ask me and find my thoughts wandering off about what Matheus said. How could I simply ask anyone here at the station for him by name and expect anyone to know where he is, or better yet, to help me find him? I am the equivalent of a prisoner here. No one will help me do anything. And who is Matheus that everyone here would know him by name?

Something isn't adding up in my head.

"Time to go," Ophelia says as she barks a direction at me to leave. "We both need our beauty rest for tomorrow, especially you."

Ophelia takes me back to my room herself and dismisses the guard. I can already tell she has a reason for doing so as she lingers inside my room, trying to flirt with me and seeing if I will bite.

"What did you think of my dress tonight?" she asks as she runs her humanlike hand down the smooth, metal side of her body.

It's definitely interesting the amount of detail that someone crafted into her mechanical pieces—right down to the perfectly formed metal nipple that pushes up from beneath the thin fabric of her dress. I wonder if she has been this way her entire life.

"Critiquing your wardrobe is not part of what I am required to do," I say flatly.

"How do you know? You are required to do whatever I tell you to. If I tell you to critique my dress, then do it." Ophelia walks closer to me and places her metal finger against my chest again.

"I'm not afraid of pain," I say as I hold her stare.

"Perhaps not," she sneers. "But you are afraid of causing Bex pain, are you not?"

I scowl at her. "Your dress is nice," I say benignly. "Now, if you'll excuse me, I will go to bed."

"Perhaps I will come to bed with you," she says with a syrupy tone that makes it sound as if her tongue is made of metal, too. "Maybe I will tell you to seduce me tonight, and you will obey my command."

"Like hell I will," I growl at her. "You can try to keep up this charade of control, Ophelia. And for a while, I might obey it in order to spare my friend, but I will never seduce you because the sheer sight of how evil and manipulative you are makes you hideous, regardless of any exterior beauty you may think you possess."

Her face turns bright red, or at least half of it does. I can tell now that her pale skin gives away her anger almost as much as Vira's translucent skin does.

"I warn you," she hisses at me. "The human girl you are trying so desperately to protect will end up being your undoing." With that, Ophelia storms out of the room and calls for the guard to stand outside my door again.

I slump down onto the side of the bed, emotionally and mentally exhausted from the day's events. I still don't understand what the Union wants me to do. I need to find Bex and get us both the hell out of here before the situation gets worse.

I lay down on the bed and rest my head against the pillow as I try to replay events in my head and see if I can figure anything out. But my thoughts keep going back to one thing until I finally decide that, in the morning, I will call on the new friend that I made tonight—Matheus.

19

BEX

"You need to get me inside the station," I tell Aerlon. Now that I know I have a contact outside, beyond the work farm, I abandon my plans of trying to escape since Aerlon made it clear that they won't let me get me far, anyway. Instead, I come up with a new plan; one that will get me closer to my goal of taking down the Union and finding Ben.

"Can you get me inside the station intentionally? Like, get me legitimate work there, or permission from one of the Union delegates? If there are four delegates, then surely Pschye can't have the final say about everything."

"I'm sure that she doesn't," Aerlon says. "But I can tell you that she carries the most weight out of all the delegates in the Union."

"Why?" Vira asks.

"No idea. Perhaps it is her brazen Spewt personality, if for no other reason."

"I need to see for myself what is going on with Ben," I

say. "And to try to find this Matheus guy and see what his take on all of this is."

"I think it's pretty obvious what his take on it is," Petra interjects. "If he is the head of all of this, then he is the one pulling all the strings."

"Not necessarily," Aerlon adds. "Sometimes those in power are actually much more manipulated by the people around them than we realize."

He might not be wrong there.

"This is why I need to go and see it for myself," I reassert. "Can you get me inside?"

"I might be able to get you inside," he says, "but it's a long shot. And if I can, it will be to a position that's much worse than working on this farm, I can assure you."

"I don't care. Just as long as it gets me in and closer to Ben and the head of the Intergalactic Union. I don't care what the position is."

Aerlon nods and gets ready to go, but then I think of one more question I want to ask.

"Aerlon, I know you said that you don't know much about Matheus, but do you at least know what species he is?"

Aerlon shakes his head.

"Why does that matter?" Petra asks.

"I'm not sure," I say honestly. "I just have a feeling it might."

"I've never seen him," Aerlon answers. "And I've never heard mention of it, so I honestly don't know. All that I know is that it is Matheus' ultimate desire to control every species, and every planet, within every galaxy."

Based on that, I am reaffirmed in my belief that I need to take him down as quickly as possible and get Ben out of the Union's clutches.

Aerlon leaves, and the three of us go back to our beds to try to get some rest while we wait to see if he is successful in getting me a transfer closer to the heart of things.

THE NEXT MORNING, THERE IS NO SIGN OF AERLON AT ALL. And the same is true for the day after that.

"Do you think that he was caught talking with us?" Vira asks as we sit over a pot of strong, bitter coffee.

"I don't see how. No one saw us."

"But there are cameras everywhere." I really hope Aerlon didn't get caught or restationed somewhere else. Not only would it ruin my chances of getting closer to the station, but it would also mean that a new assassin would be reassigned to me, one that wouldn't hesitate to shoot me.

THANKFULLY, JUST AS MY ANXIETY IS ABOUT TO GO through the roof, Aerlon reappears after three nights of being gone.

"He's here," Petra whispers to me as she pokes me in the side to wake me.

I am already awake, anyway. I can't seem to sleep anymore these days.

The two of us wake Vira, then sneak out between the shift change to meet Aerlon in the same place as before.

"Where have you been?" I ask in a bit of a frenzy. "We thought something had happened to you."

"Sorry, but it took quite a lot of doing in order to convince Pschye to change your assignment."

"Wait—you did it? She has agreed to let me work inside the station instead of here at the work farm?"

"Yes." Aerlon nods. "But don't get too excited. Like I said, it's not a good position. I convinced her that it would be a better punishment for you to be brought into the station and assigned to Ophelia. I told her that you seemed too content here at the farm with your friends, and that if she really wanted to punish you, this would be worse."

"Why would being Ophelia's assistant be worse?" I ask reluctantly, already fearing the answer.

Aerlon takes a deep breath in and exhales slowly before telling me the rest.

"Ophelia has been assigned to train Ben as a delegate. Some at the station are saying that she is keeping Ben as her pet while grooming him for his new role in the Union. The punishment that I have now successfully convinced Pschye to give you is going to be even more terrible because both you and Ben will now be able to see each other in these new roles you must now play."

It takes me a minute to realize the impact of what he is saying.

"Bex," he continues, "Ben is playing a part, or at least I think that he is. And you will now have a part to play, too. Neither one of you will be allowed to see or talk to each other alone, but I have no doubt that Ophelia will parade you both around in front of each other. She has a keen enjoyment of torment. If you truly want to get to the head of the Union and find Matheus, then you will need to keep your calm and keep your senses about you. Otherwise, you will put both yourself and Ben in danger."

"I understand," I acknowledge.

I don't like it, but it's literally what I asked for. I want to be inside the station so I can be close to finding the head of the Intergalactic Union. And I want to be close to Ben so I can see what has happened to him. No one said that this was going to be easy. Nothing seems easy anymore.

But even after all that I have already gone through, nothing could have prepared me for what comes next.

That very morning, I am brought into the station, hand-delivered by Aerlon himself, and handed over to Ophelia to be her personal servant. The look in her eyes lets me know that she already despises me. One glance at Ben standing next to her shows me why. She doesn't want to share her new toy.

Ben looks all cleaned up and seems to be obeying Ophelia's every command. I watch and listen as I pour her tea, and I try not to pay attention to all the mechanical body parts strewn across the top of her vanity tabletop.

"Let us discuss the next planet we will venture to and what your role in it will be," she says to Ben, who stands dutifully beside her without so much as looking in my direction.

"I think we should go back to Brocadia, although it might take some convincing to get the others to agree. There is a plethora of resources there, and the Fshie arguably need to be put down."

I nearly spill the tea by overpouring it into the tiny cup on the table in front of her. When I hear her mention of Brocadia and the Fshie, all I can think about is Talon and how crushed Vira will be if he doesn't survive all this.

"You foolish thing!" Ophelia scolds. "You've spilled tea on my lap."

"I would imagine that it doesn't burn metal," I say, knowing the remark is likely to only make her more irate with me.

"Ben, be a darling and fetch me the screwdriver." Instead

of coming back with an angry retort, Ophelia uses her power over the situation in a much cleverer and crueler way.

While I stand there mopping up the spilled tea, she unscrews a metal plate in her thigh so she can replace it with a clean, dry one beneath her dress.

"Can't have my wiring getting wet." She laughs as Ben acts like both servant and handyman.

I am infuriated and outraged.

"I hardly see what this training is going to do for him, in terms of preparing him to be a Union delegate," I say as I finish cleaning up the mess.

"Fortunately for you, it's not your place to know how I choose to train my new recruit." Ophelia glares. "I suppose the only thing pertinent to you is that Ben is now mine, and I will do with him what I please."

Ophelia looks over at Ben as he puts the screwdriver back in the drawer. I can see the veins in his neck bulging, something that happens when he is under extreme stress. I'm fairly certain that Ophelia can see it, too.

"Well now, this is fun." She laughs. "I need to owe Pschye an apology, I suppose. She told me I would enjoy having the both of you in my charge, and I didn't believe her. But now I am starting to see what she means. What a fun little game this all is."

I want to take the teapot in my hand and smash her porcelain face into pieces.

When Ophelia gets up from the table to change, I try to steal a minute alone with Ben to talk to him.

"Ben!" I whisper urgently before Ophelia returns to the room. "We need to get out of here!"

At first, it almost seems as if he didn't hear me.

"Ben!" I say again.

When he looks up this time, the sense of heavy heartache sweeps over me. He stares at me for a moment, and then he looks away as he carefully picks up the metal piece that Ophelia removed. He wipes it clean and dry with his sleeve, then returns it to the vanity drawer. Then, without a single word to me, he turns to leave and go to Ophelia.

I am left standing there, alone in her room, utterly shocked and heartbroken.

If I hadn't seen it with my own eyes, I would never have believed it. But it is true—Ben has changed. We were in this room alone together for enough seconds for him to have replied to me with a single word, or even a single, silent glance of reassurance that he was still him and I am still me in the midst of all this. But he didn't. Instead, he left me here and went to her. He has actually betrayed us. Ben has betrayed me and turned his back on his friends in exchange for a position of power and amnesty from his previous transgressions against the Intergalactic Union. I can't believe he is such a coward.

I try to fight back the tears because, even if half my reason for coming here has failed, another half still remains —to destroy the Union from the highest point of command downward.

I finish cleaning up, then walk outside of the room. There are guards there to monitor my every movement, and I don't see Aerlon among them.

"I want to go to my room," I say to the guards. "Ophelia and Ben have already left, and I have finished my work there."

One of the guards looks at me with disgust, as if I shouldn't have dared to even speak to them. But another one simply points to a door down the hall, which I assume is where I am supposed to stay.

I walk toward the room, peering only once at the guards who are still staring at me to make sure that I don't try to run away. And when I reach the doorway, I step inside, not bothering to close it behind me.

There isn't much that I can do today unless Ophelia comes back to get me and tow me along with her. I am not allowed to wander the station by myself. Tomorrow, I will need to come up with a reason to convince Ophelia to take me out into the rest of the station, or to let me run an errand for her so I can scout the place and try to find Matheus. I hope he's real. I hope he doesn't turn out to be just some rumor. If he is, then all of my plan will come crashing down around me.

I sit on the bed and without even meaning to, dropping my head into the palm of my hands as I cry. I've been holding the tears in for a while now, and since I am here alone in this room with nothing else that I can do, now is as good a time as any to let the tears out, I suppose.

Losing Ben like this—to betrayal, to something we both stood against together—is the worst possible thing I can imagine. It would have been less painful to be shot on the work farm.

"Are you all right?" a voice says from the doorway.

I lift my head up quickly to see a man standing there.

At any other time, I would have come up with some excuse as to why I am sitting here, bawling my eyes out. But right now, I am too emotional and not thinking, so I spit out the truth to this stranger instead.

"No, I am not all right," I cry. "But I will be once I get the hell out of this place and recollect all my friends."

The man stands there staring at me, and I can't blame

him. I am a hot mess as I try to wipe the tears from my face and clear my blurry vision so he looks more normal. Currently, the man looks as if his eyes are sunken deeply into his head and someone shined a strange yellowish light on him that makes his skin look abnormally jaundiced. But when I clear my eyes from tears and look at him again, he still looks the same.

For a minute, the two of us stare back at each other. He is probably wondering why I look like such a wreck, and I am wondering why he looks so sickly. It's hard to tell with all the aliens here whether they all look as they are supposed to or whether something is wrong with them.

After a few awkward minutes, he simply gives me a weak, sympathetic smile, then turns to walk away.

Even though it isn't yet even dinnertime, I lay down in the bed and pull the blanket up over my head. I don't feel like eating, or showering, or staying awake. I simply feel like crying myself to sleep.

BEN

After turning an agitated Ophelia away again last night, I wound up pacing the perimeter of my room until the wee hours because I couldn't stop worrying about Bex. By the time I finally collapsed onto my bed and fell asleep for a few hours, it seemed as if it was already morning.

Even now, as I wake up and try to control my anxiety over the situation, I am completely strung out.

I want the chance to talk to Bex and to tell her why I am going along with the Union and with Ophelia, and why I couldn't risk giving my plan away last night in Ophelia's room—especially since the entire place is crawling with cameras in nearly every corner. I need to tell her that our previous friend, Aerlon, is an assassin tasked with killing her if I don't follow Ophelia's every command, no matter how ludicrous they seem.

My nerves are completely shot when I think about how upset Bex looked, and to be honest, I doubt she will even listen to me now, anyway. There isn't much I can do aside from continuing to play the game until I can figure out a way to get us both out of here. At least she is here in the station building with me so I can at least try to keep watch over her, even if it is torture for the both of us.

I put on my clothes and splash some cold water on my face to try to look less fatigued, although I don't think it works. Then I head over to Ophelia's room again to see what kind of daunting activities she has planned for me today. I fail to see how any of this provides me with training unless I am simply in training to become Ophelia's personal man-slave.

But before I reach the door of her room, I can hear her screaming out into the hallway.

"Where *is she?*" Ophelia shouts with a reddened face as soon as I step inside her doorway.

"Where is who?"

"You know who! That lousy, disobedient servant that can't seem to get herself to her post to bring me my morning coffee without being late," she yells. She is obviously starting out this morning in a particularly unhinged mood. "That worthless human girl. Humans make the absolute worst servants. The whole lot of you are entirely irresponsible and disrespectful."

Ophelia shouts out into the hallway for one of her alien guards.

"Go and find Bex so I can give her a solid scolding and punishment for inconveniencing me this morning," she tells him. "Maybe if she grovels, I will refrain from setting the assassin on her."

My skin prickles at the mention of it. There is not a chance in hell that I am going to let Aerlon harm a hair on Bex's head.

"I can get your coffee instead," I offer in order to defuse the situation.

But before I can even reach for the kettle, the guard returns to the doorway, looking flustered and as if he is afraid that he is about to get into trouble for something.

"She's gone," he says.

"What?" Ophelia growls at him.

"The human girl is missing. She isn't in her room, and no one can find her in the hallways."

"That's impossible, you incompetent fool," she scolds. "Check all the cameras and find her. Get all the guards to search the entire station!"

Suddenly, the station becomes a flurry of agitated excitement as everyone tries to find Bex. But after scouring the entire station building and searching all the cameras both inside and outside, and on the work farm, Bex is nowhere to be found.

"How could you have let this happen?" Pschye yells at Ophelia in her most condescending tone as soon as she hears what has happened. "How could you have lost her?"

"I didn't lose her," Ophelia protests. "She escaped."

"She escaped on your watch," Pschye counters angrily. "You should have locked her up in her room so she couldn't get out until you sent a guard to fetch her in the morning. How could you be so stupid and careless?"

For a tense moment, I look between the two women as they glare at each other. It's hard to say which of them is more turbulent and deadly.

"Call for Aerlon," Pschye tells one of the guards in the doorway without breaking her glare at Ophelia.

The guard stands there, looking as if he wants to melt into the floor.

"Did you not hear me?" Pschye hisses at him, seeing he hasn't moved to carry out her command.

"I did hear you," the guard says in a shaky voice that is quite unbecoming of his massive stature. "But I'm afraid the assassin is missing, too."

Pschye's eyes could kill. Her double pupils narrow into thin slits that would resemble snake eyes if they were turned in the other direction. Before she can lash out at him, and likely at Ophelia again, the guard has one more thing to tell her.

"And..." he says carefully as he takes a step backward out of the doorway, seemingly ready to run for his life, "there is a ship missing from the cargo bay." As soon as he manages to get the words out, he turns and leaves without waiting for further directions.

Fortunately for him, Pschye is much too preoccupied with her rage at Ophelia and the calamity of the current situation to bother with the cowardly guard.

"Do you see what you have done?" she snarls at Ophelia as she moves her face so close to Ophelia's metal cheek that I can see her reflection in it. "You have caused us chaos."

Ophelia surprisingly doesn't say another word as Pschye pushes past me and storms out of the room. I can hear her calling for Drelax to put the entire Intergalactic Union station on lockdown until someone finds where the rogue human girl and her turncoat assassin has gone. It's a rather redundant move that makes no logical sense. If a ship is missing, then it is likely that they have already managed to get out of the station. The better question is: why would Bex go with Aerlon, and why would he be helping her escape when he is charged with her assassination?

I step out of the room as soon as Ophelia turns around

to reach for a different appendage to change out. I can only imagine she is reaching for one that can enact a murderous intent. I follow down the hallway, listening to the panicked chatter of the guards who are all trying to avoid the wrath of the highly displeased delegates.

"Two more people are missing from the work farm," one of the guards reports.

"Let me guess," Pschye says from a short distance up the hallway. "Petra and Vira? What is it you guards do if not prevent my prisoners from escaping?"

Suddenly, this all seems to make sense in my mind now. Bex, Aerlon, Petra, and Vira—it all pieces together. They have all somehow orchestrated an escape together. And this is my one shot of finding them. I know I won't get another.

I wait for Pschye to turn down another hallway, and I stride up to the nearest guard.

"I need to speak with Matheus," I say, as if the mention of his name is no big deal for me to be uttering.

But the guard's mouth hangs open as if I spoke a different language.

"How do you know that name?" he asks in shock.

I am a bit taken aback. I didn't realize my new friend's name would provoke such a reaction. I am starting to wonder even more now who he really is.

"He is a friend," I say. "And he told me I could send for him if I needed anything."

The guard stands there for a moment, visibly trying to decide whether to believe me or not, eventually deciding he would be in less trouble if he was wrong about taking me to see him than if he was to deny my request and have it been true.

He breaks his post and motions for me to follow him.

"Come with me," he says as he walks quickly down the hallway and then up several flights of stairs.

When we reach the top floor and make it to the last room in the hall, I am winded but glad to see Matheus sitting inside the room, in a chair next to the window with a book in his lap.

The guard turns and leaves, and I immediately launch into an explanation of what has happened, which Matheus seems completely undisturbed about, as if he somehow already knows all about it. He sits there calm and unfettered, still holding the book open to the page he was reading.

When I am finished, he simply looks up at me and nods.

"Why did you come to tell me all this?" he asks. "What do you need?"

I hesitate. I wasn't prepared for him to be so calm and collected while everyone else is running around like their house is on fire. Matheus looks even more sunken and yellowed today, and I am starting to wonder if this look is normal for whatever he is or if there is something wrong with him. But I remember what he told me at that fancy event with the delegates—he told me if I ever needed anything to ask him, and I certainly do need help now.

"I think I might know where Bex and the others are heading, and I need help getting to them. If I don't go after them now, then—"

Matheus lifts his hand in the air to silence me.

"No further explanation is necessary," he says. "I already know what you are going to say—if you don't go now, they will be lost to you forever. And these are your friends, are they not?"

I nod.

"Friends who you don't want to lose forever," he continues. "I understand."

His demeanor continues to strike me as odd as Matheus glances slowly out the window of his room, as if trying to take one last look at Nairu from his room. I don't even know what level of the station we are on, but it seemed like we climbed at least a few dozen flights of stairs. This building reminds me a little bit of the city buildings in Brocadia that seem tall enough to pierce straight through the sky.

I know there probably isn't much this guy can do to help me chase after Bex, but I have no one else here to ask for help.

"Come on," Matheus says as he stands up from his chair, finally closing his book but not before folding the corner of the page he was on.

He is a contradiction. On one hand, he acts as if he will never see the view from his window again with his calm and lengthy stare at the landscape amidst the confusion. On the other, he marks his page in the book as if he is planning to come right back to pick up and finish where he left off.

"Where are we going?" I ask as I follow him through the halls and down a single flight of stairs.

"To go find your friends," Matheus answers, as if that answer should have already been obvious to me.

"But we would need a—"

The staircase leads us straight into the back corridor of the cargo bay. There are several ships sitting there, looking as if they are waiting to be flown out of here, and even more guards standing around them.

As we approach, one of the guards walks up to us, but Matheus simply raises his hand and waves the guard away. The other guards seem to take a step back and let us walk all the way to one of the ships without being stopped or hassled at all.

Who is this guy?

When we reach the hatch of one of the ships, the guard standing in front of it stares at Matheus as if awaiting instruction. Again, Matheus simply motions his hand for the guard to open the hatch and step away without saying a word.

As he gets ready to step inside, I turn to look around. All the guards are still standing there in the cargo bay, watching us, but not a single one of them is calling to inform the Union delegates that we are getting ready to steal a ship. None of them are making any move to stop us or call out and report us.

"Why aren't they doing anything?" I ask.

"Like what?" Matheus asks as he turns to see what I am looking at. "Isn't standing around guarding things what they're supposed to be doing?"

"Yeah, that's my point. They aren't guarding this ship we are about to steal. They just let us right on it."

"I don't know I would go so far as to say that we are *stealing* the ship, per se," Matheus says as he plays with semantics and words. "What we are doing is more akin to *borrowing* it."

I step onto the ship with him, and the two of us both sit in the cockpit.

"You are truly a mystery," I say to him. "What did you say you do here at the Intergalactic Union station?"

"I don't think we reached that part in our conversation yet." He smiles as he looks at the control panel in front of us. "But you might want to table that for the moment, in lieu of going after your friends before it's too late. It would seem they have gotten quite a head start on us. But you said you know where they are going, right?"

"I mean, I have an idea, but I can't be certain until we go there to see for ourselves."

"All right," he says as he buckles himself in. "Do you know how to fly a ship?"

"Yes," I answer as I clip my buckle and fire up the engines. "Do you?"

"No, not a clue." Matheus laughs. "I suppose I should get out more and learn more of these kinds of things. Then again, that's what makes this so much fun right now. It's an adventure."

"You're a strange guy, Matheus," I say as I get ready to fly this ship out of here and fly it toward Brocadia. "But I greatly appreciate your help. I'm glad I had the chance to meet you at that party. Meeting you has been the only decent thing that has happened to me since I was brought back here to Nairu."

"We'll see," he says as he looks out the ship's window into the open skies that I fly the ship into. "That might change."

BEX

It was only a few minutes after that strange-looking man left my doorway last night while I was crying before Aerlon showed up to check on me and "guard" me from leaving my room at night. I know the real reason he came was to protect me and prevent any one of the treacherous people at the station from entering my room while I slept. Aerlon is a good guy, always trying to protect his friends when he can. He and Amity didn't deserve to be pulled away from each other.

But as soon as he found me there crying and asked me what had happened, I adamantly told him that we *had* to get out of there and off Nairu. We needed to find our other friends and disappear someplace the Union would never find us again.

At first, Aerlon said it was impossible. But then he looked out the window in my small bedroom and saw that the large, overhanging door to the Union's cargo bay had been left open.

It was a nearly unthinkable mistake. Those ships are always kept under tight lock and key, and someone would definitely lose their head for the oversight. But it was also an opportunity, a highly risky one.

I saw it, too, and it didn't take much for me to convince Aerlon that we needed to seize this chance—at least not when I told him that this was his chance to get Amity back.

So late last night, after he was sure that everyone had gone to bed, and that the remaining guards at their posts were drowsy and not paying any attention at all, Aerlon snuck me out of the station and we headed back to break Petra and Vira free from the work farm.

"Are you guys crazy?" Petra says in the wee hours of the morning before the light has even appeared. "You want to *steal* a ship right out from under their noses in the cargo bay? You're both mad. There's no way we will be able to get a ship and get out of here before we are caught. Even *if* the cargo bay door is open, there are still dozens of guards inside there."

"I don't think so," Aerlon says. "That section of the cargo bay is usually locked tight. I don't think there will be any guards there at all at this hour."

"This seems way too easy," Petra says skeptically.

Vira nods her head in agreement. "I definitely want to get out of here," she says anxiously. "But this seems like a quick way to get caught and killed."

"It's risky," I acknowledge. "There's no doubt. But this is our only chance. I can't stay here another minute. Are you coming with us?"

"What about Ben?" Vira asks.

I feel the tears start to sting at the corners of my eyes, but I just can't bring myself to cry anymore, so I choke them back down.

"He's changed," I say sadly. "And he won't be coming with us. He's with them now."

"Them?" Petra asks as she looks between Aerlon and me. "Are you saying that Ben has joined the Union? It's true then?"

"We don't have time to talk about this now," I snap. "We need to leave. Are the two of you coming or not?"

Petra and Vira exchange glances, then Petra reaches out to place her hand on the top of my shoulder. "Yeah, we're coming." She smiles. "You're gonna need our help."

Aerlon knows where all the cameras are located, which means he knows how to move us between the blank spaces so we aren't seen or caught on camera as we head from the work farm to the cargo bay. I know how to avoid the kill traps, and Vira easily distracts the guards by letting some of the livestock loose and waiting for the guards to run after them, fearing a punishment if they get loose.

I feel as if I don't breathe until we finally make it to the cargo bay unseen. But this is only half the battle. The hardest part is getting the ship out of here before getting stopped.

Thankfully, just as Aerlon predicted, there are no guards here.

"I still have a strange feeling about this," Petra says as we walk quietly through the cargo bay toward a ship. "You don't think it's odd that there isn't a single guard in sight?"

"No," Aerlon answers. "The guards are stationed at the active bays that are open and more frequently used. This one should have been all locked up and therefore not need to be guarded. The stranger thing is how it became unlocked and had its door wide open. I would be more worried that someone is trying to set us up, but I don't know who it could possibly be if that is the case. I've been listening and haven't heard a thing."

"All right, guys," I say as my skin starts to crawl with nervousness. "Can we just discuss all these theories after we've managed to escape out of here?"

"I agree with Bex." Vira nods. She looks as anxious as I feel.

The four of us quietly get inside the closest ship, and after a quick check that it has fuel, Petra sits in the cockpit and starts up the engines.

"That's really loud," Vira says with a worried glance out the ship's windows.

"Yeah, sorry, but that's what ships sound like when they're getting ready to take off." Petra shrugs. "Nothing I can do about it."

"Can you pilot this kind of ship?" Aerlon asks her as he looks at the control panels. "It's one of the older models. That's probably why it has been in this unused cargo bay."

"I can fly it." She smiles. "I can fly anything. Aircraft is just like language—there's a bunch of different variations. But to me, they're all the same."

As we all buckle in, Petra flies the ship out of the cargo bay, up and away from the surface of Nairu. For a few seconds, I almost can't believe that we are managing to escape. I don't think I am the only one with that thought because everyone on board is silent, as if we are all waiting for the sound of another ship to fire at us. But no shots come, and we are able to clear the skies of Nairu entirely.

"Does anyone have any idea where we are going?" Vira asks. "Did we even decide that?"

I get ready to answer her and tell her no, we hadn't discussed it, but I have a few ideas. Aerlon beats me to it.

"We need to go to the dead planet," he says decisively. "To get Amity and Clover back."

Aerlon looks over at me to gauge my reaction, and I am in full agreement.

"If they are still alive," I say, knowing that Aerlon doesn't want to think otherwise about it, "then they are going to need our help. We will get them first, then head to Brocadia."

"Brocadia?" Petra asks with a wrinkled brow. "Those bastards sold us out. Why would we want to go back there?"

"Because," Vira answers for me as she gives me a grateful smile, "Talon is there, and we need to rescue him, too. If he is still alive." Her face drops, and the color of sadness and worry washes through her veins and across her translucent skin.

"Talon is alive," Aerlon assures her as he reaches out to hold her hand. "And so are Amity and Clover. We will rescue all our friends, and then Petra can fly this ship into a galaxy where the Union cannot find us again."

"I like how this is fleshing out." Petra chuckles. "No one gets left behind."

As soon as she says it, everyone realizes that someone *is* getting left behind—Ben.

"Maybe there's still hope for him," Vira says gently to me. "Maybe he will come around."

"No," I say harshly because it is much easier to be angry with Ben than to dwell in the sorrow of having lost him. "He's gone."

Petra pilots the ship to the dead planet, and when we get there, there is a strange mix of both relief that we have made it here and also dread at what we might find. Inside my head, I make a silent wish that Amity and Clover are still alive and haven't been eaten by the giant beasts that prowl the surface of this place. Thankfully, we see their faces coming toward us almost as soon as we step off the ship.

Without reservation, Aerlon immediately runs toward them, scooping them both up in his arms and hugging them with fierce relief as the three of us stand around with smiles on our faces.

It's good to see my friends reunited and happy, even if I can't enjoy the same sort of reunion with Ben myself.

"What are you all doing here?" Amity asks in surprise as she buries her face against Aerlon's perfectly formed chest. "I feared we might never see you again."

"Well, you can thank Bex for this bold and brazen move. It was her idea to escape from the Union station," Aerlon says with a smile. He lets go of them and stands back to look into their tear-filled faces. "I'm so glad to see the two of you are safe and well. Did the creatures here not return?"

"No, not yet," she answers. "Clover and I have heard them prowling about off in the distance, but we have kept quiet and close, and have been able to avert detection so far. It hasn't been easy, though. Staying hidden and safe meant we couldn't go far for food and water. We are nearly out of both. You've arrived just in time."

She looks around as if she is searching for something among us. "Where's Ben?"

I can feel my face tighten, afraid I will crack and fall apart if I don't make an effort to hold myself together. I can also feel everyone staring at me as they wait for my answer.

"He's not coming with us," I say with a matter-of-fact tone that makes it clear I don't want to elaborate.

Amity nods with a solemn look in her eyes, as if she understands that something bad has happened but doesn't press me further.

"Let's get you both out of here," Aerlon says as he ushers them both back onto the ship.

"Wait!" Clover calls out as she glances up at Amity. She waits for a nod of approval before running back to the small hovel where they've been sheltering.

"Where is she going?" Petra asks. "We aren't really in a rush, but I don't want to chance another impromptu run-in with one of those giant beasts without Talon here to help us."

Before Amity can answer, Clover is back, holding a small handful of something.

"Look," she says to us as she opens up her hands to show us what's inside.

There, resting on her turned out palms, is a small pile of shells. They look almost like the same kind of seashells that used to be on the beaches back on Earth. One of them has a fleshy colored pink middle to it, and a shell that twists around in a spiral. Another looks like nothing more than a white crustation on the outside, but inside there is a beautifully delicate lavender color.

"I think something used to live in these." Clover smiles with appreciation of her found treasures.

"Undoubtably," I agree with a nod. "Where did you find them?"

"Just around." She shrugs. "I was digging in the dirt right outside the shelter we made, and I found them buried there. Aren't they so special and pretty?"

"They are lovely," Vira adds, in awe.

"And important," Aerlon adds as he lifts the lavender one from her hand to take a closer look at it.

"Important how?" Amity asks.

"This is proof of sustainable life here," he says. "Not just predatorial life like we saw the last time we were here, but the basis of an ecosystem. If there are shellfish, fresh water, and plants, then this is definitely not as dead of a planet as we were told."

"Didn't we already know that?" I ask.

"We knew there was life here, but only the kind of life that devoured everything around it. We didn't know there were sustainable conditions for prolonged survival," Aerlon explains. "That is a much different matter."

"Whatever." Petra shrugs. "We still need to leave."

Everyone boards the ship with Amity clutching Clover's hand and Clover clutching her handful of precious treasures.

"Where are we going now?" Clover asks as everyone gets settled on the ship.

"Brocadia," I answer. "We are going to sneak into the city and rescue Talon."

"Isn't that going to be hard?" she asks.

"Yes, impossibly hard," I answer. "But we're doing it, anyway. No one gets left behind."

When we get to Brocadia, I am grateful to see there are still no defenses around their planet. Apparently, they are still foolish enough to place their trust in the Intergalactic Union and the agreements they made. What fools. I almost feel sorry for them since I know what the Union plans to do to their entire civilization and world. Then again, they betrayed us, and they deserve what they have coming.

They aren't even bothering to monitor the skies around their planet for possible intrusions anymore because they so foolishly think they are under the protection of their deal with the Union. That means Petra can land the ship without even being seen. It couldn't be any easier to sneak onto the planet. Now we just need to sneak into the city and find Talon.

"Do you think he's still alive?" Petra whispers to me in a voice Vira cannot hear as we get off the ship.

"I surely hope so," I answer. I don't know what Vira will do if he isn't, but the hard truth of it is that sometimes we lose the ones we love the most. I should know.

"The two of you should stay here," Aerlon says to Amity when he sees her and Clover getting ready to come with us.

"No, we should all stay together this time," she says. "I don't want us to get pulled apart again."

"I agree," Clover says with conviction. She shoves the shells into her pocket and gives one hand each to Amity and Aerlon as she stands between them.

For a second, I stand there and look at them. They are an unusually beautiful sight. A tall, perfectly symmetrical alien with a long ponytail of hair that stretches down his back, standing between two human girls. They look happy together, like a family—an unexpected and beautiful family. And they look fiercely protective and devoted to each other.

The Intergalactic Union has it all wrong, as most giant conglomerates of corruption usually do. They're trying to destroy this—this beauty, love, and perseverance—all so they can have control over life that doesn't belong to them.

All six of us head into the city, sticking to the corners and shadows of things and trying not to be seen. It seems like most of the Fshie are preoccupied today, and we are able to slip into the center of the city unnoticed. I'm not sure if that is a good thing or not because it feels a bit like we are walking into a trap. I don't think we really know where we are going or how to even find Talon, but Vira seems to walk ahead of the rest of us as if she somehow knows or can *feel* where he is. The rest of us follow her, assuming that maybe she has some sort of alien ability that is tracking him down somehow.

We wind up at the bottom of a dungeon cell beneath the main building in the city center, the building where the Minister of Life presides. And there, sitting in a dank and unguarded cell, is Talon.

For a second, I definitely feel as though we have walked right into a trap. Why would he be kept here in this cell without a single guard in sight? But as we get closer and I see the condition he is in, I can tell he is much too beat up to be able to shift into his more vicious form and attempt to break free. His hands are chained to the wall behind him, and his ankles are shackled to the floor. Every portion of skin on his body is covered with gashes and bruises.

I glance over at Vira, whose veins have turned an almost luminous shade of light blue. She looks as if she feels the pain she can see in Talon.

She runs over to him and cups his battered face in her hands as she kisses the side of his cheek. I guess when the person you care about is on the brink of demise, you no longer care about holding back affections.

Talon opens his eyes and smiles at her. "You're here," he says weakly. "You came back for me."

"No one gets left behind," Vira whispers as she repeats my sentiment, and a stream of tears runs over her clear cheek, making a shimmering trail over her exposed cheekbone.

Talon might be in rough shape, but he is alive, and that

is all that matters for now—that and getting out of here alive.

Aerlon manages to break his chains and shackles with a few tools he had the foresight to bring with him from the ship. But as soon as the chains are released, Talon crumples to the ground.

"He's too weak to walk," Vira says as she looks up at us helplessly.

"It's okay," Aerlon says as he reaches down to help Talon stand and wraps his arm under his shoulders to support his weight. "We'll help him."

The trek out of the dungeons is much slower than the pace we were able to sneak in with, and it makes me edgy to move so slowly while we are trying to escape.

"We're almost there," Petra says as she helps Aerlon support Talon between them.

I am constantly in awe of her strength, and I don't think it's just a species trait. I think Petra must have gone through a lot of her own shit in life to be so strong both in character and in physical perseverance.

I look ahead of us and can see that we are nearing the edge of the city. Just a little farther to go, and we will be under the cover of trees and almost back to the ship. But no sooner do I let myself think that maybe things will be fine than we are apprehended. This time, the Fshie aren't playing nice.

Instead of their beautiful forms, a small pack of them has spotted us and are encroaching around us in their transformed, deadly, nightmarish forms.

There is no sense in putting up a fight because not only are there more of them than there are of us, but we have a child and an injured alien. There's no way we can stand up against them without someone getting hurt, or worse. So, we let the Fshie drag us all the way back to the minister's building in the city center, without them saying a single word or transforming back into less visually disturbing forms.

As we trudge slowly back, I feel a sense of hopelessness set in. *We were so close to getting out of here and finally being free.*

BEN

I steer the ship straight toward the dead planet. If Bex is with Aerlon, I know that is the first place they will go so he can rescue Amity—assuming that Amity and Clover have survived.

"We're going to the dead planet," I tell Matheus as he stares out the ship's window in amazement. I get the feeling that he has never flown in a ship before. This guy is definitely strange, but helpful. "A couple of our friends were left there to perish, and I have a strong feeling that Bex and Aerlon would go there to see if they're still alive to save them."

Matheus nods and continues to stare out the window. "The dead planet is named such because life cannot live there. At least, that is my understanding of it."

"Yeah, but I think the Union tends to underestimate the persistence of life that wants to be lived."

"What do you mean?" he asks.

"Well, even though that planet is indeed a harsh one, not suitable for sustaining life, there is still life there."

"What kind of life?" he asks. "Like plants and animals?"

"Yes, there are plants, and fresh water, and some sort of creatures that I had the displeasure of coming across. But there are also fish and things to forage for in order to sustain life," I explain.

"So, you don't think the planet is uninhabitable?"

"I didn't say that. I just said that everything on it isn't truly dead. At least, not yet."

Matheus seems to ponder my thoughts on the matter, and he is mostly quiet for the rest of the ride. But when we get there and step off the ship, he looks nothing short of fascinated.

"This is absolutely remarkable," Matheus says as he looks around.

I leave him near the ship as I go in search of the others. I can see the small shelter that appears where Amity and Clover were staying in, but it is empty now. I scout a small radius around the area and call out their names, being careful not to be too loud and risk drawing the attention of the giant predator again.

But after several minutes pass with no answer, I realize that no one is here. Since I don't see any bodies or signs of death, I presume that Amity and Clover are still alive. Bex and Aerlon must have already been here and gotten them. That means they are heading to Brocadia to rescue Talon.

I know Bex, and I know she will do everything she can to save everyone, especially if Vira is there, too. There was a definite connection between Vira and Talon, strong enough that they will risk themselves to go back for him. It's a stupid move, though. The Fshie are in a brokered deal with the Union now, which makes them even more unpredictable than before. I wish I was with

Bex now because I would tell her not to go there at all. As much as I sympathize with rescuing Talon, it's a suicide mission—one that I am now getting ready to follow to reach Bex.

"They aren't here," I say as I return to the area where Matheus is touching the plants and dirt around the ship. "We need to get back on the ship. I know where they are heading next."

"Oh no, not yet." Matheus shakes his head. "This is all much too interesting and marvelous to leave already. I want to look around a bit more."

"We need to go," I repeat. But Matheus doesn't listen to me at all. Instead, he just wanders farther off, seemingly enthralled by the dead planet and the signs of foliage and life that are still here. "Matheus, wait!" I call as I follow after him.

He walks along as if he has no fear at all, and as if we have no reason to hurry.

"Where is the fresh water?" he asks. "I want to see the water here."

I can tell by his determined expression that he isn't going to leave until I show him. So, I quickly lead him to the stream, keeping an eye on our surroundings the entire time in case one of those massive, lumbering beasts sneaks up on us. Without Talon, there would be no defeating one of them this time.

When we reach the stream, Matheus bends down and cups his hand to scoop up a small handful of water that he brings to his lips.

"It's good," he says as he looks up at me, as if he is shocked by the discovery. "This water tastes clean and unpolluted by waste or chemicals."

I don't really know what to say in response to him

because it strikes me as odd that Matheus seems to be so astounded by the conditions of the surface here.

"Have you ever been here before?" I ask.

"No, but I have heard about this place. It would seem that what I have heard isn't the truth, though. There is life here."

"Yeah, well, there's some pretty deadly and seriously scary life here, too, in the shape of giant and violent predators that will eat us as soon as they figure out we're here," I say as I try to urge him once again to get back onto the ship.

He seems shocked by that information as well.

After a short period of looking around, I am finally able to convince Matheus that it is time for us to leave so we can go to Brocadia.

Once we've taken off again, I can see that the look on his face has changed. He seems lost in his own thoughts, his eyes full of questions.

"Am I to guess that you've never been to Brocadia before, either?" I ask to try to make the silence less awkward and heavy.

Instead of answering me, Matheus asks me a question of his own, one that is strange and deep.

"Ben, what would you do if you thought your time to be alive was running out?" he asks. He looks at me with a serious face that awaits a serious answer. I find the question to be strange and random, but I answer him, anyway.

"I would want to spend every last minute I could with Bex and my friends," I say.

"But why wouldn't you try to spend all of your time and resources trying to look for a way to prolong your life?"

That thought hadn't even come to my mind.

"Why would I want to waste the time I had left looking

to prolong my life instead of actually *living* the time that I had?" I ask in return. It seems like a no-brainer to me, but then again, I don't understand much of what the other people on Nairu prize as being valuable to them. To me, my freedom and my time with Bex is all I really care about. The rest of the stuff is irrelevant. I could have all the time in the world on Nairu, as Ophelia's slave and a member of the Union, but without Bex and my freedom, I would wish it all away. It would feel like an imprisonment worse than death to live a life that makes me unhappy.

Matheus is silent again for a long while.

It is a longer ride to Brocadia. After some time, and what appeared to be a lot more thinking, he asks yet another question.

"What do you like most about being human?" he asks thoughtfully.

I am almost ready to answer him, but then I stop myself short.

"Before I answer any more of your questions," I say, "there is something I would like to know about you."

"Sure," he says with a half-hearted smile. "Ask me whatever you would like."

"What species are you?"

Matheus looks hurt by the question initially, and I start to feel bad and get ready to apologize. It is sheer curiosity on my part, and the desire to understand who this guy really is, but I can see how the question would come across as being rude.

"I can understand why it might be difficult for you to tell," he says with a kind tone. "I used to be human...like you."

Used to be? What does that mean? I haven't ever heard of someone being able to change species, unless that's a species ability that I've never come across before. It certainly would pose limitless possibilities if that was the case, but something tells me it's not as great as that.

"What do you mean that you *used* to be human?" I ask, now feeling even more curious than ever.

But before he can answer me, if he had even been willing to or not, Brocadia comes into view. Our conversation will need to be tabled for now because I need to focus on making sure we aren't seen landing here in the remote wilderness outside the city. The last time I was here, the Fshie betrayed us, and I have no doubt that they will do the same again.

I point out the window at a thicket of trees in the forested area ahead, just beyond the towering buildings of the city. "I will land there, and then we can sneak into the city to find them. It is dangerous, though. The Fshie are traitors and are in league with the Intergalactic Union. You can stay safely hidden here in the ship once we've landed, if you'd like. I will come back for you after I have my friends."

"No, I don't want to stay on the ship," he says. "Land the vessel right there." He points straight at the city.

"I can't land there. We'll be seen and caught if I land inside the city."

"Trust me." He smiles. "Land the ship right there in the center of the city, right in front of the tallest building."

"That's the Minister of Life's building," I say. "He's the leader here and won't hesitate to ship us right back to Nairu to meet with punishment."

"Ben, I haven't steered you wrong yet, have I?"

"No, but—"

"And without my help, we wouldn't have even been able to borrow a ship, and you wouldn't even be here right now, would you?"

"Again, no, but this is different," I say. "This is a suicide mission if I land this ship in the middle of the city."

"I think you'll be surprised at how things might turn out differently than you expect," he says. "If you want my continued help, you need to trust me. And if you want to be able to find and rescue your friends, you will need my help."

I'm not sure what to do. I know if I land this ship in the city, it is a kamikaze mission. But I also know Matheus is right about my needing his help. Against my better judgment, I do as he asks, already regretting the decision and feeling crazy for thinking we're going to make it out of this in one piece.

"Matheus, you are an enigma," I say as I shake my head at this foolish idea. "A very frustrating and fascinating enigma. And if we make it out of here alive, then you still owe me an answer to that question."

I land the ship smack-dab in front of the minister's building, which towers over the height of the ship. And even before we make it off the ship, I can see the Fshie coming to surround us. When we disembark, the fearsome Fshie, in their most intimidating and wild-looking forms, greet us with gnashing teeth and enough numbers to surround the ship entirely.

"This was a bad idea," I say under my breath, knowing I should have landed the ship out in the forest. We're as good as dead, or at the least captured and returned to Nairu to face the consequential punishments for our actions.

Instead of cowering in fear like I would expect any normal person to do in the face of such terrible aliens, Matheus doesn't look the least bit worried. He simply waves his hand in the air and talks to them as casually as he was talking to me.

"Change back," he says. "No one wants to see that side of you. Change back to your more pleasant forms."

If Matheus trying to command the Fshie to change back from monsters to men wasn't shocking enough, the fact that the Fshie actually listen to his command and turn back into men is beyond unbelievable.

"How did you do that?" I ask in a hushed gasp. "Why did they listen to you?" I now know that Matheus has at least been to Brocadia before, because he seems to already know about the transformative ability of the Fshie.

"Matheus," the Minister of Life says as he walks through the crowd of gathered Fshie and comes toward us. He stops right in front of us, gives me a solid glare, and looks at Matheus with a polite and welcoming smile. He greeted Matheus by name, as if he personally knows him.

I stand there, at a complete loss for words as I watch Matheus reach out his hand to shake the minister's.

Who the hell is this guy?

23

BEX

As soon as we are brought back into the center of the city by the horde of hideous Fshie, likely to be handed over to the minister to decide our fates, I am shocked to see a Union ship parked just in front of the Minister of Life's building with a crowd of people standing around it. At the front of the crowd is the minister himself, and standing right in front of him are two men, one of which is Ben.

What in the world is Ben doing here? What on Earth is he doing parking a Union ship in the center of the city? And why the hell is that strange guy from the Union station with him?

I exchange a nervous glance with Aerlon and the others. They look every bit as confused and surprised as I am.

All the Fshie around us immediately transform out of their violent forms and back to their more palatable appearances as soon as the minister sees them and waves for them to change back. It's much easier to see what's around once there aren't all those huge, deformed bodies to try to look past.

Ben spots me and, for a second, we lock eyes. I expect the same reaction from him as before—for him to turn away and disregard me entirely. I'm not even sure why he is here unless it is on Union business, and I suddenly get the dreadful thought that he was sent here to find us and drag us back to Nairu. That would explain why the guy who was at my doorway while I was crying in my room at the station is here with him, too. He is probably one of the Union guards or assassins.

Instead of turning away from me or ordering someone to come and grab me and toss me back onto the ship, Ben runs up to me alone, as if he can't even help himself. He stops in front of me and reaches out to hold me. I am too stunned to pull away from him because I have no idea what's going on. Ben's behavior has been erratic and unpredictable, and I don't know what to make of it.

Before I can even summon words to my mouth, he starts apologizing and a flood of words and explanations push out of his mouth as he quickly tries to explain everything he did. I try to decipher what he is saying, but his speech is flurried, and my eyes are filled with tears as I bury my face against him and let my emotions consume me. I manage to make out only a few of the things he says, but it's okay because I think they are the most important points.

"I was only doing those things in order to try to save and protect you," he says. "I had to go along with Ophelia. She would have had you killed if I hadn't. Please forgive me, Bex. I stole a ship and came here to find you once I heard you were gone. I was only trying to protect you; you have to believe that. I would never, *ever* turn my back on you, Bex."

This all feels like a dream. It feels too good to be true. Granted, we are in the middle of the Fshie city and we likely won't live to see another day, but at least now I can die knowing that Ben didn't betray me. It almost makes this all worth it.

"I believe you," I whisper against him as I feel his grasp tighten around me.

We stand there together for another moment, blocking out everyone around us until I hear Petra clear her throat, reminding us that we are still in the middle of a dire situation.

Ben lets me go, and I look around. Behind him stands the strange man with the sunken eyes and yellowed skin.

"What is going on here?" Talon asks weakly as he tries to stand on his own.

The sentiment is echoed by everyone. We are all completely confused about what is happening and who this guy with Ben really is. The Fshie aren't attacking. The Minister of Life looks rather politically placated. And even though we have managed to reunite everyone, there is one new addition that no one seems to know.

"Matheus, how lovely that you dropped by to pay a visit. It's been quite a while since you left the station, has it not?" a voice calls from just inside the door of the minister's building.

I know that voice.

Sure enough, everyone turns to look, and I see Pschye step out of the building and into view.

"What is *she* doing here?" Petra growls from beside me.

"I don't know." To be honest, I don't think any of us know.

Ben reaches down and holds my hand at our sides, and we watch as Pschye stands before Matheus.

"I had a feeling you were coming unraveled at the Union," she says to him. "And I had a feeling that eventually, we would all end up here on this resource-rich planet of Brocadia."

"Hello, Pschye," Matheus says as he greets her with a face that indicates he doesn't care for her too much. I don't blame him—she's as wicked as they come. Whether he's a guard, a slave, or even a delegate that none of us knew about, I am sure he has reason to hate her, too. Everyone has reason to hate her—even her own peers, like Ophelia. I wonder if the person at the top of the Union feels as poorly about her as everyone else seems to, and if so, why in the world she was offered a position of power.

The Minister of Life takes a step back and out of the way so that Matheus and Pschye can address each other. All the other Fshie are simply awaiting direction. At least they aren't so scary-looking for the time being.

"You really should be home in bed, my friend," Pschye tells him in a subtly condescending tone. "It would be terrible if your condition were to worsen and the Intergalactic Union were to lose its leader."

A bitter taste rises in the back of my throat as simultaneous gasps are heard around me and as I notice the veins on Ben's neck bulge with a tightening jaw. None of us knew. This man, with his strange features that, based on Pschye's comment, now seem to point more toward sickness than species, is the head of the snake. Matheus is the leader of the Intergalactic Union, the man in control of all the delegates, including Pschye, and the person responsible for overseeing all that has happened. This is the man I set out to kill. How in the world did he end up on a ship with Ben?

I turn my head to look at Ben, and he looks both furious and betrayed. I wonder for a moment if he considered this man his friend, an ally, only to now learn that he is the evil behind all that has happened.

Suddenly, everyone realizes that this sickly, strange man is the prime leader on Nairu.

He waves Pschye aside, and she makes a disgruntled expression. He completely ignores her as he turns to address to the Minister of Life.

"Let us go inside and talk like civilized people instead of standing out here on the streets," Matheus says to the minister. "I feel we have much to talk about now."

The minister nods obediently and bows deeply in respect to Matheus before leading him toward the doorway into the building.

"Oh, and all these people," Matheus says as he turns and waves at Ben and the rest of us standing there with our mouths still hanging open, "bring them, too."

"What is happening?" Vira asks as the group of us are all shuffled in behind the minster and Matheus.

"I'm not sure," Petra tells her. "But just stay quiet and alert."

"I think that's good advice for all of us," Ben says as he looks around while we walk inside.

The inside of the building is incredible. I didn't stop to take a look when we were slinking down the stairwell to the dungeons in order to rescue Talon, but now I can see every inch of it. The building is taller than anything I have ever seen. There is no ceiling in the front entryway, so I can tilt my head all the way back to look up past the sky where the spire seems to touch.

If I were to compare this sight to anything even remotely close to the architecture on Earth, I would have to say that it most reminds me of a cathedral; one of those old and beautiful cathedrals with the tall spires and richly colored stained-glass windows. But even then, nothing on Earth was ever built to be this tall. I don't even think we had the technology to do it.

The windows are reminiscent of stained glass, except for the fact that the colors are all varying shades of the same hue. Everything is a deep purple, or blue, or green. The colors overlap and blend, and their jewel tones on the windows cast a light inside the building that makes it feel like twilight even though it's midday here.

The minister leads us down a long hallway, and then toward one of the rooms that line the side of the corridor. Inside the room, there is a wide table with room enough for all of us to sit. For a second, I thought Pschye disappeared or ran off somewhere because I haven't heard her voice for the entire walk inside, but then I see her take a seat at the table close to Matheus.

Once we are all settled, Matheus talks first.

"I am sure that you all have quite a lot of questions for me," he begins. "And I am sure that some of you might have feelings of distrust for me now as well." He looks right at Ben as he says the last part. "But I can assure you that I don't mean any of you harm."

This time, everyone is surprised by the fact that it is Amity who makes a small grunting sound in response to his claim.

"How could you profess that?" she asks. "Do you know how many lives have been lost due to your thirst for power?"

Matheus looks genuinely confused by her choice of words.

"Hope was carrying the first unborn child of the new human race that you dumped onto the dead planet," Amity continues. "And your assassins shot her dead."

Matheus shoots a furious glance over at Pschye. "Is this true?" he asks, acting as if this is the first that he has heard of it.

"There are many things the Union delegates have handled for you in order to ease your burden," she replies. It's basically a "yes" but with some extra fluff to make her response sound better. "These renegades, as they would call themselves, have done nothing but undermine the goals of the Union since the start of their involvement."

"Involvement?" I ask, harping on the word as if we had some choice in the matter. "None of us wanted to be involved with this at all."

Matheus removes his eyes from Pschye and looks at the rest of us instead, as if he doesn't have the time or patience to deal with her right now. For some reason, he seems to think that we are the more important audience.

"The term 'renegades' has a certain appeal to it," he says. "As if you are on some noble and dangerous mission to topple the unjust."

Pschye rolls her eyes and pushes her back against her seat.

"Well, renegades, let me explain to you why I created the Intergalactic Union. The Union was to be a project used in order to explore scientific discoveries across the galaxies and return home with the information collected. I consider myself a bit of a philanthropist."

"A murderous philanthropist," Petra mumbles.

"Not at all," he continues. "In fact, I used to go on all of the ventures myself just so I could meet new species and learn from their ways. I've been to Brocadia several times before. But somewhere along the way, in one of the many places I had journeyed to, I became infected with an alien DNA that caused me a crippling and debilitating illness."

He looks straight at Amity and Clover, whose wide eyes are watching him warily as he speaks.

"I am every bit as human as the two of you," he says with a smile. "But you'll have to forgive my wretched appearance. It is, I'm afraid, one of the disturbing realities of my deteriorating health. When I fell ill, I repurposed the Intergalactic Union to find a species and a planet that seemed resilient enough to help me find a cure for my otherwise inevitable death sentence and a quickly shortening lifespan. It appears this may have been a bad decision on my part."

"You cannot possibly pass judgment on that." Pschye laughs rudely in the face of her superior. "You haven't seen anything the Union has done in years. You couldn't possibly know what is actually happening on the planets we have helped."

"You haven't helped anyone," I say sharply. "All you do is murder, and imprison, and destroy."

"This is all my fault," Matheus says as he shakes his head. "The sicker I got, the less hands-on I became. I allowed the Union delegates to take over for me as I took a seat on the sidelines and waited for them to find a discovery that would heal me. But now I can see—between talking with Ben and seeing how things truly are on the dead planet, and even here—that the delegates have abused their positions in an attempt to seek control and riches for themselves. They have turned a once noble cause into a power-hungry force being used to control instead of discover."

There are whispers between some of us at the table, and even the Minister of Life doesn't seem to know what to make of it all.

"I know none of you have any reason to trust me," Matheus says, "but I hope you will give me a chance to earn your trust back. I have decided to disband the Intergalactic Union."

No one looks more shocked than Pschye.

"I will enjoy the last of my days doing what I love most —talking with other species and learning about other discoveries in the world. A new friend recently helped me see that I should be making the most of the time I have left, instead of watching it slip away from me."

Matheus smiles at Ben, and I finally see Ben relax a bit, as if he is starting to trust Matheus again.

Matheus might have made a mistake, but at least he now seems to see the error he has made and wants to make some changes with the time he has left.

"If you are giving up on trying to prolong your life," the minister says, "then you will meet your demise one day, and then who will preside over Nairu if both you and the Intergalactic Union are no more?"

"I understand your concern," Matheus says with a nod toward the minister. "And I am sorry that it seems Brocadia and Nairu have had diminished relations since the last time I was here. But I think it is within my power now to see things clearly and set them right."

Much to Ben's surprise, Matheus stands shakily on his feet and reaches across the table to extend his hand to Ben.

"This man has reminded me of the best qualities about being human, and I believe that he honors life and freedom as much as I tried to do when I first started the Union. In my error, I have also found something good. Although the Intergalactic Union will no longer exist, Nairu will still need a good leader in my absence, one who can hold diplomatic relations with other planets and bring the people of Nairu into a free and peaceful future. Ben is the person to do that."

Ben looks stunned and speechless, but not nearly as shocked as Pschye. She squirms in her seat as if she knows what is about to happen next and doesn't like it.

"Ben has impressed me with his determined sense of compassion and his level-headedness in times of chaos— both of which are qualities of a true leader. For this reason, I will proclaim my successor here in front of the Minister of Brocadia as being—"

Matheus is a mere moment away from making the decree in front of all who are gathered and the leader of another planet. He has the beginning utterances of Ben's name forming on his lips, but the word never comes out of his mouth. Because in an instant, Pschye pulls her gun from beneath the table and shoots Matheus squarely between the eyes, killing him instantly and dropping his body onto the table in front of us.

There are screams and chaos as panic erupts. The minister calls for his guards, and the Fshie attempt to surround Pschye to take her into custody. But Pschye will never surrender, especially when she can continue to leverage those around her.

She grabs the person closest to her—me—taking me as the one hostage that she knows will give her the most control over the situation because Ben would do anything to prevent her from hurting me. These Spewt may be evil, but they are also extremely intelligent.

24

BEN

Instantly, I jump to my feet as fast as I can and try to grab Bex from the clutches of a completely unhinged-looking Pschye.

"Get away from me!" Pschye screams as she pulls Bex against her chest and holds the gun to the side of her head. "You will all back off and let me leave here in a Union ship back to Nairu without any interference. Or I will gladly blow this human's head from her shoulders. Believe me when I say that I have been looking for a reason to kill her."

I can tell by her two narrowed pupils in each eye that Pschye isn't bluffing. She means what she says, and undoubtably wants to kill Bex if given a reason. The only thing keeping Bex alive right now is her value to Pschye as a hostage to leverage her safe passage off Brocadia.

"Please, everyone stay still," I say as I hold my hands up toward the Fshie guards and stay in my place.

They listen to me, and I'm not sure why, but I'm thankful they do. Perhaps it is because the things Matheus said about me were enough to impress the Minister of Life.

Everyone remains motionless as Pschye tries to inch her way toward the door, dragging Bex along with her.

"Why would you kill Matheus?" I ask her. "What could you possibly hope to accomplish with this act? Everyone here has seen you murder the leader and creator of the Intergalactic Union. Do you really think that will simply be overlooked? Even on Nairu, by the people and the other delegates there?"

"The new Union didn't need Matheus anymore," Pschye hisses in response. "We outgrew that sickly man years ago. We were all just waiting for him to quietly die off in his bedroom on Nairu where he wasn't a problem. If he had stayed closed up inside his room and remained all weak and sickly without venturing here to wave his voice around, then he could have lived out his final days staring out his window in peace. But you filled his head with all sorts of ideas of grandeur, and so if you want to blame anyone for his death, then you can blame yourself. I am simply reclaiming all the wasted power and resources he had at his disposal."

"So now what?" Talon asks with a scowl of disgust on his battered face. "You will appoint yourself as the new leader of your planet?"

"Nairu doesn't need a leader. The four Union delegates will assume control over Nairu, and we will continue to further our reach throughout the galaxies by conquering planets and species and harvesting their resources. This was never about finding a cure for the old man for us. This has always been about assuming the power that the strongest of us were meant to have."

I watch as Bex tries to wrestle away from Pschye, but cannot. The Spewt are much, much stronger than humans.

I want to reach out and grab her, but the gun is pressed firmly against Bex's temple, so I don't dare try.

"What could you possibly want with all that power?" Aerlon asks. I can tell that he is trying to stall her, hoping one of us will come up with a way to prevent Pschye from leaving with Bex on a ship back to Nairu.

"Why can't you just be satisfied letting other civilizations live in peace? You have all you need on Nairu. You don't need to go around terrorizing the other worlds."

Pschye looks around at all of us and bursts out into a fit of maniacal laughter. "You are all fools for not being able to see the bigger picture," she scolds. "Since you are all so inferior and daft, I will give you a few pieces of the puzzle and see if you can figure it out for yourself."

It's working—Aerlon is stalling her. But the problem is that none of us have a way to get Bex away from her.

"Matheus sat right here and told you that he discovered an alien DNA that was causing his descent into death. Tragic, truly," she says sarcastically. "But on the other hand, Ophelia discovered an alien technology that allowed her to enhance herself to the point of becoming nearly indestructible."

I had wondered that—whether or not Ophelia was born as a half-cyborg or if she made those modifications to herself. Her alien form could probably handle it better than a human could.

"So, what do you think could be possible if the Union was able to have a sample of every species of DNA and every unique resource in the entire universe?" she asks. She pauses as if she is giving us a moment to think before answering. Pschye's weakness is her desire to make people feel inferior to her in any way possible.

Talon is the first to speak up.

"Whoever had all of that, and whoever could find a way to merge varying species of DNA together like that, would theoretically be able to control life and death."

"Bravo." Pschye grins. "Not only a strong brute, but a smart one at that. You're not quite as stupid as some of the others, except that your theory is very much not hypothetical."

"There's no possible way that you could collect all of that DNA," Petra interrupts. "No matter how many populations you enslave or planets you conquer to steal it from. It wouldn't be possible to keep that much alien DNA viable without a host. And obviously the DNA that used Matheus as a host wasn't successful since it was destroying him. You'd be making the same mistake."

"You're not as smart as you think you are," Pschye chides before turning to look at me and smiling. "We already have a host."

Before anyone can say anything else, Pschye pulls Bex with her through the door. Everyone jumps from their seat and follows behind them, but no one interferes because the gun is still pressed against Bex's skull.

As soon as Pschye reaches the Union ship that I landed right in front of the building, I start to think about how to prevent her from getting Bex on that ship. But just as she is about to step inside the hatch, Pschye tosses Bex out toward us, then closes the hatch and takes off.

Bex stumbles from the force of the push, and I reach out to grab her.

"How the hell does that bitch know how to fly a ship?" Petra asks as she glares up at the sky to see Pschye making a clean escape back toward Nairu.

I hold Bex in my arms for a minute and press my lips against the top of her hair. I was worried that Pschye was going to take her all the way back to Nairu as a hostage, so at least Bex is here. But everyone else is worried.

The Intergalactic Union is now being governed by a team of four volatile lunatics, with no halfway sane leader above them to answer to. And if previous experience serves as a model for the hierarchy of the delegates, Pschye will be calling most of the shots.

"Who is the fourth delegate?" Vira asks as we all stand there, still reeling from what happened. Matheus' blood is still spilled across the table inside. "I don't remember ever seeing a fourth."

"Clyde," Aerlon answers her.

"That's a strangely human name," Amity remarks.

"I suppose it is," Aerlon says. "But trust me when I tell you that Clyde is no human. He has godlike strength, is covered in thick fur, and has a tail that I've heard can double as a whip. He rarely ever attends the delegates' meetings."

"Why not?"

"No idea." Aerlon shrugs. "I have a feeling there are some dynamics among the four of them that we don't know about."

When I let go of Bex, she looks startled, and I try to reassure her that she is safe now after that harrowing experience. But that isn't at all what she is worried about.

"What did Pschye mean when she said that they already have a host?" she asks me with eyes full of panic. "She looked right at you and smiled when she said it."

I know that. It wasn't lost on me that Pschye seemed to make an effort to single me out during that sentence and vague proclamation. But I don't want Bex to have anything else to add to her pile of worries right now. I know how she can get when she overthinks things and worries herself into a downward spiral, and we all have more than enough to deal with right now without trying to decipher the Pschye's gibberish that Pschye. Still, it does give me pause.

I remember Ophelia mentioning something about how I am special, and I can't help but wonder if it has something to do with this.

"I don't know what she meant by that," I say, trying to calm Bex's nerves. "But I wouldn't read too much into the rantings of a crazy woman."

"She might be crazy, Ben, but she's also very smart and powerful. What if she has done something to you?"

Suddenly, everyone is staring at me as if I am some sort of mutant being.

"Do you feel okay?" Petra asks.

"Yes," I say as I brush the question off as being ridiculous. "I feel perfectly fine."

"Did anyone do anything to you while you were assigned at the Union station with Ophelia?" Aerlon asks. "Drink anything or eat anything that tasted weird? Wake up and feel different after a dead sleep? Any sort of testing or injections that they tried to give you?"

"No, none of that," I answer him honestly. "I kept to myself as much as possible when I wasn't having to tend to Ophelia's whims or attend Union events. There wasn't any sort of experimenting on me, and I can't remember having any moments of blacking out or lost time. I think you guys are reading into this too much. She could have just been lying, and she didn't even refer to me specifically. She's probably just trying to get in our heads."

"What about before you were ever picked up by the Intergalactic Union?" Amity asks.

I'm surprised that she is joining this conversation, but I

guess she would know as well as any of us what it was like to be "processed" by the Union delegates.

"I don't remember anyone doing anything at all to me," I say. "At least, not anything that was different than what everyone else went through in the containment pods. Did they do anything to you?"

"No." She shakes her head. "Same as everyone else. I mean, they did seem to stare and marvel at me for a while, which was unnerving. But they did that with all the humans I saw."

"Yeah," Bex adds in. "They seemed to have a fascination with humans. I noticed it, too. I wonder if it has something to do with the fact that their leader, the creator of the entire Union, was human?"

"See? Now that part still blows my mind," Talon says.

He is standing on his own now and looking much stronger than when I first saw him.

"Why, and better yet, *how* was a human able to rise to such a position of power within this immense galaxy of alien civilizations? No offense to those of you here that are human, but you guys aren't the strongest or the most advanced species."

"None taken," I say. "I agree that as a species, we are lacking. As is evidenced by the destruction of Earth and the demise of our kind. But there are a few of us every now and then who stand out as being exceptional. I think Matheus was one of the exceptional ones."

While everyone breaks off into their own small discussions about what to do now, I zone out for a minute. I try to think about my first days at the Union station after being taken from Earth, especially anything that stands out in my mind as being odd or "special," but nothing does. I suppose it's possible that both Pschye and Ophelia are just trying to mess with my head. Then again, it seems like a lot of effort to go through, and I haven't really seen the two of them get along well enough to do any successful collaborating.

Still, why did they choose me to bring back to the Union and try to assimilate me as a delegate? I know Ophelia said it was for punishment, which definitely made sense, but what if there was more to it than that? What if there really is something disturbingly "special" about me? And what if they did something to me I don't know about? If one species of alien DNA could cause as much destruction on a human as it had on Matheus, then I can't even imagine the sickness that would be caused by several species' DNA. I wouldn't even know what symptoms to look for.

I try to give myself a quick health assessment without overthinking it, causing myself to have phantom feelings of being unwell. But just like I answered a few minutes ago, I feel fine. The only thing that doesn't feel good right now is my mind that is racing in a bunch of different directions, trying to think about what to do, where to go, and what the hell I'm supposed to do if I am a living DNA farm. When I stop to think rationally, I really do feel just like I always have —tired, but fine.

"You okay?" Bex asks as she tugs at my hand.

"Yeah, sorry, I was just thinking."

"About what?"

"All of it."

"Wouldn't it be nice if we could just go back to Earth and live normal lives before the planet broke down and before we were tossed into all this craziness?" she asks as she rests her head against my arm. "I didn't even know most of this existed back then."

"Yeah, me neither," I say. "But I also didn't know that

you existed before all this and before we met at the Union station. I'm not so sure that I would trade it all back if it meant I didn't get to be with you."

She looks up at me and beams. "Really? I'm not sure I am worth all this trouble."

"You are," I say as I lean down to rest my temple against hers. "You definitely are worth all of it."

I leave my head resting against hers for a minute while we watch the others still engaged in worried conversations.

At some point, I need to tell Bex that I love her more than I can possibly say. But for the moment, I need to make sure that I am not a walking petri dish of alien DNA. She has already lost a lot, as we all have, and Bex has already warned me not to make any promises to her that I can't keep. So, I need to make sure before I tell her that I am not at risk of meeting the same fate as Matheus before I tell her that I love her and will never leave her.

BEX

Pschye may be gone, but I am still worried. I don't like the way things are right now. We are still here on Brocadia, and even though the minister has realized his mistake in having made an agreement with the Intergalactic Union and is no longer hostile toward us, I still don't feel comfortable here.

The minster offered all of us his apology and a place for us to all stay unbothered and safe within the city for as long as we need. We all kind of stand around and check over each other as we try to wrap our minds around everything that has happened. In the course of a few short hours, we found out there was a leader of the Union, that he was human like us, and then watched him get slaughtered at the hands of the true evil behind all that has been going on. At least we are all together now; those of us who are still alive, anyway.

"We can't just run and hide on some faraway planet anymore," Petra says as she voices the thought that we are all thinking. "Not anymore. The Union won't stop at destroying everything in order to get what they want. We can't just sit by idly while planet after planet and species after species are hunted down and used like lab rats."

"I agree," Ben says beside me.

I agree with them, too. In fact, we all do. Even Clover doesn't want this evil to go unpunished and the culprits behind it to do what they did to her family, to more innocent people. We are all in agreement that we need to at least try to stop them.

Before we can even think about how to stop something as powerful as a completely off-the-rails Intergalactic Union, we need some rest. None of us has gotten a solid night of sleep in days.

The minister shows us to rooms inside his own building this time, and they are exquisite. Every convenience is afforded to us, and we are all much hungrier and more tired than we even imagined. After a good meal and the chance to freshen up, we are eager to get some sleep.

"Are you sure it's safe?" Vira asks Talon as we all walk together down the hall, breaking off into separate rooms. "I mean, these people are the ones who beat you nearly to death and had you chained to a dungeon wall not more than a day or so ago."

"Yes, I know," Talon says as he wraps his arm around her. "But if there is one thing I know about my people and the minister, it is that they never admit they are wrong unless they feel it deeply. I have no doubt that the Minister of Life has become made wiser by his mistake and that we are safe here now. The minister is devoted to the sole protection of his planet and his people at large, and he expects the complete obedience and loyalty of his people in return. They will do as he says, and I believe he is now our ally—this time, a genuine ally.

MATTHEW THRUSH

I watch as the two of them walk into one of the empty rooms, and I really hope that Talon is right. At this point, there isn't anywhere safer for us to go now, anyway. There is still one Union ship here, the one that Aerlon and I landed just outside the city. Eventually, we will figure out where to go next. For now, with full stomachs and tired muscles, we will all get some sleep.

Amity and Clover stay in the same room as Aerlon. I think they feel safer in numbers. Petra is the only one who chooses a room alone.

"Do you want to stay with me?" I ask as I see her get ready to step into a bedroom.

She glances quickly between me and Ben and smiles. "Nah. Thanks, anyway, but I am most comfortable when I'm alone." At that, Petra walks inside a room and closes the door behind her.

This time, Ben stays in the same room as me. I almost forgot about the last time we spent the night here on Brocadia and how jealous I was that he and Petra went back to stay in the ship together. That incident feels so small and petty now, considering all that has happened since then. I am no longer jealous of Petra, and I'm glad that we've become friends. I'm also no longer angry at Ben for what happened on Nairu. I know he was just trying to protect me, even though it hurt at the time.

To be honest, I am so emotionally drained that I can barely think straight anymore. And I am glad to know that Ben and I will be right here together tonight, just like we were before all this craziness happened. We've been separated enough, and I don't think either of us is quite ready to let go again just yet, even if it's just for a night.

We lay down right next to each other in the bed, but even though things seem comfortable once again, there is a worry hanging in the air between us that is nearly palpable. I look over and see him staring up at the ceiling. I can tell there is something he isn't telling me.

"What is it?" I ask.

"What is what?"

"The thing you are keeping from me. And before you try to tell me there isn't anything, just remember that I can always tell when you're lying."

Ben chuckles, knowing I'm right.

"Ophelia said something that is sticking in my head."

"What was it?"

"She kept making reference to me being special and saying that the Union had some sort of future plan for me. It was all very vague and cryptic, and at the time, I figured she was just trying to mess with me."

"But now you're starting to wonder if it has something to do with what Pschye said about the alien DNA, aren't you?" I ask.

"Yeah, a little."

At least he's being honest with me about it now. I hate thinking that Ben would keep things bottled up inside instead of talking to me about them out of fear that he would worry me. We are in this together.

"I just can't shake the feeling that maybe I might have been somehow exposed to alien DNA and not known about it," he says.

"But when could that have possibly happened?" I ask.

"I don't know. Maybe when we got those tattoos in the containment pods just before we started our mission? I mean, I know we all got them, and the antibacterial injections to go along with them, but—"

"Wait a second—what antibacterial injections? You told Aerlon you didn't get any injections," I remind him.

"I guess I forgot about that one. But it was so small, and just the routine antibiotics to prevent a skin infection from the tattoo. Everybody got one."

"No," I say with concern as I shake my head, "I didn't. I got the tattoo, which I still don't know what those were for, but I didn't get any injection to go along with it. We need to ask the others."

Ben and I get out of bed and go door to door to ask everyone else. Amity, Clover, and Talon don't have any tattoos, of course; they weren't at the Union station with us or part of any missions. But Aerlon, Petra, and Vira were, and none of them got injections to go along with their ink. Now I am definitely worried.

I don't say anything as Ben and I walk back to the bedroom together. But as soon as we get behind a closed door, I can feel myself start to panic.

"Ben, all signs of this point to you being the host that Pschye was talking about," I say as I start to pace the room.

"Bex, come on, try to relax. Come lay down with me."

"No, you can't just brush this off. This is serious."

"Okay but pacing around the room isn't going to solve anything. At least come lay down with me. We're both tired."

He's right. I go back to lay down with him on the bed, but I'm not done talking about it.

"What if the same thing that happened to Matheus happens to you?"

"I think you're worrying prematurely," he says in his usual calm demeanor that he gets when he's trying to talk me down off the ledge. "We don't even know if Pschye was telling the truth or not. And she's definitely not the most honest person I've met. She could've just said that to spin us up."

"But what if she was telling the truth?" I ask. "What if they really have been dumping a bunch of alien DNA into a host in order to see what happens, and what if you are that host?"

"Look, even if it was true," he says as he wraps an arm around me and pulls me up to lay against his chest, "there's nothing that we can do about it now, anyway, so there is literally no sense in worrying about it. All that worrying will do without being able to have access to a viable solution is mentally exhaust us more. Besides, that was one very tiny injection that happened only one single time. There couldn't have possibly been a whole universe of DNA in that single shot."

I frown. "Wasn't it only one species of alien DNA that was killing Mateus?"

"I'm going to start calling you a doomsayer," he teases as he squeezes me around the shoulders and tries to lighten the mood. "We need to use our energy to focus on more productive and pressing matters, like how to stop Pschye and dismantle the Intergalactic Union."

He's right about that part. I had thought that finding the "head of the snake" and killing off the Union leader would take the whole corrupt system down, but boy, was I wrong. Instead, the corrupted system took their own leader down, and now they are running out of control.

We talk for a while longer, and then my eyes eventually start feeling too heavy to keep open any longer, and I fall asleep to the sound of Ben's steady breathing against my ear. I can't even remember which part of our conversation I fell asleep on, only that we both suddenly stopped talking and that was the end of it.

I had hoped to be able to have a deep and restful sleep,

but there is something I forgot about being so tired that you fall into a deep sleep—you dream.

This dream isn't just any dream; it's a nightmare of epic proportions. In my dream, I see myself waking up, and the worst part about it is that I actually feel like I am awake and that everything I am seeing in my dreamscape is real.

At first, I feel a bit disoriented, because I think that I have only been asleep for a couple of minutes and am now suddenly awake again. I expect to find Ben still lying beside me, but he is gone. I get up from the bed and go to look for him, still feeling foggy but also still thinking that I am actually awake.

"Hey, have you seen Ben?" I ask Vira and Talon as I peek in through their open doorway.

They both look like they are sitting on their bed, talking, and I wonder what time it is and if anyone has actually gotten any sleep.

They don't answer me. They simply shake their heads in silence as they look at me. This should have been the first sign that I am still dreaming. In my worst nightmares, no one ever speaks. They are always eerily silent, and communication is always done in gestures or expressions. But I still don't yet realize that I am trapped inside my dream.

For a while, I wander around asking everyone if they have seen Ben, but no one has. I walk down into the main entrance of the building and see the Minister of Life standing there, surrounded by several Fshie in their most attractive forms. I ask all of them if they have seen Ben, too, but no one has seen him. That is when I finally start to get the feeling that something isn't right.

I walk out into the city, barefoot for some reason, which also should have clued me in that I am still asleep and dreaming. I search the streets for him. The city seems empty, and there are only a few stray Fshie walking off in the distance.

When I still can't find him, I decide to walk out into the wilderness where we left the other ship. For some reason, I start to feel as if I can hear his voice calling me in a soft whisper that sounds as if it is coming from inside my own head. The closer I get to the ship, the louder his voice becomes until I am finally standing right in front of the hatch.

I open it and step inside, fully expecting to see Ben there, but again, he isn't. The ship isn't big, and there aren't too many places to be hidden in, so I can tell almost right away that he isn't here, either. His voice in my head has stopped, and I can't think of anywhere else to look for him. Since the ship is still here, I know he hasn't left the planet, not that he would have reason to.

"Where are you, Ben?" I say to myself as I stand inside the empty ship and try to think of where he might have gone and what to do.

Then I hear a noise behind me, and I see him standing with his back to the hatch just outside the door. He is unmoving and faced away from me with his head tilted slightly up, as if he is looking at something in the sky.

"Ben?" I ask as I walk toward him. "What are you doing out there? What are you looking at?"

He doesn't answer me, and it suddenly dawns on me that no one has spoken to me with voices or words this entire time. *Come on, Bex, think—think…this is a dream, and you know it.*

I walk to the hatch of the ship and step outside. "Ben?"

Still, he doesn't turn around or move in the slightest. So, I reach my hand up to touch the back of his shoulder.

As soon as I touch him, he turns around, and I feel a momentary wash of relief...until I see what he looks like.

His shallow eyes are sunken into his skull, as if they are so loose that they might rock right out of their sockets. His skin is a sickly pale yellow that looks covered in sores that are starting to flake off. And when I look closely at his face, it looks as if there is something moving beneath his skin, and a sick realization comes over me that Pschye was telling the truth and Ben is a host for a whole range of alien DNA experiments.

As soon as the thought hits me, my eyelids fling open, and I am awake, lying in the bed next to Ben, who is still sound asleep, and shaking as if I have seen a ghost.

BEN

I*t's all in my mind*, I tell myself when I wake up and think that I am feeling unwell.

After Pschye's verbal gameplaying, and the worried conversation I had with Bex before bed, it makes sense that I would wake up and feel ill. I was feeling totally fine until I started worrying that I had possibly been infected with some sort of invasive and foreign genetic material. This is all just nothing but nerves and overthinking.

When I wake up, Bex isn't there. She must have already gotten up and gone to see the others or get some of the Fshie's equivalent of coffee. I felt her move around a few times during the night, as if she was having a restless night of sleep, so maybe she just needed to get up early this morning and clear her head. I don't blame her.

I head out into the hallway and notice that the rest of the rooms are all empty. Either everyone got up early, or I must have slept later than I thought. It hardly feels like I slept at all because I am still tired.

When I find everyone, they are all sitting around a

round table in one of the downstairs meeting rooms, already heavily engaged in talking about our options.

"Hey." Bex smiles at me when I walk into the room. "You must have been beat."

"Why?" I ask, still feeling a bit confused about why I was the only one left sleeping. "Did I sleep late?"

"Late?" Petra chuckles. "It's late afternoon here already."

That's definitely odd.

Talon hands me a cup of Fshie coffee, and I sit down to join their discussion.

"What did I miss?"

Aerlon fills me in on how they have been continuing the discussion from last night, about how running away and hiding is no longer an option that anyone wants to consider, not after seeing how the Union was going to lay waste to everything. It doesn't sound like they have come up with any truly viable options yet.

"Our only choice now is to try to stop the Union," Petra reiterates. "But how?"

"Can I suggest an idea?" a small voice calls from the beside the window in the room. Clover, who has been sitting and listening quietly, is staring over at the table of us with an innocent and eager face.

"Did you have something you wanted to say?" Amity asks her gently.

"Yes," the young girl says as she walks over to the table to stand beside Amity while she speaks. "You have all been talking about this for a long time, but you aren't coming up with any answers. I think the answer is very clear."

"Oh?" Aerlon smiles at her. It's easy to see that he cares for the girl almost as a father would, even though the two of them are completely different breeds of beings. "And what is this *very clear* answer that you see?"

"You should just start a war on Nairu to stop the bad guys and free the people there who are their slaves and prisoners," she says.

There is something about the way that Clover says it, something that is so clear and smart, and so full of conviction, that it seems much more mature and viable than anything the adults have been babbling about this entire time.

"It usually works in the fairy tales," she continues. "My parents used to read me fairy tales before they died, and my mother told me that it didn't matter if the hero was a prince, or princess, or even a dragon. It only mattered that they fought against the mean ones. That's how they always win. I think that's what you should do, too."

"She's right," Petra says.

I have to admit to being surprised that, out of everyone here, one of the toughest ones seems to agree with this child.

"It's a simplistic child's viewpoint," Petra continues, "but Clover is right. There is no other way to stop the Union than to oust them from control and defeat them where they stand. We need to put Nairu back into the hands of people who will care for all the refugee species there instead of trying to manipulate and control them."

Petra turns to Bex as if she has suddenly had an idea come into her head. "Do you remember what I said to you about how everyone can be broken?" She doesn't wait for Bex to answer before she continues on. "The Union has already been fractured. Their leader is gone, and the delegates are already at odds simply because they all want to be at the top of the food chain. Now we just need to know where to hit the Union to make it break wide open. They must have a breaking spot."

"Hang on," I interrupt. "You seriously want to go start a war on Nairu? That is their home turf. They have all the advantages, are already dug in, and have cameras, guards, and weapons literally everywhere on that planet. Not to mention the fact that they have enough numbers between all their guards and slaves to form an army. We don't have any army."

Everyone is quiet for a moment as they think about what I've said. It's a nice fantasy to think that our small little band of renegades can go riding into Nairu on white horses and start a war that we can somehow win against all odds, like one of the fairy tales in Clover's books. But the reality of it is that wars take armies to fight them, and with sheer mathematical numbers alone, there is no chance in hell that we would ever prevail.

"We do have an army," Talon says as he looks up and interrupts the quiet at the table. "The Fshie."

"You can't be serious. I know they are your people, but they betrayed us, nearly got us all killed, and beat the absolute shit out of you. What makes you think they would even want to risk getting involved in this fight?" I ask.

"They're unprotected," Talon says. "They have no defenses around Brocadia. And obviously no standing agreement with the Intergalactic Union anymore. The only thing that they do have is an army. Helping us take down the Union is the same as helping ensure their own safety and protection from any future actions the Union might take against the Fshie."

"I still think it's a bad idea. Even if they would agree to help, which I don't think they will, I wouldn't trust them."

Despite my protest, Talon goes to get the Minister of

Life and bring him in to join the discussion. Just as I expected, he is not eager to offer up his forces to fight a battle that we want to wage against the powerful Intergalactic Union.

"But Minister," Vira says as she tries to help support the point, "don't you see that if you don't help us stand up against the Union now, you will be vulnerable to any cruelty and invasion that Pschye might decide to wage against your planet in the future? Brocadia could very well end up just like my home—destroyed."

Vira's words give the minister pause, and then Aerlon jumps in to drive home the point.

"I know it seems like a scary risk to send your people into a war that you have tried to avoid. And you are right to be wary and cautious. All wars result in deaths, and this one will be no different. You will lose some of your people, and the Fshie will suffer losses. But the question that you should ask yourself as a leader is whether to take a smaller loss now, or a bigger one later. Is it worth it to buy yourself a few days, weeks, or months of peace if you sacrifice your entire way of life in the end?"

It takes some more convincing, but the minister eventually concedes to help us with his army. He is swayed because he realizes that if the Union isn't stopped, they will inevitably come for his resource-rich planet and destroy his civilization. As a leader, he is making the right choice to act now, but I still don't think this is a course of action that can succeed. Even with a Fshie army—of what size we don't even know—the Union still has the upper hand on Nairu.

"I will agree to letting Talon train and take as many of the Fshie men with him to Nairu as you need to create an army to fight against the Union," the Minister of Life says before turning to Talon. "You have proven yourself to be worthy and honorable, even in spite of how we have treated you. And for that reason, I will give you this great and heavy responsibility."

Talon lowers his head in respect and thanks the minister for this honor. It baffles me how suddenly we all seem to be friends again. I hope that Talon isn't wrong to put his trust in the minister again, and in the Fshie.

"The Union is not just the four delegates," Bex says as we begin trying to assemble an actual and tactical plan now that this idea is taking off. "It is all the people on Nairu who are under the control of the delegates. Those people are afraid, and rightly so, because they have been threatened with terrible things. They will do as they are told, which includes fighting on behalf of the Union."

"Bex is right," Petra says. "Just think about Ransor and Soro. Those are the type of guys that will be bullying the meeker and more timid people on Nairu into taking up arms. Think about what happened on the dead planet. It was Jabber—a blue emissary—who shot and killed Hope simply because he was too afraid to defy Ransor. And Lily-bet, that sweet winged woman with the face of an angel, who stood by and did nothing to protect her friends.

"The Union has a powerful influence over the people on Nairu—fear. They aren't afraid to manipulate it to the fullest extent. This will not be an easy battle, even with the help of the fearsome Fshie to help us."

There is more discussion as Clover goes back to play near the window and the minster remains at the table to help us flesh out some of the logistics in getting his people trained to work with us. There is talk of how to disable monitoring systems, and how to reach some of the people on Nairu before they can be enlisted to the aid of the Union's defenses. There's also talk about how to breach the station and what to do with the four delegates. After a while, the conversation starts to blur in my head and my temple begins to throb.

"Are you okay?" Bex asks as she taps me on the shoulder.

"Yeah, I'm fine. I think maybe I slept too much and got a touch of a headache," I answer as the conversation comes to a close at the table. Everyone is going to take a short break to eat some food, and that suits me because I think I'm hungry, too.

I watch as everyone stands up from the table, and Clover swings around in circles as she plays by herself excitedly in the corner of the room, now eager for some lunch. I feel as if my head is suddenly much too heavy. My mouth tastes dry and chalky, and my muscles feel shaky. I go to stand up with the others, hoping that some food will help, but before I can even push the chair out from beneath me, I abruptly collapse.

The last thing I remember is the sharp thud of my head hitting against the table and the echo of pain it sends through my skull. The tabletop feels cold against my cheek, and there is an undercurrent of voices that all sound shocked but are too indiscernible for me to make out what they are saying. Then everything goes black.

When I feel myself starting to wake up, I can already tell that I am no longer downstairs sitting at that table. I feel myself lying down against a soft cushion, and I can feel something cold pressed against my forehead. I hear the soft, gentle voice of a single person talking to me—Bex.

For a minute, I can't open my eyes. It feels as if I want to wake up, but my body is boycotting the idea. I can feel her hand holding mine, and I can feel the small drips of a damp cloth rolling down the side of my face, or maybe it's sweat—I can't really tell. I feel as if I can't move anything at all because every part of my body is too heavy and weak, including my eyelids that remain firmly shut.

"Ben?" Bex's voice asks quietly. "Ben, can you hear me?"

I want to tell her that I can, but my mouth doesn't want to cooperate, either.

"How is he?" another voice asks. It's a male voice, but I can't tell who it belongs to. How weird that I'm having trouble recognizing any voice but the one belonging to Bex. It's almost as if I've forgotten everything I used to keep inside my head.

"He's burning up," Bex answers.

There's a pause filled with quiet, and then the sound of her sobs.

BEX

To say that I am beside myself with concern is an understatement. I am absolutely worried sick over Ben. While Petra and Aerlon help Talon get started training an army of the Fshie, and Vira and Clover work with some of the native Fshie to help them build a defense system for this planet since we will be using it as a home base for our war operation at the moment, I sit beside Ben.

He is sick—*really* sick. And I know that it can only be the alien DNA.

He has been in and out of feverish sleep, burning up, shaking, and mumbling gibberish to himself as he sleeps fretfully.

When he collapsed at the end of the meeting, Talon carried him to the bed, and this is where he has been ever since. Hours have passed, and he still hasn't opened his eyes.

Everyone keeps coming in to check on him, and I think they are also checking on me to make sure that I've stopped crying.

"You have to be all right," I whisper to Ben as I hold his clammy hand in mine. "We've made it through too much together already, and I am not going to lose you now. We need you. You're a leader among us, and we can't do this without you."

I wonder if he can hear me. I feel like I am mostly talking to myself.

While everyone else is preparing for the biggest fight of our lives and carefully planning every move with precision to mitigate the chances of this idea blowing up in our faces, I should be helping, too. But all I can bring myself to do is sit here beside Ben until he wakes. I can't do any of this without him.

Then, finally, after much of the following day has already passed, he wakes up.

"Ben!" I say with so much excitement that I nearly jump out of my chair beside him.

His eyes open slowly, as if looking at things hurts.

"I'm so glad you're awake! How are you feeling?" I ask. I can already tell just by looking at him that he must feel terrible. He looks even sicker than Matheus did— sicker than in my dream, too. His eyes are not sunken, and his skin is not yellow, but his cheeks are a burning bright red with fever and his hair is matted to his head in sweaty clumps. He is shaking so furiously with chills despite the fever, and I can hear his teeth clattering against each other.

He looks like he is suffering.

"How long have I been asleep?"

"A while."

"Did I miss anything?"

I dodge his question because I don't want him trying to get up and overdo things, which he will want to do when he hears about how steadfastly everyone is preparing for the war that we are getting ready to launch on Nairu.

"Ben, do you remember if you received any other injections besides the one with the tattoo?"

"I don't think so. Why?"

"Because your sickness has come on so suddenly, and your symptoms are rapidly getting worse, faster than Matheus' illness seemed to be. We think that perhaps you received a recent injection, which would have prompted this to take such a speed of infection over you."

"I don't think that I—" He stops himself mid-sentence and reaches down to touch his shirt, just below his ribcage.

"What is it?" I ask.

"Ophelia," he says with a scowl. "She and her stupid mechanical fingers. She sliced me with one of them as a punishment. There was a blade hidden inside one of the fingers of her mechanical hand. I wonder if maybe it wasn't a blade but was instead a—"

"Syringe."

Ben lifts his shirt, and there, right at the top of his torso, is a fresh scar that is festering with infection. I clasp my hand over my mouth to keep from gasping and try to make my face look not as horrified as I feel.

"That good, huh?" Ben asks with a light laugh before looking down at it himself.

The gash is bubbling over with a strange infection, the likes of which I have never seen before. Painful-looking blisters filled with a strangely colored fluid.

What Ben assumed to be a blade was really a tool used to implant more alien DNA into his system. Thank goodness he got out of there before they could inject him with even more.

"I guess I should have paid more attention," Ben

mumbles as his last couple of words turn into a quiet sigh. He falls back against his pillow again and, within seconds, is back in a feverish sleep.

I sit there, staring at the infected area of his chest before I pull his shirt back down over him to cover it. I have absolutely no idea what to do or how to treat an alien infection like this. I wrestle with what to do.

On the one hand, if we don't stop the Union before they decide to come back and pummel us, then we are likely all dead. But on the other hand, if I don't do something to cure Ben, he will wind up sicker and dying even faster than Matheus. The onset of his symptoms seems to be happening much, much faster with Ben, and I don't know how much time he has left before this becomes irreversible. I need to save him.

I stand up and look out into the hallway, seeing only Clover there as she heads back to her room to get something.

"Clover," I call to her, "can you please come and help me?"

She is sweet enough to want to help everyone here and has no problem sitting with Ben to keep an eye on him while I go try to find some helpful answers about what to do.

"Just don't lift up his shirt, okay?"

Clover looks down at his shirt, and it's impossible not to notice the seeping puss starting to soak through it.

"I'm not afraid of scary, gross things," she says with indignance. "I've already seen some."

"I know you have," I tell her with a gentle smile.

It's terrible to think of all this young girl has already witnessed. Watching a pregnant woman get gunned down in front of us had to have been one of the worst. Although,

I realize that she also watched her own parents get slaughtered by the Union, so Clover has been through more than any child should have had to endure.

"How old are you, Clover?" I ask.

"Twelve."

"Well, you are by far the bravest twelve-year-old I have ever met," I say as I put my hand on her shoulder. "Just don't lift his shirt because I don't want it to cause him pain or wake him, okay?"

Clover nods, even though that isn't really the reason why. I simply don't want her to have to see what it looks like under there, no matter how brave she might be.

I go to ask all of my fellow renegades for help first, starting with Aerlon because he is always so calm and grounded. But he has no idea how to help Ben. Amity suggests some ground medicinal packs and maybe a tincture or two, but this is not a normal illness or injury, and it isn't something that crude first-aid or holistic medicine is going to fix.

I go around asking all the rest of them, yet no one seems to have an answer. They are all saddened and worried, but no one knows what to do about it.

Finally, I go to seek help from the Minister of Life.

"I'm afraid I cannot help you," he says.

"Why not?" I ask angrily. "Not only are we supposed to be on the same side and trust and help each other now, but we are trying to save your damn planet."

"It's not that I *won't* help you," he says. "But that I cannot. I have no idea how to cure Ben of an alien DNA infection."

"But your whole civilization is built upon technology, and innovation, and scientific advances," I argue in disbelief that there isn't something they can do to help Ben.

"Surely, with all this advanced progress that you have here on Brocadia, there must be something you can do to help save him?"

"All our progress has been discovered and understood through countless hours of research," the minister replies. "We are only able to solve and cure things that we have had experience with. We have no idea what kind of DNA Ben has been injected with. If we knew what was infecting him, then yes, we could cure him. But we cannot hope to understand or provide an effective remedy for something that is still a complete mystery to us."

As much as I hate that answer, I can understand it; it makes sense. But it doesn't do anything to help, and right now, Ben needs help.

"So if you knew what it was that Ben has been injected with," I press the minister further, "then you could help him?"

"Yes, but I don't think that we have any way of knowing what—"

"Thanks," I interrupt as I quickly turn and walk away.

My mind is racing with the possible options that I have right now, and there is only one. I have to find out what Ophelia had in that syringe. I need to know what was hidden inside that mechanical finger of hers, and there is only one place that has the answer to that—the Intergalactic Union on Nairu.

If I wait until we launch the war, it will be too late for Ben. It also risks the chance of Ophelia, Pschye, or one of the other delegates who has the answers getting killed. I need to find out the information before that happens and before Ben can't fight the infection off any longer. I need to go back to Nairu and talk to Pschye and Ophelia to find out what they injected Ben with, even though I know they won't be forthcoming and will probably just take me prisoner instead. But if I can get an answer, and maybe even a sample of the genetic material they used, then the Fshie could whip up an antidote.

I have to try.

I walk past the others who are all still talking and training, but I don't stop to talk to any of the other renegades about this. None of them will agree with me or be on board with the idea of me going back to Nairu. In fact, they will likely try to stop me, and I can't have that happen. My best chance of doing this is to leave now, while they are all occupied and while I still have a chance to get to the Union before something else happens.

When I arrive back at the bedroom, Clover is still dutifully sitting there with Ben. I stand in the doorway for a second and listen as she recites one of her fairy tales out loud to him.

"And they all lived happily ever after," she says. "The end."

I smile at her as I walk inside the room.

"He likes stories," I tell her. "I'm sure he can hear you and that you are making him feel better while he sleeps."

Clover smiles at me, but it is a sad smile.

"I don't think he's going to live," she blurts out.

I can't help but make a horrified face.

"Sorry," she says. "But it's the truth. I have a sense about these things, just like I knew that Hope wasn't going to live."

"Well, we just need to keep hoping for the best," I say, realizing that it's a shallow and uselessly positive remark. "Hey, I need to run an errand for a little while. Would you be able to please stay here with Ben for a little bit longer until I return?"

She looks at me with her eyebrows scrunched up. "Where are you going?" she asks suspiciously.

"I just...well, I need to..." Dammit, I suck at lying under pressure. "I need to make a tincture." Thankfully, I remember that being one of Amity's suggestions. "Amity told me a recipe for a tincture that might help Ben feel better, so I am going into the city market to see if I can find the ingredients for it. I might be gone a little while. Can you stay with him?"

"Sure," she says, seemingly appeased by my quick lie.

"Thanks." I smile as I ruffle her hair in my fingers. "Be back soon."

I grab only my jacket because I don't want to raise her suspicions any further, and then I head out into the hallway. I make a quick stop in Petra's room, which is thankfully empty while she is helping the others. She has weapons—a few pieced-together guns and a blade or two—that she made herself. She always seems to have a tool to pull out at just the right time. And since I know it's a real possibility that I might get captured and imprisoned on Nairu again, I want to be a little bit more prepared this time.

I grab one of the guns and one of the blades and shove them both inside my boot. Then I slide past everyone in the building and out into the city. I walk toward the edge of the city where the wild overgrowth begins and head toward the Union ship that is still waiting for me there.

The Fshie have ships, too, but they keep them all carefully tucked away inside large, covered buildings in the city, on shiny landing pads that look like giant silver platters. I tell myself that I'm not *really* abandoning the other renegades here, because they still have a way off the planet if they need to escape. Granted, they would have to use a Fshie ship, but still, I am pretty sure that Petra can fly nearly anything. She's a walking owner's manual for anything mechanical.

As I look down at the control panel of this ship now, I find myself wishing I had her skill.

"How hard can it be?" I ask myself aloud. "It's just like driving a car."

I take a minute or two to acclimate myself with the controls, and then I decide that this is all just wasting time. Pretty soon, someone will notice I am missing.

I start the engines and overzealously bring the ship off the ground and up into the sky, nearly thrusting myself out of my seat before remembering that I need to buckle in. But once I am in the air, the navigational system is user-friendly enough for me to set it on autopilot back to Nairu. Landing there will be another issue, but I'll think about that later.

I sit back in the seat and think about Ben.

I've taken a big risk in doing this, especially doing it completely *alone*. And there are so many things that could go wrong, I start to second-guess whether this was a smart move. What if I get captured and stuck on Nairu with no way out and no one knowing where I have gone? What if Ben dies before I can make it back to Brocadia with a sample of the alien DNA? What if they launch the war, and I find myself smack in the middle of it, unprepared and trapped on the other side?

I am almost consumed by my downward spiral of worrying when I hear a noise coming from the back of the ship. Since the controls are on auto pilot, I unbuckle myself to walk back there and see what is making the sound.

"Hello?" I ask, thinking that maybe a wild animal from the forests on Brocadia's surrounding wilderness took refuge inside the ship while it was parked there.

I get ready to reach into my boot for the blade in case whatever it is isn't a friendly creature, but then a person steps out from behind the tall pile of blankets that had been folded up in the corner of the ship.

"Clover?" I gasp in surprise. "What are you doing here? I thought you were watching over Ben liked I asked you to."

"I was," she says as she steps forward. "Please don't be mad. Ben is safe with Amity looking over him. I told her I needed to take a nap because I was tired, and she offered to sit with Ben."

"What are you doing here on this ship?"

"I knew you weren't running an errand in town," she says. "And I knew that you were going to try to find a cure for Ben. It just made sense that you would try to go back to Nairu to find a cure for him, and since this is the ship that you came in on, well...I figured it would be the one you flew back to Nairu."

"But—"

"I snuck in here as soon as you left the bedroom because I want to come with you."

"Why in the world would you do that?" I ask angrily. "Don't you know I am heading this ship straight back to the Union? It's so dangerous, Clover. You shouldn't have come!"

"I had to," she says with another one of her innocent, blunt statements. "You need help."

I don't even know what to say in response to her. It's too late to take her back now, so she will have to stay. I sigh, not wanting to be angry at her, and motion for her to come with me as we both go back to sit down in the cockpit and buckle up.

"It's pretty up here." She smiles as she looks out the window at all the space around us. There are moons and stars and planets for as far as the eye can see. "Is it true that new planets are constantly being made?"

"Yeah, I think so."

Her eyes are filled with wonder, and I hope desperately that she doesn't wind up getting herself killed with her unfettered sense of fairytale-like bravery. If she manages to survive all this, then I have no doubt that Clover will one day be the hero of someone's story.

As we get closer to Nairu, I start to prep for landing this ship. I don't have any preconceived notions that I will be able to sneak the ship in. I will be spotted and apprehended for certain, and that is fine because I want to be taken to Pschye or Ophelia, anyway. They are the two people I want a chance to talk with. I have every intention of surrendering myself as soon as the ship lands in one of the cargo bays that the auto pilot is carrying it toward. But I don't want Clover to be captured.

"Okay, so listen carefully," I say as I see the Union station on Nairu come into view. "You need to stay here on the ship and stay hidden, do you understand?"

"But what about you?" she asks. "What if you need—"

"No. You stay here on this ship. You need to hide because the Union guards will come to search the ship, and you need to stay hidden."

I can see her face looking deflated, and I know if I don't give her some illusion of having an important part to play in this mission, she will do something reckless again, like try to leave the ship and come find me.

"Clover, it's very important that you follow my directions this time. You're the only other person who knows I am here. I need you to remain hidden on the ship, and if I am not back in a few hours, then you can use the comm link to contact the other renegades for help, okay?"

"Okay." She nods.

"Good." I smile. "Remember, stay hidden. The last thing we want is for one of the red assassins to find you here. They are ruthless killers, and they won't care you're a child. They will slaughter you just the same."

"I know," she says quietly as she looks at me with sad eyes. "Just like they slaughtered the tiny new human."

"What tiny new human?"

"The one that was never born back on the dead planet."

Hope's baby. It's a terrible thought, but a true one.

"Yes, just like that," I say. I want to make sure that she is too scared to get off the ship. In this case, fear will save her life.

I get ready to leave, waiting for her to get into a hiding place again before I open the hatch because I know there will be guards on the other side of it. I call back over my shoulder and see her face disappear behind the blankets. "Stay hidden."

BEN

I can feel myself wade in and out of fever dreams. Sometimes I am stuck between a state of waking and sleeping, a state that seems to be an existence all its own.

Mostly, I feel tired, and there is a numb sense of pain that I can tell is there but cannot really feel. Everything is dull, and blurred, and confusing, and there is no sense of how much time is passing by.

Sometimes, I try to open my eyes enough that they are thin, little slits I try to see out of. When I do, I can see Amity, Aerlon, or Vira caring for me and setting cool clothes on my head as they talk to me as if I can understand what they are saying. But I don't understand any of it at all. It almost feels like I am losing the thoughts, the words, the languages in my head. I get angry and sad, and I want to know where Bex is and why I can't see her through my barely open eyes anymore.

But most of the time, I don't have to worry about it because I cannot wake up, anyway. Most of the time, I am stuck inside my feverish dreams that seem to bleed from one thing into the next as if they are trying to form one big moving picture playing out in my mind.

In one dream, I see an alien species that I don't recognize. It's not one I have ever seen before, so I figure that it must be part of my fevered imagination just going wild with surreal imagery.

The aliens in my dream look like dark shadows. The only bright, light thing about them is a pair of glowing pure white eyes shaped like horizontal eggs that come to points at both corners. The aliens look thin, like matches, and they have long, dark hair that floats around them in tendrils, seeming to move in an invisible breeze.

I try to talk to them and ask them who they are and why they've come into my unconscious state, but they don't answer back. I suppose that even in my feverish madness, I know better than to expect dream aliens to hold a conversation with me.

One dream leads to the next, and they are all exploding with saturated surrealism. But they all eventually converge on the one with the dark aliens. Every time I see them, there are more and more of them until finally, it looks like a whole forest of dark, wispy aliens with their glowing white eyes staring back at me. They look intent, like they have a purpose here or a message to bring me. I wish I knew what they wanted to tell me.

All the aliens look like females, although a few look a bit androgenous. But there are no distinctly male-looking aliens among them. Since I am trapped inside my own head with nothing better to do than dissect the dreams I am having, I ponder how their species replicates itself if there are no males among them. Maybe they have evolved past the point of reproduction. Maybe they just create themselves at will. Now that would be a cool premise for a story. If I ever get to feeling better again, I will be sure to tell Clover about that idea. I bet that she could turn it into some sort of fascinating fairy tale.

But as my dreams continue, and as my sleep becomes more and more fitful, I start to notice that the aliens are coming closer to me, and that their thin, twisted fingers are all pointing toward my chest, over and over again. I look down in my dream and see myself, and I can see my shirt soaked in sweat and oddly colored goo.

Gross.

At that same moment, I have a second or two of slight alertness, and I try again to open my eyes.

I see Vira there, and her face looks horrified as she lifts my shirt to tend to my infected wound. Talon is behind her, and I can hear him talking.

"The infection is spreading," he says. "It's spread all the way up to his chest and is nearly to his collarbone now."

"But what are all those black lines in his skin?" Vira asks. "It looks like a web."

"His circulatory system is carrying the infection and whatever toxins are inside that alien DNA throughout his body," Talon answers her.

I have a single moment where I feel more awake than I have since Bex left, and I feel as if I can open my mouth to try to talk. But when I do, nothing but an agonizing moan comes out. I am suddenly swept over with so much excruciating pain that I can hardly stand it.

That moment is fleeting, and within seconds, I find myself falling back asleep again. I tend to think that is the human body's way of deflecting the agony; it's a pretty miraculous thing, in fact. The human body throws itself right back into an unconscious state to avoid one's mind from processing a pain it cannot handle. And a painful, lucid moment is instantly exchanged for a pain-free dream.

I want to stay awake because I want to see Bex. I wanted to utter her name instead of that groaning sound of pain. I want to know where she is and why she isn't here with me, but I can't. Now I am too tired to wake up at all.

So, I resign myself to my dreams again and watch as the dark aliens start to fill my head back up with their presence, as if they are overtaking my thoughts with their inky faces.

I wonder if these figures are the aliens whose DNA now runs rampant throughout my system. It would make sense that they would be. If alien DNA is in my body, then it is in my head, too. Maybe these are the thoughts and images of this species' own people. Maybe this is what I am turning into now.

One of them comes closer to me than the others, and she points again toward my chest. But this time, she touches the tip of her finger to my skin. And this time, I can hear her say something.

"Help," she whispers.

I look at her face, and she looks calm and undisturbed. It doesn't look as if she is fearful or under duress. So why is she saying *help*?

"Help," she repeats as she taps her finger to my chest a second time.

Then suddenly, all the other aliens touch their fingers to my chest, too, and I find myself surrounded by the swarm of them. They aren't hurting me, and they aren't scaring me, but they are definitely trying to tell me something.

"Help."

"Help."

"Help."

The word repeats throughout all of them, as if it is echoing throughout my dream. There are so many thin, dark fingers tapping my chest; too many to count, too many to even distinguish.

I look at the alien standing the closest to me. Her eyes seem to glow the brightest, as if they are the most urgent.

What are you trying to tell me? Is this a threat? Are you trying to help me? Or are you trying to ask for my help instead?

I know that I am dreaming, but there is something different about this, something that feels too real to be a dream. And I can't help but wonder if they are trying to give me some sort of warning. But what could it possibly be about?

What could aliens in my dream possibly have to warn me about? Especially if it is their DNA that is the cause of my sickness? None of it makes any sense, and the only thing I want to see or even dream about now is Bex.

Wherever she is, I hope she comes back soon before it is too late.

BEX

Of course, it has to be Ransor who apprehends me as soon as I step off the ship. His deviant grin hasn't changed one bit since the last time I had the displeasure of seeing him. And he seems to take great satisfaction in the fact that I have willingly landed myself right in his lap for capture again.

"You really are stupid." He laughs as he waves for two of the other guards in red jumpsuits to put my wrists in cuffs and drag me along between them while Ransor leads the way. "I would ask what you were thinking that would possess you to fly a ship right to your own funeral, but I have a feeling it would be some emotionally inept reason that would just make me laugh until my sides hurt."

I keep silent, but in my head, I think of a thousand ways I would like to smash Ransor's face in with the heel of my boot. Which reminds me that I still have weapons inside my boot that the guards were too arrogantly foolish to even think about checking.

As we walk off the cargo bay and into the station building, I can see out of the corner of my eyes that two guards are going onto the ship to make sure that I came alone. I can only hope that Clover stays well-hidden.

As we walk down the halls of the station building, with me sandwiched between Ransor who is leading our little parade and the guards behind me bringing up the tail, I decide to start a conversation that might help me get a bit of insight into what is going on here since the incident on Brocadia involving Matheus' assassination.

"Why do you and the others still serve the four delegates of the Union, even after the head of the Intergalactic Union has been killed?" I ask plainly.

Behind me, I can hear the guards breaking into whispers. And in front of me, I can see Ransor's shoulder muscles tighten.

"What are you even talking about? Quit your incessant rambling. Your mindless chatter will not spare you from consequence," he growls.

His response indicates that he has no idea what I am talking about. And just as I thought, Pschye has been lying to everyone here, even about the death of their leader. Everyone believes her unquestionably because the four delegates are supposed to be the vessel through which the Intergalactic Union leader works. But now the leader has been murdered, and no one even knows to ask about it. If it all weren't so disturbing, it would be rather intriguing, like a social experiment in which all the people are sheep who blindly follow what they are told to do without question, even though they know inside that it makes no sense.

When we reach the delegates' meeting room inside the Union station, all four delegates are already inside as if they had been in the middle of some other business.

Ophelia grins. "Look what the cat dragged in."

I pan around the room and see them all sitting there with their smug faces and eyes full of malice. I see Clyde, and I'm reminded of what Aerlon said about how his tail doubles as a whip. It's no wonder that he sits a lot of these the meetings out. He is so fearful to look at that it's almost impossible to concentrate on anything else. But I collect my thoughts and look at each of them firmly in turn before finally settling my gaze on Ophelia.

"Tell me what you have infected Ben with, and how to cure it," I demand.

Ophelia simply looks at me and laughs.

"You do you realize that you have no bargaining power here, right?" she asks. "You can't possibly be as dumb as Ransor makes you out to be. You must at least know that you have walked into our hands with this brazen move to return to Nairu."

"Oh, she knows," Pschye interjects as she pours herself a glass of water at the table. "Bex isn't at all stupid. It would do you some good, Ophelia, to stop listening to stupid guards about who they deem unintelligent. Trust me, it only makes you look like a fool."

Ophelia huffs and frowns at Pschye, then she rubs her metal fingers against her mechanical thigh as if she is running nails on a chalkboard. One day, these two ladies will engage in a fight to the death. They are that level of mortal foes, and I hope they wind up killing each other and ridding the world of two evils at once.

"Pschye," I say as I turn to her, hoping to play their rivalry against each other and get one of them to slip up and tell me something that could help. Sometimes, power-hungry people like these two accidentally stumble into a monologue to stoke their egos that divulges more information than they had intended. "Tell me how to cure Ben before the sickness consumes him."

She is entirely unmoved.

"Why? He must be in bad shape if you were desperate enough to fly a stolen ship back here and grovel on your knees in front of us, knowing full well you have nothing to offer us and no leverage to use in exchange. Why would we want to tell you anything at all?"

"Because he is dying," I plead. I don't care if I have to grovel. I need an answer that will save him, something that I can take back to the Fshie.

"The only thing I will tell you is that the species that the DNA came from is like no other," she taunts. "I have neither need nor desire to tell you anything more."

"And you will never figure it out on your own," Ophelia chides as she adds fuel to the fire.

My plan is backfiring. Instead of being at odds with each other, they are doubling down on me.

"We have only managed to capture one of its kind before the entire planet became unavailable to us."

"Honestly, Ophelia, shut up!" Pschye scolds as I wonder what "unavailable" means. It was a carefully chosen word, one that suggests that the planet they are talking about still exists somewhere.

"Why?" Ophelia shoots back. "Why shouldn't I tell her everything and be able to bask in our success? It's not as if she is ever going to leave this place again, or ever be able to tell anyone else."

This is the perfect thing that I was after. *Go ahead, Ophelia. Monologue a bit and spill your secrets without realizing.*

"Unless you're afraid that you actually don't have things as under control as you would like to think?"

"I have things exactly as I want them," Pschye says.

"They couldn't be more perfect." She glares at Ophelia and looks out the corners of her eyes at the other two delegates sitting with them.

Ophelia thinks she won that battle, and so she continues.

"Ben is our experiment," she says, strictly to show off and defy Pschye on purpose.

I imagine that all four of them think they are equal on this little board of delegates. Little do they know that Pschye considers herself a queen.

"And as our experiment, we will wait to see what happens to him because that human might be the solution to everything we are trying to achieve."

"So you think he is special?" I ask directly, using her own words against her that Ben told me about.

Ophelia picks up on it, which honestly surprises me, and gives me a dirty look.

"We think that Ben could be the solution to all that we are trying to achieve. If his body is able to absorb and integrate the alien DNA into his own existing system, then we have found the cure for every ailment, even death."

"I doubt that highly," I scoff. "There is no cure for death because death is not an illness. And none of your species is immortal."

"It doesn't matter," Pschye says as she resigns to talking to me about it. I have a feeling she was just getting sick of Ophelia getting all the attention in the room. "It could be the discovery that leads to being able to master life and death."

"Why don't you just talk to the Fshie and get the technological advancement that you desire from that species instead? If you truly don't have access to this other planet for some reason, then why would you take such a risk as hedging everything on a single human instead of just using the collective genius and resources the Fshie have?"

"This is even beyond the knowledge of the Fshie," Pschye answers. "A discovery like this could not only make what was once mortal immortal, but it could make us completely impervious to injury and disease. For every species, even humans."

It does sound like an impressive feat, but it also sounds wrong. And not just because of what it is doing to Ben, but also because of what the Intergalactic Union likely did to the alien species they harvested it from.

"Did you destroy their planet, too?" I ask bitterly. "Is that why it is unavailable? Because you simply decimated it and kept one of their kind as a trophy?"

I feel disgusted, and angry, and above all else, I feel as if I am running out of time to save Ben. All I care about right now is him. Nothing else matters to me if he dies, not ever again.

"Tell me what kind of alien DNA you used on him," I snarl at the entire panel of them.

"She certainly is a spunky one," Drelax says. "You have to give her that."

All four of them break into laughter at my expense.

"You are amusingly brave to have come here and demand an answer from us," Pschye says. "But you have walked right into our building, surrounded by our guards, and with no hope at all of escaping. Tell me, did you have a plan for what to do if we didn't give you the answer that you came in search of?"

"No. I just hoped that you might for once take pity on someone who doesn't deserve to die at your cruel hands," I answer.

"Pity? On Ben? There is much you don't know still,"

Pschye scolds. "You are foolish and naïve, and it's a shame to think you are unintelligent, too. We have no reason to let you go."

I glare at her, and the moment she killed Matheus plays out in my memory. That gives me another idea. I turn to face the others and try to ignore Pschye entirely.

"Are the rest of you aware that Pschye killed the head of the Intergalactic Union, Matheus?" I ask.

Based on their immediate reaction and shocked faces, I can tell that they had no idea. All three of them look flustered, and no one answers me.

"You didn't know that, did you?" I ask. "You didn't know that Pschye has been lying to all of you this entire time."

I can feel a small moment of discord, and I try to seize it.

"It would seem that you now serve her instead of Matheus," I say, looking straight at Ophelia because I know she will despise the thought of bowing down to Pschye the most out of all of them.

All three of them look at Pschye, who acts aloof and dismissive of my claims.

"She's lying. This human girl has been lying ever since I met her," Pschye says. "Don't fall prey to her attempts to get you to sympathize with her."

As I stand there in front of them and wait for their reaction, I wonder what Pschye could possibly hope to accomplish by the end of this. She is obviously lying to everyone around her, and they will, at some point if not now, find out. Every single person in the Union, both delegates and subordinates, will hate her for having betrayed them. Even if they stand by her now, and she is able to buy herself a bit more time of being in charge of things, it won't last. Eventually, the truth will bleed out, and she will be discovered as having manipulated them all. She can't hide Matheus' death forever.

"Do you really expect anyone here to believe you?" she hisses at me. "They already know how you killed Matheus."

"What?" I blurt out in shock. "Me? But I—"

"Everyone here already knows how you took that ship to Brocadia with the intent to stir up trouble with our allying alien neighbors, and how you kidnapped the Union leader to use as a hostage to barter."

"You're out of your mind!" I scream at her. It is the most frustrating thing to be made out as the bad guy by the actual villain. I turn to look at Ophelia. She might be evil, but she isn't dumb. "Ophelia, you know she's lying, don't you? You know a meager human like me couldn't hope to take down someone as powerful as the leader of the Intergalactic Union. You said so yourself even—how daft and helpless I am."

"Matheus was an easy target," Pschye interrupts. "He was weak and sickly, and the other friends of yours that escaped Nairu with you helped you to do it. I saw it all happen right in front of me."

I shoot my eyes back to Pschye.

"Then how do you explain why you were there on Brocadia?" I ask, trying to trap her in her own lie.

"I was there for the same reason that I am very frequently on that planet—to check on our allies and secure more resources for the Union's purposes. There is nothing unusual about why I was on Brocadia at the same time that you and your renegade friends happened to be there to carry out this heinous act of assassination." It is rather astounding how effortlessly Pschye lies and how willing they all are to believe her. "And it's a good thing that I was there.

Otherwise, I might not have made it just in time to hear Matheus proclaim me as his successor to reside over both Nairu and the Intergalactic Union in his absence."

"That is absolutely untrue!" I scream. I try to wrestle free of my cuffs and the guards so I can lunge at her and try to knock the wind out of Pschye's infuriating baseless claims. She is literally twisting it all around, and there is nothing I can say or do to prove it. I know the truth because I was there, but my words mean nothing here.

"Silence," Clyde says as he stands up from the table. "I almost pity how pathetic you are." He looks at me and shakes his head, and I can now see his tail wrapping around his ankles as he stands. "You came here thinking we would all believe your lies and that you would be able to walk free with the answers to saving your friend. Instead, you have simply doomed yourself to being tossed back into a prison cell."

"He's right," Ophelia adds with a jeer as she fiddles with the top of one of her mechanical fingers. I wonder if that is the one that hides a syringe inside the hollow of it. "Now, if Ben really does end up dying, then you won't even get to spend the last few minutes of his life with him because you will be here rotting away in a prison cell. You are a fool to have come back here."

Pschye gives Ransor the command to toss me into a cell, which he savors being able to do. He drags me out of the room and down the hall by my cuffs, meeting up with Soro when we are almost there.

"Whoa, is that—"

"Yes, it's Bex." Ransor beams with satisfaction about having me as his prisoner as he roughly shoves me against the wall so that Soro can have a better look at me.

"I thought she was gone," Soro says.

"She was, but she apparently has a death wish, so she came back."

Soro laughs and walks with us for the rest of the way to the prison cell. When we arrive, Ransor tosses me inside so hard that I stumble over my feet and fall face-first onto the ground. Since my hands are cuffed behind me, I have nothing to break my fall. My chin splinters against the ground with a sickening cracking sound, and both men stand there smirking as if I am their newest form of entertainment now.

"I'm surprised that Ben didn't stop you from coming here," Soro says. "Wasn't he kind of like your boyfriend?"

"He's almost history," Ransor says. "He's sick and dying, and she stupidly thought this little stunt of hers would somehow save him."

Between the two of them, there are eight dilated pupils staring at me with ridicule.

"I bet you're wishing you had thought this out a little more now, aren't you?" Ransor laughs.

"Yeah, so much for being the brave Bex," Soro says as he jumps in on the taunting. "What is it that you guys called yourselves? The renegades? What a totally stupid name."

Instead of saying anything in response, I simply grin back at the delegates as if I have a secret that they don't know about, because I do—Clover.

CLOVER

When night falls and Bex has still not returned to the ship, I know something has gone wrong. The people that she came here to talk to probably didn't listen to her like she had hoped they would. I could have told her that wasn't going to work—the evil ones never listen to the good ones in all the stories. They are probably holding her captive again, and she is going to need my help.

I did exactly as she said when the guards came aboard the ship and checked that no one else was here. Hiding behind a pile of blankets was too obvious. So, while Bex was just outside the hatch talking to them, I changed my hiding place and crept into a small open panel in the floor that led into the mechanical belly of the ship. I am good at hiding, thanks to all the games of hide and seek that me and Hope used to play together on the dead planet.

When the guards came, I could still peek out of a crack in the floor to see them. Sure enough, they knocked all the blankets down, and I would have been caught if I had hidden there. But even though they walked right over the top of the portion of floor that I hid beneath, they never found me.

I waited for a while in hiding, and then I eventually came back out to sit in the cockpit and wait for Bex. It's been too long now, and I know it's time to do what she said she needed me to do.

I turn on the comm link onboard the ship, just like she showed me, and set it to the dial she pointed at when she was explaining how to use it.

"Hello?" I ask quietly into the little microphone. "Hello? Is anyone there?"

When there is no answer, I start to wonder what I will do next, but then, after a few minutes, I hear a familiar voice answer me back.

"Who is this?" Petra says through the speaker.

"Petra!" I exclaim excitedly. "It's me—Clover!"

"Clover, what in hell's name are you doing on that ship? Where are you?" she booms through the comm link.

"Petra, shh…" I say to her in a panic. "You're going to make me get caught. They will find me if you are loud."

"Oh, geez, okay," she says much quieter. "Clover, tell me where you are."

"Okay, but don't be mad. Promise."

"All right, I promise," she says. "Tell me where you are."

"Me and Bex took the ship back to Nairu to find a cure for Ben. I think she loves him, and it made her sad to think he was going to die. I came along to help her because I knew she would need someone."

I can hear Petra cursing softly under her breath. I don't think she's really angry, just more worried than anything else. She takes a few breaths to calm down before saying, "Where is Bex now?"

"I don't know. But she has been gone a really long time, so I am pretty sure that she's a prisoner again."

"Has anyone seen you?" she asks.

"Nope. I hid."

"Okay, good, good girl. I need you to stay hidden, okay? I need you to stay out of sight. We are coming to help you. Can you do that?"

"But I think Bex needs my help," I protest.

"Clover, stay hidden," Petra says again, this time a little more strictly than before. "We are coming to help get you both out of there. Promise me that you will stay hidden on that ship."

"Okay," I say reluctantly.

But when we disconnect the comm link, I don't want to stay hidden any longer. I am tired of always having to run and hide from the bad guys. I want to help Bex.

I search all around the ship to see if there are any weapons on here I can use. Since Petra has flown this ship before, I figure that she would have some stuff stashed around. She always has stuff hidden and stashed around in case she needs it, and this time is no different. I find a small gun jammed inside one of the cockpit seats, and even though I'm not sure how to tell if it's loaded, I'm betting that it has at least one shot left in it.

I carefully tuck the gun in the waistband of my pants, and then I slip off the ship.

The cargo bay is dark, which is good for hiding and slinking around without being caught.

Inside the building, it is a bit more difficult since there are guards and lights, but I still manage to avoid running into any of them…for the most part.

Soro is standing at the corner of one hallway, and it takes everything I have not to want to go up to him and use my bullet to shoot him. He and his assassin friends helped kill Hope. But I bite down my anger and wait for him to pass before I continue down the hallway.

At the end of the hall, there is an open bedroom with huge windows that look out onto the landscape of Nairu. It is pretty with all the moons and stars outside, and something about the room draws my interest. I go inside and look around.

This room looks like it belongs to someone really smart. There are a ton of books and sketches that look like diagrams. There are also a lot of photographs. I look at some of the stuff, not wanting to take too long and risk being seen, and I come across a letter that is addressed to Matheus. I wonder if this was his room. It would make sense, I think.

Right before I get ready to leave the room, I spot two leather, weathered-looking journals on the side of the bed. They look like they have been used a lot, and when I flip through them quickly, they look like they are filled to the brim with information and notes on important things. One of them has a bunch of writing on different alien species, and a drawing of some really strange-looking aliens that look like shadows with glowing white eyes and long fingers. I feel like these might be important, so I tuck them into my jacket to take with me.

After some more searching, and descending down a few flights of stairs, I finally find Bex.

"Bex!" I call out in a hushed, excited voice. "I found you!"

She looks pretty shocked to see that I have made it all the way here to her. She jumps up to her feet to stand on the other side of the cell bars to see me.

"Clover, what are you doing here?" she whispers. She looks upset. "I told you to stay hidden on the ship!"

"Yes, I know. Everyone told me to stay hidden, but I didn't want to. I came to help you."

"What do you mean *everyone*? Did you use the comm link to call the others?"

"Yep." I nod, feeling pleased with myself for having at least followed that part of her directions.

"Good. But you still shouldn't have risked yourself by coming all the way here through the station. You need to go back on the ship where you can stay safe until—"

"Hey, you!" a guard calls from a few paces away as he rushes up and grabs me by the back of my shoulder.

It's definitely too late for me to go anywhere now as he opens the cell and tosses me inside with Bex. At least we are together now.

"No idea who you are, kid," the guard says, "but I'll let Pschye know she has a new visitor in the morning when she wakes up." He walks off as if he has done something good, but really, he's just a mindless pion. I hate those kinds of guys in the stories—the minions of the evildoers. I think sometimes they are even worse that the villains themselves because they stand for absolutely nothing.

Bex gives me a hug, and I am glad that she no longer acts like she is mad.

"Okay, everything is going to be okay," she says in a nervous voice that sounds more like she is trying to convince herself than me.

"I found something cool that I want to show you," I say as the two of us sit in the corner of the cell by a small window that looks to the outside. "I think they are from Matheus' room."

"How did you find Matheus' room?" she asks.

I shrug as I dig the journals out of my jacket pocket.

"I dunno, I just kind of stumbled on it." I hand her the journals, and Bex cracks one open. "I thought they looked like they might be something important."

"Clover," she gasps. "These are Matheus' personal research journals. There might be a clue inside their pages that could help save Ben." Bex looks up at me and smiles while her eyes get all watery. "Thank you," she says as she reaches out and gives me another hug.

Adults are weird. One minute, they're crying because they're sad or angry, and the next, they're crying because they're happy and hugging you.

We sit and look through some of the pictures and notes together for a few minutes, but then there is a thunderous, loud noise that comes from outside. It is so loud and so powerful that it shakes the walls of the cell and makes dust fall from the bricks.

"What was that?" I ask as I feel my eyes widen. A rumbling sound continues as we both get to our feet and look out the small window to see if we can spot anything outside.

I stand on my toes to see out, and we both press our faces into the small space to look out into the dark but moonlit night to see a Brocadian ship landing on the surface of Nairu.

Once it lands, the massive hatch opens and an army of Fshie soldiers come pouring out of the ship and onto the ground of this planet.

"They've come to rescue us," Bex says. "And to try to take down the Intergalactic Union at the same time."

We watch in awe as Petra is the first to stand in front of the army of Fshie. She leads them forward toward the station, with all of the other renegades behind her. Aerlon and Talon are there, and Vira is there, and even Amity. The only one who isn't there is Ben, probably because he's still sick, if he is even still alive.

The renegades are all clad in armor, which the Fshie must have given them. To me, they look like heroes.

Behind them, there are too many Fshie to count, more than I even saw on Brocadia when we were there. They pour out of the ship without ceasing in an endless stream of synchronized steps. Talon must have taught them how to organize like that, and it is impressive, to say the least.

They march toward the Union station, and as soon as they get close to its doors, the Fshie all transform into their beastly and nightmarish forms. They are huge as they thrash their claws around and gnash their teeth so loudly that I can hear them even from inside this prison cell.

Petra and the other renegades look behind them to make sure they are ready, and Talon changes into his terrifying form, too. Then, with a single, powerful thrust of her hand in the air, Petra signals the start of the war and they descend upon the station.

THE CLONING OF EDEN

CHAPTER 1 (BEX)

At the first sound of the crash, the station guard takes off down the hallway, forgetting to care that he is leaving me and a young girl inside this prison cell. It suits me just fine —I prefer to fend for myself, and I would rather protect Clover from a war than from the guards.

"Why did he run off?" Clover asks with apprehension. She's the bravest girl I think I've ever known. Most teenage girls I knew back on Earth would be crying or screaming in terror by now. Clover just seems to take it all in stride.

"I think that everyone in the Intergalactic Union is probably terrified of the Fshie," I answer. "Admittedly, they *are* a fearsome sight. We should probably back away from the window before something gets shot into it. Wars are a dangerous thing."

"Aw, but I want to watch!" Clover protests as she sits back down on the floor of the cell and scoots closer to me, still holding Matheus' journals in her lap. "I like the Fshie," she says. "They're good friends."

I can't help but laugh. "You think a species that can

transform into terrifying creatures with two rows of bulging black eyes and white, bristly fur sharp enough to pierce your skin are *good friends?*"

"Of course I do. Scary friends are the best kind. They keep you safe from those who want to hurt you."

"You're a strange girl." I chuckle. "And I mean that in all the best possible ways. And you're also not wrong."

Clover smiles again, as if she has decided that the two of us are now kindred spirits.

"Shouldn't we try to break out of this cell so that we can go and join them?" she asks. "They might not find us all the way up in here."

"Don't you worry about that. Petra doesn't give up when she's on a mission and, from the looks of it, she and Talon are leading the pack. She's like a rabid dog with a bone. She'll make damn sure that they find us. Besides, I want to take a look at those journals some more."

For a few more minutes, I skim the pages of the journals. I figure that we might as well use this time of solitude since there might not be any soon, depending on how the battle plays out.

A lot of what is in the journals is gibberish, the signs of a mad man losing his grip on reality, or maybe finally *discovering* it for the first time. Either way, it's dangerous. *Knowledge* is dangerous here. I've finally come to learn that.

It's a rather surreal feeling to be sitting inside this stone cell with the sounds of a crashing battle outside the window below, and the contradicting sound of Clover's rhythmic humming as she sways back and forth on her knees and tries to draw pictures on the walls of the cell with a stub of charcoal that she fished out of her pocket.

Matheus' journals are overstuffed with pages, as if he sewed more into the binding when he ran out and still had more that he wanted to document. There are drawings crawling toward the edges of the pages and notes written in words so tiny that I can barely make them out. But regardless of how unconventional or *insane* the books seem, they are brimming with precious, secret knowledge. Not the least of which might be the answer to curing Ben, I hope.

"If the Fshie win the war…" I start to say to Clover as I look up from the journal with a thought to share.

"They will," she interrupts me quickly, with unwavering certainty.

I envy her blind confidence. The Fshie are definitely fearsome, but the Union somehow seems to always be one step ahead of things.

There's a loud boom that shakes the station building and lifts dust into the air from the stone bricks of the prison cell walls.

Clover dashes to the window to look outside, even though I told her it was dangerous. "Don't you want to see what's happening?" she asks as I stay seated on the ground with the journals spread out in my lap. "They're at the gate and, from the looks of it, they're breaking through the Union's defenses. Almost all of the Fshie are coming in, and there's a mountain of dead guards in their wake."

I visualize a literal mountain comprised of shredded corpses, torn apart by the Fshie's sharp fangs. I hope that Ransor's and Soro's bodies are among them. It would serve them right for how much damage they have caused.

"Where is Petra and the other renegades?" I ask.

"I don't see Petra. I think she might already be inside since she was leading in the front. I don't see Talon or Vira, either."

"Not even among the dead?"

I wait as Clover squints and pushes her face against the

bars of the window, trying to make out the bodies down below.

"Nope, I don't see their bodies."

That's good, at least.

"But I do see Aerlon and Amity," she says. "They're standing at the hatch of the ship. That's weird."

"What is?" I ask.

"Why are they just standing there with weapons in their hands but not fighting? Everyone else is moving the fight inside the station, but those two, they're just standing at the entrance to the spacecraft as if they're guarding something."

Instantly, I feel my eyes widen, and I scramble to my feet. If they're guarding something, then there is only one thing on that ship of importance that they would have brought here with them, something that *needed* to come in order to have a chance at staying alive—*Ben.*

I reach down into my boot and pull out the small knife that I still have stashed inside the leather. Then I use it to pry open the lock on the cell door.

"Hey! You had that all along?" Clover says as she turns away from the window to see what I am doing. "Why didn't you use it to break us out of here before?"

"Because I wanted some time to look through the journals."

"And now you don't?"

The lock pops open and drops to the floor with a loud clatter. I turn around and grab the journals from the floor, shoving them into the inside pocket of my jacket, then reach my hand out for Clover to take.

"Now I need to get to Ben."

"Ben? But he isn't even—"

"Yes, he is," I interrupt. "He's on the ship."

"How do you know that?"

Instead of stopping to answer her, I pull Clover along with me as fast as her legs will carry her. Thankfully, the corridors are empty because all the guards have gone to try to defend the station's entrances on the main level.

Knowing what I do about Petra, she likely has already found another way in.

"Bex, look out!" Clover screams as I slide to a stop before nearly crashing into a guard who appeared suddenly at the corner of the hallway.

He's not one that I recognize, and for a second, he stands there, visibly trying to figure out which side of this fight we are on.

"What are you waiting for? Kill her!" a voice snarls from behind him.

That is a voice that I recognize immediately—*Ransor.*

"She's a traitor, and the one who prompted the Fshie to attack the station in the first place! *She* is who they are here to get!" he hisses.

The other guard draws a weapon and starts to move toward us.

I force myself to let out an insulting laugh, which makes me sound a bit crazed, to be honest.

"Ha! I would expect nothing different from you, Ransor—you spineless, sniveling coward! The fight is down on the ground, and here you are, hiding up on one of the higher levels with your own personal guard to protect you. Since when do guards get to have their *own* guards?"

"Since I became someone of importance and value." He glares as he spits his words back at me.

I make him furious because I speak the truth. I insult his ego, and it disarms him because he isn't at all as strong as he tricks everyone into thinking. He's *fragile* on many levels, and he knows it.

"Valuable and important are things that you will *never* be," he says.

The guard and Clover both stare at the two of us, as if they are watching our little spat play out before making a move in one direction or another.

"Wait. If the Fshie are here for her, then doesn't that make her valuable as leverage?" the guard asks naively. He obviously doesn't know better than to question Ransor. If we were stuck in any other moment of time instead of in the middle of a war, I have no doubt that Ransor would give him a swift slap across the face.

"She's more trouble than she's worth." Ransor scowls. "She's better off dead. Kill her."

The guard doesn't look as if he's entirely keen on the idea, but he moves to carry out his command. Before he manages to take more than two steps towards me, however, a shot is fired, and he drops to the ground. All of us look around to see where the shot came from, even Ransor.

There is no one visible in either side of the intersecting hallways, but after a couple of seconds, the metal grate pops off the top of one of the air vents in the ceiling.

"You guys always have a tendency to try to start the party before I get here," Petra says as she drops down from the open air vent in the ceiling. "It's okay, though. I don't mind. It gives me an opportunity to make an entrance."

I have never been so happy to hear her dry, sarcastic sense of humor. Ransor, on the other hand, is filled with absolute hatred. He stands there for a moment, waging whether or not to try to fight or run. As predicted, he runs. Ransor is only a tough guy when there are people around to either help him or watch him.

"How did you get in here?" I ask as I run up and throw my arms around Petra.

I can tell that my action catches her by surprise because she stiffens as if she wasn't expecting it. To be fair, it caught me by surprise, too. I guess I'm just happy to be getting out of here...and worried about getting back to Ben.

"There's enough calamity in the lower levels to provide a good distraction," Petra says. "It was easy to slip away and duck into the vent system to crawl up here and find you. I heard your voice and knew you were in this hallway."

"Is Ben here?" I ask abruptly. "Did you bring him with you on the ship? Is he still alive?"

"Yes to *all* three of those questions," she says with a smile. But I can tell by the halfhearted, upward turn of her lips that he isn't doing well.

"We have to hurry," I say. "What is the position of the war?"

"The Fshie are kicking ass." Petra laughs. "They've killed almost all of the guards and Union members. I think they even managed to kill one of the four delegates, the one with the disturbing number of teeth."

"*Derlax*," I say. "Good riddance."

"Yeah, he was super creepy." Petra shivers theatrically. "But to be honest, I wish they would have been able to kill Pschye or Ophelia instead, or even the one with the whip for a tail."

"Clyde?"

She nods.

"Why couldn't they kill all four of them?" I ask.

"We can't find them," Petra says. "It's as if they all disappeared at the first sight of our ship landing at the station. Not sure how they got away anywhere, though, because we haven't found a missing ship or pod yet."

"There must be some answer for that," I say as I think aloud. Then I remember that time is not on our side.

"Come on," Petra says, recognizing the worried urgency in my eyes. "I'll take you to Ben."

"Aren't you guys in sort of a fight?" Clover asks as we sneak around the hallways, making our way down to the lower main level.

"Huh?" I ask, trying to pay attention to not getting spotted and killed.

"You and Ben; isn't he going to be mad at you for having come here and leaving him behind?" Clover is wiser than her years.

"Yes, probably. But I don't really think that any of that matters right now," I answer. "The only thing that matters is saving his life."

"How do you know that's the only thing that matters to *him*?" she asks.

I actually stop walking for a second and turn to look at her because her question is so profound and unsettling. It's just the kind of thing that Ben would say—trading his own life to ensure that I don't put mine at risk.

"Look, sometimes adults do things for reasons that don't make sense right away, but you'll see later on that I've done the right thing, and so will Ben."

Clover lets out a small, sarcastic snort. "You guys are *barely* adults."

"Looks like she's come out of her shell more than a little since the last time I saw her." Petra laughs as she grins at Clover.

We finish our descent down the stairwell since all of the electrical in the station has been knocked out from the blasts of war, except for the emergency lights, which cast everything in a foreboding red hue that makes everything look like it has been doused in blood.

As soon as we reach the main level, there is carnage everywhere. But even more so, there is still a bloody battle raging on. I grab Clover and hold her tight against me to make sure she doesn't get struck and I don't lose her in the fight.

All around us is a sea of bulging, black Fshie eyes, arranged in double rows on their deeply pigmented skin. They are the perfect killing machines when transformed. Their entire bodies are covered with the pale, bristled fur that would make porcupine quills feel like feathery down in comparison. Even a pinprick could levy a fatal wound, depending on where it stuck on its victim. That means that by merely *moving* through the crowd of opposition, they have a chance of killing. On top of that, they are fitted with high-tech weaponry and trained to wield them with extraordinary precision.

Petra jumps back into the fight briefly, and I want to join her, but I don't because I also want to keep Clover from getting herself killed. As it is, the girl is brandishing the nub of her charcoal stick as if it's a sword in the faces of the guards. Bravery might be her strong suit, but moderation is *not*.

The Fshie are difficult to tell apart when they are transformed, at least to my eyes—I'm sure they can tell each other apart. Regardless, one of them does stand out more than the others—*Talon*. I can tell it's him because Vira is fighting so closely at his side that she almost impales herself on his fur a couple of times. I've never really seen Vira fight before, and for some reason, I figured that she wouldn't be great at it. But as she gracefully whirls around, dodging strikes from the remaining guards and slicing through a few of them with a curved blade grasped firmly in her hand, fierce emotions play out across her skin that give her a shimmering, golden gleam. She looks like a star princess made out of pure light and power. And Talon has one set of his beastly eyes watching over her at all times. Anytime a guard or Union member gets too close to her, he intervenes and brutally removes a few limbs from the opposition.

There are so many of the Fshie that the Union never stood a chance. Soon, every last guard and Union operative is either dead or on their knees, begging for mercy.

I use the palm of my hand to cover Clover's eyes as soon as I see that the Fshie, or at least this transformed version of themselves, don't entertain mercy. Every last guard is slaughtered, even the ones on their knees, begging to be spared.

I remove my hand when I realize I don't even know why I covered Clover's eyes. It's not like she hasn't already seen death and destruction. I'm pretty sure there isn't anything that could be more traumatic for her to witness than what happened to Hope and her unborn child.

"Look there," Petra whispers to me as she tilts her head toward the corner of the station's main hallway.

I look and see a handful of emissaries and ambassadors slipping quickly into other rooms to hide. Some of them I recognize as our former teammates from our original Intergalactic Union-sanctioned mission. I wonder why she isn't alerting the Fshie to their escape. Surely the Fshie would hunt them down instantly and kill them. But maybe that's exactly why Petra is *not* ratting them out. It seems unlike her to take pity on those who have betrayed our trust, but I also don't think she's a fan of needless blood-baths. Besides, if there are hostages here, maybe they can be useful when we try to hunt down the four Intergalactic

Union delegates who somehow managed to evade the battle entirely. They're such a despicable crew that I imagine they did something heinous, like using their own people for living shields in order to save themselves.

When it's clear that the battle has been won and the Fshie have been victorious, the aliens change back into their more palatable physical appearance.

Talon's long white hair falls down against his shoulders, no longer in braids but hanging wildly against his skin as he reaches to hold Vira in his arms. Everyone checks to see who has been injured or killed. Thankfully, most of the losses were on the Union's side and not ours.

"The four Union members are gone," one of the Fshie calls out. "Our mission has not been an absolute success."

"*Three*," Talon corrects him. "One was killed in the fight, and we will find where the others have gone and go after them. First, we have quite a mess to clean up here if we want Nairu to remain a functional planet."

"What about Ben?" I ask as I step forward into the remnants of what moments ago was a huge fight scene.

"Yes, *and* we have someone to save," Talon adds, looking over at me with a nod. "For the moment, we will take this as a victory, and we will reclaim Nairu for its rightful people and liberate it from the Intergalactic Union's tyranny. Let's go bring in Ben and see what we can do here to cure him."

As soon as we get within several yards of the ship, Amity spots Clover and runs toward her. The two of them practically smash into each other in their excitement to be reunited and give each other a hug.

"I assume this means we've won?" Aerlon asks when we reach the hatch.

"Yep, we won." Petra smiles from ear to ear. "For now,

anyway. We still have a few snakes that slithered away in the grass, but we'll deal with them after we've seen to Ben."

I practically sprint through the ship until I find him, lying unconscious and soaked with sweat. The black veins covering his skin look like a roadmap and are now bulging as if they are about to burst. Whatever alien DNA this is, it's brutally *killing* him. All I can hear inside my head are Ophelia's words about how the species that did this to him had been down to the last one of its kind. I want to know what alien this is that is filling his body with inky blood. I want to find it and force it to make Ben's suffering stop.

ABOUT MATTHEW THRUSH

Matthew is the founder of EMPIRE Publishing, which is a premium publishing service agency that assists experts, practitioners, thought leaders, business owners, and entrepreneurs turn their knowledge and experiences into bestselling books.

He has personally written over 200 bestselling books since 2005, and he and his team collectively over 1,000 bestselling books.

In addition, his partners and he have launched more than 1,500 authors and books to the *Amazon, Barnes & Noble*, the

Wall Street Journal, USA Today, and the *New York Times* Best Seller lists, and he's on a mission to help one million people share their knowledge, expertise, thought leadership, or breakthrough stories in a book to impact one billion lives.

His work has been awarded Editor's *Pick of the Week*, been published in multiple online magazines and blogs, literary journals, and even used to promote Blockbuster movies. His one story has grossed over 1,000,000+ reads and used by Hollywood producers and directors to promote Season 8 of *The Walking Dead*, *Pride & Prejudice: Zombies*, and *The Boy*.

He even had a story that won Top 35 Finalist in one of TNT's competitive horror writing contests where the winner won a $20,000 **GRAND PRIZE** and had their story adapted to TV & film. Those two stories alone quickly brought in a flood of new avid readers tallying over 54,000+ in less than a few months and sealed his legacy as a top storyteller.

Some other cool accomplishments...

- 200-Time Bestselling Ghostwriter
- Multiple *USA Today* & *WSJ* Bestselling Author
- Funnel, Webinar, & VSL Expert
- Million Dollar Book Coach
- Multi-Award Winning Author
- Top 35 TNT Horror Writing Finalist
- Multi *Editor's Pick of the Week* Recipient
- Founder of Author Hacker Academy
- Founder of Full-Time Ghostwriter

Expert Speaker & Guest on...

- Kindlepreneur
- Author Platform Rocket
- AWAI
- Make Money While You Sleep
- Your First 10k Readers
- Wordslinger Podcast
- Fearless Success Summit
- Draft2Digital
- Wattpad
- 6-Figure Ghostwriter
- Perfect Funnel System
- Legacy Builders Mastermind

However, Matthew gauges his success by how well his clients' books perform. He's fortunate to have worked with many of the best minds, talents, professionals, and world changers.

One of his client's *based on true events* Science Fiction Thrillers was adapted into a graphic novel with artwork by Marvel, DC, & Image designers, and is in talks for adaptation to the big screen and/or a video game.

Others have gone on to generate multiple seven-figure income streams for multiple experts, coaches, speakers, consultants, and thought leaders, which opened the floodgates for them in ELITE partnerships and joint ventures with some of the biggest TITANS in the world, like Tony Robbins, Dean Graziosi, Jack Canfield, Russell Brunson, Kevin O'Leary, and Kevin Harrington.

If you want help writing, publishing, launching, or leveraging your book for greater impact and profit, reach out to Matthew and his team.

You can use the link below to schedule a free strategy call to go over your book idea.

https://calendly.com/matthewthrush/bestseller-brainstorm-call

p.s.

When Matthew isn't helping clients change the world with their books, he enjoys writing science fiction, fantasy, thrillers, and self-help/authority books within his own brand to entertain and educate people for breakthroughs in their own lives.

He lives in Houston, TX, with his two sons and wife, and their pets.

ALSO BY MATTHEW THRUSH

Intergalactic Alliance

The Emissary Of Nairu

The Cloning Of Eden

The Chosen Of Straella

Total Gut Makeover

Total Gut Makeover: Ulcerative Colitis

Total Gut Makeover: Irritable Bowel Syndrome (IBS)

Total Gut Makeover: Crohn's Disease

Total Gut Makeover: Chronic Inflammation

Total Gut Makeover: Diverticulitis

Total Gut Makeover: Leaky Gut

Total Gut Makeover: Migraines

Total Gut Makeover: Celiac Disease

Total Gut Makeover: Diabetes

Total Gut Makeover: Chronic Fatigue Syndrome

Total Gut Makeover: Sinusitis

Total Gut Makeover: Allergies

Total Gut Makeover: Inflammatory Bowel Disease (IBD)

Total Gut Makeover: Small Intestinal Bacterial Overgrowth (SIBO)

Total Gut Makeover: Cystic Fibrosis

Total Gut Makeover: Gut Health & Immunity

My Blessed Life

My Blessed Life

Debt Free Life

Tax Free Retirement

Debt Free College

Debt Free Car

Debt Free Mortgage

Fund Your Life

Build Your Bank

Legacy Wealth Blueprint

Tax Free Capital

11 Months to Debt Freedom

Call of the Wolf

Silence of the Wolves - Prequel

Call of the Wolves

Path of the Wolves

Music of the Wolves

Whisper of the Wolves

Spirit of the Wolves

Ballad of the Wolves

Fate of the Wolves

Alpha of the Wolves

Order of the Moon

Secrets of the Moon

Shadows of the Moon

Blood of the Moon

Darkness of the Moon

Magic of the Moon

Light of the Moon

Legacy of the Moon

Keeper of the Moon

Uniting the Clans

Awaken

Magic

Fire

Air

Water

Earth

Light

Darkness

Uniting the Covens

Curse

Alchemy

Grimoire

Rune

Charm

Spell

Hex

Enchant

Uniting the Legions

Conjure

Summon

Hellfire

Omen

Possession

Wicked

Condemn

Purgatory

Uniting the Fae

Faerie

Darkling

Glimmer

Spark

Shadow

Glow

Whisper

Shatter

L.A.R.S Protocol

The Lazarus Protocol

The Lazarus Gene

The Lazarus Experiment

The Lazarus Covenant

The Lazarus Effect

The Lazarus Revolt

The Lazarus Plague

The Lazarus War

The Blade

Before the Blade

Into the Blade

Against the Blade

Nebula Hendrix

Binary Collapse

Supremacy Warp

Autonomy Shift

Smoke & Ashes

2136

Amber Skies

Risen

Demon Hunter

Chosen

Born Again

The Fell

The Calling

The Sectarian

Raifen

The Search for Truth

A Call to Evil

Atomic Planets

Outer Rim

Deep Space

Oracle of Mars

Red Plague

Sirens of Mercury

Rebels of Babylon

Shadows of Earth

Bones of Earth

Standalone Books

Rapid Debt Crusher

Deactivated

Three Shades of Black

All is Lost

Nemesis

Red Planet

The Busy Entrepreneur

The 3 Factor Key

Kiss of Death

The Bestseller Generator

The 6-Figure Ghostwriter

Full-Time Writer

Book Sales Revealed

www.ingramcontent.com/pod-product-compliance
Lightning Source LLC
Chambersburg PA
CBHW011716240626
47153CB00009B/2885